Born in Carshalton, Surrey, Kevin Michael Hall spent his childhood in Bath, Somerset. He attended the City of Bath Grammar School, then moved to Isleworth in Middlesex to study at Borough Road Teacher Training College. Kevin and his wife, Lindsey, settled in Hounslow, where they brought up two daughters, Keeley and Lucy. He taught for thirty-eight years in two local boys' secondary schools.

This book is dedicated to my wife, Lindsey, a class act in her own right.

Kevin Michael Hall

CLASS CONFLICT

AUSTIN MACAULEY PUBLISHERS™

LONDON * CAMBRIDGE * NEW YORK * SHARJAH

A CIP catalogue record for this title is available from the British Library.

ISBN 9781035858712 (Paperback)
ISBN 9781035858729 (ePub e-book)

www.austinmacauley.com

First Published 2024
Austin Macauley Publishers Ltd®
1 Canada Square
Canary Wharf
London
E14 5AA

Lin Evans' assistance with this second novel about Biggsy's teaching escapades has been a constant reassurance. I thank her for the many hours she spent proofreading the book twice and the timely suggestions relating to storyline development.

Chapter 1

"I've messaged Ella that I've brought you to casualty. She's on her way."

Biggsy winced by way of response.

Dr Manoukian drew open the side cubicle curtain and entered. He was busy dealing with several patients on his evening stint, some in a far more serious condition than this middle-aged teacher.

He knew what was wrong with the patient. The method of treatment, however, was an issue. The hospital couldn't cope with any additional emergency admissions over the Christmas period, which left him with one alternative. The man was in serious discomfort, but there was a way to deal with his problem which would mean that he could return home. The treatment method would be undignified but effective. His wife had driven him to the hospital, and there was no reason why she couldn't take him back home. Gentle persuasion might be necessary. Once the inflammation had subsided, within a week or so, Mr Biggs could return to the hospital as an outpatient in the new year. A further assessment of the severity of his condition could then be arranged.

"The X-ray image clearly shows that your prostate has become abnormally swollen, Mr Biggs, resulting in acute urinary retention. I can assure you that this inflammation is temporary and will subside in the course of time. But we do need to sort out your urine flow as quickly as possible."

Myra, standing by the bedside on which her husband writhed, clutched his hand. The constant contortions were doing little to alleviate his distress. Struggling to cope with the abdominal pain as best he could, he was reassured to hear that surgery would not be necessary to sort him out. Pain relief was what he now craved. The trauma of the rectal examination had resulted in him screwing up his face to the extent that he was finding it difficult to unscrew it.

"One course of action would be for you to become a hospital admission. Here we could provide the required medication and palliative treatment over the next few days, then keep you in for a further period for observation and tests. We know from your recent PSA check and my own examination that you are clear of any serious infection."

"Is there any other possible way to sort him out, doctor, that doesn't involve him being admitted?" Myra queried. "He's seriously hospital phobic. I work here and he doesn't even like it if he has to drive into the car park to pick me up."

Dr Manoukian was tired. His shift still had several hours to run, but he allowed himself a smile.

"You are suffering from acute prostatitis, Mr Biggs. A bacteria may be responsible for the inflammation of your prostate gland. This is a fairly common complaint for men of your age. Should you wish to return home, rather than become a hospital patient, I can recommend a course of action to relieve your discomfort."

"What's that, doctor?"

"It's an unusual one, but it will enable you to empty your bladder. You must run a bath with the water as hot as you are able to tolerate. Then lie in the bath, for as long as necessary, and attempt to urinate. The urine flow will eventually return, I assure you."

"Haven't peed in the bath since I was a kid."

"Are you sure that will sort him out quickly, doctor?"

"I can guarantee it, Mrs Biggs."

"We'll do that then. Come on, my little love. Let's get you home."

"You shouldn't talk to the doctor like that," Biggsy muttered through his pain.

"You can't be so bad if you can still crack jokes," Myra said, relieved that there was something to be done for her husband that wouldn't involve a hospital stay.

"Your husband will need to remain here a little longer whilst I sort out an antibiotic prescription for him. I'll go and organise it so that you can get him home. The hospital will, in due course, send details of a toxicology appointment. If you'll excuse me, I'll leave you both for a moment whilst I sort that out."

As the doctor pulled back the privacy curtain, Myra spotted Ella talking to a nurse. Her daughter looked more agitated than she'd ever seen her. Myra attracted her attention with the loudest whisper she could manage.

"We're in here, love."

Ella looked in her direction, gave a wide-eyed look, offered cursory thanks to the nurse, then hurried into the cubicle. Her jaw dropped when she saw her distressed father on the gurney.

"Whatever's wrong with you, Dad? He looks terrible, Mum."

"Well, you know what it feels like when you've had a skinful of alcohol and you desperately need to pee. That's half your father's problem. The other half is that his bladder's blocked and he can't."

"Oh, my God! Oh, Dad!"

"It's nothing to joke about," Biggsy groaned. "Don't scare her to death."

"His prostate is unusually enlarged, I'm afraid. We've got to get him home as quickly as possible to try out palliative treatment the doctor suggested. You can give me a hand with him when the doc's sorted out his paperwork."

"What sort of treatment?" Ella asked, confusion exacerbating her anxiety.

"I'll save that for when we're in the car."

******

Mother and daughter got him onto the back seat of the car, where he lay on his side in an effort to ease his distress.

"So, what's happening when we get home? Will Dad be OK?"

"He's in pain, as you can see, but I promise he's going to be fine, love. He's suffering from a prostate infection that's interfering with his waterworks. It will sort itself out in time, but first he's got to pee."

"Prostate! That's serious, isn't it? It's one of the most dangerous cancers for men."

Ella's panic rose. She turned from her mother and looked at her father, who was preoccupied with his contortions on the back seat.

"The doctor gave us no reason to believe he's got cancer, love."

"Anything I can do, Dad? How bad is it now?"

"I'm still in pain, but I'm hoping the emergency's over. I'm relying on the hot bath to put me right."

"Hot bath? What does he mean?"

"The doctor says if he lies in a hot bath he'll eventually manage to urinate. The alternative was a hospital stay, but I think we can avoid that. He's had a prostate check recently, which came back normal, so there's no serious problem."

"Ugh, peeing in the bath! And that's supposed to sort it out? Are you just saying that to calm me down?"

"No, it's true. Last night's Christmas Day tipple might have something to do with the state he's in. I don't think you'll be overdoing it with Grandad's hooch again for a while, will you, dear."

"Does he really have to pee in the bath?"

"Don't worry, Ella. You can use the shower instead for a while if it bothers you," her mother reassured.

"It's the bloody job that's the cause, I keep telling you. Teaching seriously damages your prostate."

"Dad will be fine once we get him home. I'm used to him going down with some illness or other every Christmas once term ends. He's just being a bit more imaginative this year."

"Oh, don't be horrible, Mum."

"You know what I mean. It's usually his back going or man flu. Once the adrenaline stops flowing after a hectic term, his physiology collapses. No, he'll be fine. You wait and see."

"Sorry to have spoilt your Boxing Day fun, Ella."

"Don't be silly. You're more important than any arrangements I might have had."

"I've just remembered that I told Mum I'd ring her as soon as there was any news. Can you give your Nan a call and explain the situation, Ella? If you do that, I can concentrate on the road and then your father when we get home."

Her daughter took her mobile phone from her handbag and began working on the keypad.

"Are we there yet?" came a strained voice from the back seat.

****

He wondered what others would be doing up and down the country in the early hours of the 27th of December. There would be those sleeping off the excesses of a second day of holiday celebrations, whilst others would still be hard at it, imbibing and gorging to traditional excess. Putting on extra pounds of fat to protect one against the physical demands of the winter months was probably a sensible idea. He decided to do some catching up in that direction as soon as he felt better.

He lay in the bath waiting to urinate, recalling the doctor's instruction not to exert excessive pressure on his bladder when he eventually did attempt to do so. Myra had run him the hottest, deepest tub possible. Used to showering quickly to save time, there was rarely the opportunity for a good soak these days. The ancient Romans had never bothered with showers. He could see why at this moment. The pain had eased, and he began wondering why he didn't make time for a bath more often.

He'd given his urethral sphincters the gentle nudges suggested by the doctor, but nothing so far. The doctor had assured him it was just a matter of time. He reached towards the hot tap and gave himself a top-up. Myra was reading the Christmas television supplement in bed, looking to see what they'd missed.

"That Al Pacino film was on while we were at the hospital. I love Al Pacino," she called in his direction.

"Many apologies, but we have seen it before," he called back.

"There are a lot of things we've done before, but we keep doing them."

"Fair point."

"I hope you used some disinfectant as well as the bath foam. Any joy yet?"

"Not yet. Keep your voice down, love. If the neighbours have put a glass to the wall, they could be listening in on our conversation."

"Oh yeah! Didn't think of that. A Christmas treat for next door. 'We've opened all our presents, had a good feed and boozed it up for the past two days. Why don't we finish up by putting a glass to the wall so that we can hear what the Biggses are up to? Well, I'll be! Mr Biggs is pissing in the bath.'"

"Very funny. Hey! I think something's happening."

"Heaven be praised!"

There was, indeed, reduced resistance when he applied gentle pressure down below. If he could only maintain that level, there was hope. He resisted the urge to strain, thus avoiding the much-feared irreparable damage to the urethra. He'd been told that his urine flow could be permanently reduced, with the result that he would take even longer to empty his bladder for the rest of his days.

The sensation of a slow but steady release of fluid into the bathwater was at once disconcerting and joyous. Urination continued for two minutes.

"I've done it. What a relief."

"Yep! That's the word. Well done, love."

He felt exhausted. After pulling the plug, he climbed out of the bath into the shower cubicle to rinse himself down.

"Don't bother cleaning the bath. I'll do it with bleach tomorrow. Get yourself washed and dried, and then we can get ourselves off to bed. Oh, the joys of Christmas!"

****

This wasn't a conversation he was looking forward to, but he'd decided he would have to deal with the matter at the earliest opportunity on the first day of the spring term.

Subject leader and second-in-department were alone in the English office.

Over the Christmas period, Biggsy had thought at length about how he might explain to Andy that he'd agreed to a change of post within the school. He could have given a call over the holiday period but had lacked the enthusiasm to do so. There was always the excuse that he was unwell to explain why he hadn't. Justifying the decision to switch from leading the English department to taking charge of the sixth form would need delicate handling.

The reason he hadn't called Andy was that he continued to be disturbed by the events that had concluded the staff Christmas party. Having picked out the name of the deputy head for a Secret Santa gift, Andy had thought it amusing to buy Ms Toner a vibrator. The anonymous Christmas gift had not gone down well with her, although her expression of disgust on unwrapping the sex aid had been the perfect end to the term for many on the teaching staff. Andy was no longer a person to be trusted implicitly. The crude prank had done permanent damage to their relationship. Biggsy wished he'd never shared his feelings of contempt for the deputy head's management style. They might have been interpreted as a thumbs up for the chosen method of humiliation. Holding a member of staff up to public scorn was an abhorrent act, whatever the provocation.

No. An intelligent person could never condone such behaviour. Biggsy was resolute in his belief that professional detestation did not justify sexual ridicule. It would have been easy for him to have taken a similarly vindictive course on accidentally discovering the deputy head in flagrante delicto with Aaron Aimes, her young PE amour. But this knowledge would remain his secret, one that would never be used as a weapon against her. He'd not even told Myra. He felt sure that, if she knew the information he was withholding, she'd find the whole business a hoot and consider his reasoning 'precious', but no matter.

"The head's offered me a new role in the school, Andy. I've been giving it serious consideration."

He wouldn't divulge the incidental detail that he'd already accepted the offer. There was no need. Fingleton had not yet informed anyone he'd found his replacement for Dave Wheelhouse, the outgoing head of sixth form who'd be retiring at Easter.

There were too many professional secrets bothering him lately. Openness was his preference, but this approach wasn't an option here.

Andy looked up from the pile of GCSE course books he'd stacked on a table in the English office.

"This sounds serious, mate."

The word 'mate' jarred.

"It came as a surprise to me. I thought management was angling to see the back of me. But I appear to be the solution to one of its problems. Fingleton wants me to pick up the head of sixth form job at Easter when Dave retires. The offer took me completely by surprise."

He paused to let the implications of this news sink in.

Andy would be considering himself the obvious fit for the head of English. The kudos of a middle-management leadership role and a welcome pay rise to afford a new car would be very welcome. The ramifications for the running of the department would become uppermost in his mind. He looked at his boss, awaiting confirmation that he was the English heir apparent.

In light of his disillusionment with Andy, Biggsy considered Sarah Clifton to be the better candidate for the job. However, she was still hoping for the pastoral post for which he'd been lined up. One very good reason for taking the sixth-form job and no longer leading the English team would be that he'd not have to manage a colleague with whom he'd become disenchanted.

Secrets.

"It's certainly not a move I'd envisaged, and there's a host of reasons why I shouldn't take it. But I seem to be the one he wants."

"I could never have imagined a bombshell like this, mate. I assumed you'd be leading us for years to come. I thought a pastoral role would always be a no-go area for you."

"It's come as a shock. I've thought long and hard about it and talked it through with Myra. She thinks it might be good for me. Sarah's going to be really disappointed, though, if I land the job for which she's been angling."

"Perhaps Fingleton wants you to do both jobs to save a bit of cash."

Biggsy could see where he was being led. He had no choice but to broach the business of who would be the new English head.

"Not a chance. I couldn't do both. You'll have to prepare yourself for interview."

His smile masked the concern that the department might not benefit from the leadership change to which he was referring. He'd have to ensure he had Sarah in the loop before Andy got to her first. But registering his form group would have to come before that.

****

"Happy new year, sir. Did you 'ave a good Christmas?"

Christopher Colley, legs sprawled under the table before him, appeared genuinely interested as he awaited his tutor's response.

"As it happens, Chris, it could have gone better. Everything went downhill from Boxing Day. You could say I was a little under the weather."

"Can't 'andle the Christmas spirit anymore, eh, sir! I s'pose you must be getting worried about your 'ealth at your age," Bellchambers smirked. "Come to think of it, you 'ad a fair bit of time off last term."

This was an unusual experience. His sixth-form group was discussing his health in detail. The default conversation usually involved him probing the intricacies of their illnesses and resulting school absences. The tables had been turned.

"Yes, I have to admit that I've seen more of my GP lately than is good for a teacher."

"Never known you to be as ill as you've been this year, sir," added a concerned Jermaine Gibson.

Retaliation was called for.

"I'm sure you're all worrying unnecessarily. I'll be fine now I've got you lot on my case again. I may be a physical wreck, but at least I don't suffer from the emotional difficulties with which you all have to contend."

Colley looked up from his phone, a look of suspicion etched over his features.

"What's that then, sir?" he queried.

16

"Well, my GP is concerned about you lot because he believes the younger generation suffers from information overload."

"What overload's that then?"

"Oh, he was just confiding to me how pleased he was he'd never considered a teaching career, having to deal with tormented teens. He mentioned the full gamut of adolescent anxieties ranging from how you're supposed to dress and communicate with each other, to finding time to cope with your education. That was just for starters. He put it that you can't move for social networking instructions on everything from what you're expected to spend your money on to how you must behave in any situation. I worry that he may be right."

Biggsy was pleased that he'd managed to assign his own concerns about his adolescent charges to another party.

"Come on, sir. You make it sound as if we 'aven't got minds of our own," Colley argued.

"Would I ever suggest something like that, Chris? But I think you've put it better than I could. Even so, there may be a minority amongst you who are not affected by such young adult tensions."

"Hope that includes me?" Gibson mused.

"I think it probably does. But too many young people can't see beyond ideas of expectation, entitlement, and boredom," returned Biggsy, getting into his philosophical stride.

"Come again, sir?" Bellchambers asked, sitting upright.

"I can explain it more clearly by comparing my teenage years with yours. I grew up at a time when the media was in its infancy. I was not assaulted twenty-four hours a day by persuasive voices telling me how empty my life was because I didn't have expensive trainers, designer clothes, a mobile phone, and five hundred Facebook followers. None of that was around. My mind was comparatively uncluttered by such dross. By contrast, you're being targeted without let-up by an unscrupulous media machine."

"Bet you're glad you got that lot off your chest," Colley chuckled.

"It's a serious problem, one that you may see as more of a threat when you're older."

"How old exactly?" Padfield asked, lifting his head from the table top. He preferred to start most school days attempting a surreptitious forty winks in the corner of the room.

"When you have children of your own. They'll have to cope with even more virtual clutter in their heads than you do."

"I know someone who self-harms," Colley said. "She says she can't stop herself. There's even online stuff telling 'er 'ow to do it."

"I'm staggered to hear that, Chris. The expression 'virtual clutter' is a euphemism in her case."

"Now you've lost me again, sir."

****

Pondering the notion that self-harming was becoming a lifestyle choice for teenagers, he walked along the corridor towards Sarah's classroom. He wouldn't be teaching until after break and she was also free first thing. In all likelihood, she'd be working at her classroom desk. Through the glass panel in her door, he saw her busy marking. *Here goes,* he thought, tapping on the door and entering.

"Morning, Sarah. Have you got time for a chat?"

"Ooh! The word 'chat' sounds ominous," she said, with a playful shudder.

"You could say that. Something's come up out of the blue."

He sat on the edge of a table facing her, his lips forming a pout. She rested her chin on one hand, fixed her eyes on his and waited.

"Fingleton approached me just before we broke up at the end of last term with an offer. He said he wants me to fill the vacancy for sixth-form head."

It was his turn to wait. He gave her time to register the information.

She'd imagined the vacancy would be advertised within the school and that she would apply. She'd be wondering why the head hadn't followed standard procedure. There were two probable reasons. He didn't want to risk the 'wrong' applicant getting the job or, viewing his motive in a more favourable light, he may have wished to pre-empt unnecessary disappointment for applicants he respected but didn't want. The first was the more likely, she decided. The governors ate out of his hand and would go along with whatever decision he made. They wouldn't want to give up a whole day interviewing candidates if it could be avoided.

On the one hand, she felt deflated, but she also knew that this was often the way things happened in schools. Her boss must have been sitting on this over Christmas. She felt sorry that he'd been placed in this predicament but was irritated that he hadn't spoken to her as soon as he'd been approached. She was also annoyed that he stood in the way of the promotion that had been her objective for this academic year. Such was life. She needn't be upset. The fatalism in which she believed told her that good fortune and misfortune come one's way in equal measure. For the moment, however, she couldn't help but feel aggrieved.

"Everything you're thinking has already gone through my mind. I'm sorry to be the cause of such disappointment to you."

"I can't pretend that I'm not disappointed. I really thought it was the job for me. Never imagined you'd turn out to be my main opponent."

"I didn't. It's true. Fingleton's put me on the spot. Situations change. I can't tell you how sorry I am to be having this conversation with you, Sarah."

He could have confided further but chose not to. She was put out, as she had every right to be, and should be left alone to assimilate her feelings. Expressions of further sympathy would only jaundice this delicate situation.

Changing his mind, he risked broaching the possibility of a solution to the problem he'd created.

"But perhaps a different promotion could come your way, if I've anything to do with it, that will equally suit your leadership qualities."

"What do you mean?"

"Assuming that Andy gets head of English, I'd make your promotion to second in English a condition of my acceptance of Fingleton's offer I can't refuse."

Sarah's expression changed to one of quizzical mischief.

"Me working as Andy's second? Could be done, I suppose."

Biggsy wanted to tell her that, in his view, the assumption of Andy taking over was not the one he wished for. Although he'd have a new school role, he would still be teaching almost a full English timetable, and he'd prefer Sarah as the department head.

"But, then again, promotion within the English department may not be my preferred career path. I genuinely feel that pastoral progression would suit me better."

The realisation dawned that he'd been unwise making assumptions about someone else's professional ambitions.

"Sorry, Sarah. I understand. Your choices are your own, of course. I'm meddling here."

****

The first English faculty meeting of the spring term had been a good-natured affair. Andy and Sarah may have been wrestling with professional issues, but everyone seemed to be in the best of spirits. Bridget had spent the first few minutes bubbling over with stories about the wonderful time she'd had visiting her family in Wicklow.

Beth had confided to her department head before the meeting that she felt sure Nick was now in a romantic relationship that was doing wonders for his self-esteem. She'd picked up on the tell-tale sign that he and Angela Davies were spending less time in their own classrooms during breaks and could often be found chatting together in the staff room. The thought that Angela would not fall into the clutches of the PE department heartened Biggsy. Thankfully, the previous term's problem of unwanted online attention from her adolescent admirers had been sorted out and all but forgotten. She was growing in confidence professionally and personally, no longer the department's nervous newbie.

The meeting proved productive, analysis of mock examination results the main business of the day. Biggsy was reluctant to sour the positive mood of the moment, but no good would come from further delay.

"One final word before you all get off home, everyone. What I have to tell you needs to remain confidential until a formal announcement is made. The head could change his mind about this, but here it is. He requested I fill the vacancy that will be left when Dave Wheelhouse takes his retirement at the end of term."

He paused, looking in turn at each colleague's face. Andy and Sarah remained composed, but the general reaction of the others was one of wide-eyed silence. He wondered if those unaware of the information could detect that two amongst them seemed to be taking the revelation in their stride.

"I'd never expressed any interest in becoming head of sixth form," he continued, glancing at Sarah, "but Fingleton made it clear that I was the person he wanted. Not sure why exactly, but that's it. So, I've provisionally accepted his offer. I could have refused, but I do have personal reasons for taking this opportunity to change my role in the school."

"I can't imagine anyone else leading the department," Beth said, to Biggsy's relief. "I'm sure I speak for us all when I wish you good luck."

"Thanks, Beth. That's kind of you."

He folded his arms, looked down at his feet and crossed one leg over the other.

"Yes," Andy added. "You'll have your work cut out with that job."

He hoped that Sarah would also offer an encouraging comment.

"It's the end of an era for us all then," Bridget said, with a nervous laugh. "We've been lucky to have had you in charge for as long as we have."

"The sixth form will be such a different challenge," Hazel observed. "Do you think it will suit you?"

"If it doesn't, I'll have a rethink, Hazel. There'll be loads of admin, which I'm used to. I think the head imagines that an English specialist in the post will be useful with that workload. I know he's thinking that it will help with the university application process."

"You'll still be in the English department," Angela said, "so we won't be losing you. That would be awful."

"Most definitely."

Who was going to raise the issue of his successor?

Sarah decided to help him out at this point. Looking in Andy's direction, she expressed the conclusion that everyone must have been drawing, but which he could not utter.

"We'll be looking to you then, Andy, to do your best to fill the boss's boots. It's going to be a tough act to follow."

Turning towards Biggsy at her final words, she presented him with a smile, a gesture of which he felt wholly undeserving.

"Whoever gets the job will be only too aware of that, Sarah. Believe you me," Andy intoned with gravitas.

"Now that I've told you, I'd prefer to put the business to one side and concentrate on the present, if that's OK? Let's take advantage of this early finish to our first meeting of the term and get off home."

Pleased to do his bidding, everyone made a hasty exit.

As he rearranged the tables and chairs for the following day's lessons, he found himself thinking about Angela and Nick. He hoped that Beth's intuition was correct. The two were well-matched, in his opinion. His thoughts about them were akin to paternal concern. It would be comforting to think that the fates of two colleagues he'd had a hand in appointing might become linked. There was a vulnerability to both, he imagined, that may have drawn them together.

He began doubting whether an enduring relationship between two teachers was possible. For him, it would not be an ideal arrangement. There was the advantage of sharing school holidays together, but the thought of being attached to someone experiencing the same all-consuming pedagogical preoccupations – the emotional claustrophobia – of term time didn't bear consideration. Then again, maybe teaching wasn't that way for other professionals. He'd keep up to speed with Beth on the progress of the attachment.

****

"I'm not making the decision to try to save you and Mum money, Dad, or on avoiding having to take out a massive loan for accommodation over three years. I really want to study for a degree locally."

"St Mary's is only a mile down the road, Ella, so you couldn't be more local if you went there. But Mum and I thought you'd be keen to have a change of scenery."

He'd no intention of making his daughter change her mind but had to be sure that her new plan wasn't founded solely on financial considerations. These were, of course, significant. Only having to find the money for tuition fees and living at home did make economic sense. But there were more important factors to consider than reducing her parents' future outgoings. He and Myra had assumed that campus life for Ella would be well away from Twickenham. In anticipation of her spreading her wings and becoming more independent, they'd assured her that they'd provide whatever additional funds she'd need to supplement the student loan.

"I'm not mad keen, like so many of my friends, to escape from home. Some of them have parents you wouldn't believe – like something out of 'Eastenders'."

"I'm pleased to hear you feel that way about your home, love. It's quite a compliment. As you say, I come across so many students who can't wait to put a bit of distance between themselves and their parents once they enter higher education. But don't you want a taste of life in a totally new environment?"

"No. I don't. I love living where I am. Nowhere else could provide everything I have here, and that includes you and Mum."

It was a colossal compliment.

Fate was making certain that he would not be able to take himself and Myra off to the south coast to live out the remaining years of their lives. He might be able to put up stiff resistance against Fingleton's underhand school appointment schemes and Myra's resistance to moving anywhere, but he didn't have a chance against fate. Fate ties you in knots and stuffs you wherever it wants to, and for however long it likes. Fancy using his own daughter as yet another of the agents against him, to make sure he remained rooted in Greater London. Fate could be a bastard. Just as he'd been beginning to think that Ella's philosophy of being in control of one's own destiny might have a bit of mileage for himself, she'd made this decision. Despite his conviction that teaching was not the career for her, and suggesting ad nauseam that he hoped she'd study for a degree in a healthier part of the country, she'd countered him.

Then the idea hit him that he could be open to the accusation of being as devious as Fingleton in seeking to engineer Ella's future to suit his own ends. A part of him had reckoned that if the family home were no longer her base, it might still be possible to persuade Myra to uproot her life and head south, despite her expressed antagonism to that prospect.

"So, you really don't mind me continuing to live here with you and Mum for the next three years, Dad?"

"Of course not, Ella. Why on earth should you think we would?"

Ella danced towards her father, a broad grin on her face, pecked him on the cheek then thundered off upstairs.

****

Chapter 2

He believed in the importance of going through A-level students' mock examination papers in one-to-one conversations. The boys appreciated this personal touch, which gave them the opportunity to ask questions about their performance that they might have been embarrassed to voice aloud in a classroom setting. Suspending formal English Literature lessons for the first morning session of the spring term, he'd reorganised his timetable, with a fifteen-minute interview arranged for each student.

The perennial problems had come up: the failure to work out exactly what the question meant; a tendency to dwell on the storyline instead of answering the question; the inability to focus on significant themes; a failure to include relevant quotations to support points made; and, most important of all, a lack of personal interpretation.

Padfield, the last boy on the rota, had performed as well as expected. He was pleased with the praise offered for the positive elements in his written responses and accepted criticism of faults in good grace. There was one final area that needed clearing up.

"I'm pleased with the supporting quotation in most of your answers, Ian, but there's one little query."

"What's that then, sir?"

"You've used blue biro throughout the exam but when you write out quotations you've included, you use a different colour. Not only that, but you've adopted the sequencing colour pattern of red, green, and black, which you repeat in that order to the end of each essay. Was there any reason for doing that?"

"Just thought I'd add a bit of colour to my answers, like you told us. Thought it would cheer you up when you were marking my papers."

"What makes you think examiners need cheering up?"

"Come on, sir," Padfield laughed. "You spent ages telling us how boring the job is and how examiners get paid peanuts. You even told us that trained monkeys had to do some of the marking because they couldn't get enough teachers to do it. Seemed like a good idea to me."

"It's true that marking examination papers throughout the summer holiday to earn a bit of extra cash isn't every teacher's idea of fun."

The thought occurred to him that he may have inadvertently misinformed one of his students. However, uncertain as to whether he was the victim of a wind-up, he determined to give Padfield's initiative a fair hearing by pursuing the matter.

"The point you've just made about trained monkeys does raise interesting questions. In fact, I think I read somewhere that most simian species are colour blind. So, if you were a candidate whose paper was being marked by a chimp, your mix-and-match colour scheme would go unnoticed. Assuming that a human did the job, you shouldn't personally feel the need to lift that person's spirits. You could only do that by writing original responses to the questions set."

"You reckon, sir?"

He studied Padfield's face, searching for the merest tic or twitch.

Nothing.

"Yes, it's the unimaginative quality of much of what they have to read that makes the job tedious, not the colour of the ink. I obviously should have expressed myself more clearly when I said that you need to add colour to your writing."

"No worries, sir. Easily sorted. Anything else I need to know, sir?" the student asked, shifting in his seat.

"No, Ian. Thanks for coming along and well done with your result. See you tomorrow."

Padfield stood up and made to leave. He swung the door open then hesitated and turned around.

"I wish I'd known monkeys were colour blind, sir," he smiled.

He exited, closing the door behind him. Seconds later, there was the sound of raucous laughter in the corridor. Biggsy leaned back in his chair and laughed until his sides ached.

****

"Fukkem!"

The Yale lock clicked behind him.

"I think I'll make a late new year's resolution," was his cheery greeting to an empty hallway.

"You've never bothered with any of that in the past, love. What's so different this year?"

From within the lounge, he heard the ruffling of newspaper pages. Kicking off his loafers, he slipped his feet into leather slippers. As he hung up his jacket, he waited for Myra to start laughing. She didn't.

"I know, but I am this year."

"What plans have you got lined up then? Something nice for me? An exotic holiday?"

Shuffling into the lounge, he realised he'd have to interrupt before her mind ran away with itself, setting up the possibility of profound disappointment.

"I'm going to join a gym. My body's starting to disintegrate, and I intend to do something about it before I peg out."

"That does surprise me. You've done nothing of a violently physical nature all the time I've known you, unless you include the occasional upstairs stuff."

"What do you mean – 'occasional'? No, that comes under relaxation. I was talking to my form, and they think I'm one step away from the knacker. I used to be a fair athlete in my teens, but I've let my body go."

"I can see their point," she laughed, "but don't you think it'd be a waste of time and money? This is the time of year when people feel a bit porky after Christmas, sign up for gym memberships, and four weeks later decide never to set foot in the places again. It could be a five-minute wonder."

"I'm aware of that syndrome, but I really want to give this a go. I don't want to be a shambling baggage in my old age. I used to be super fit in my younger days – school rugby and all that. I remember one PE lesson in my first year of secondary school, we had a press-up competition. We had to see how many we could do in a minute. I won it, knocking out sixty. Jim Hardy, our teacher, couldn't believe it."

"You must be one of the lucky few blessed with natural fitness."

"I don't know about that, but I really think I should get into better shape."

"I lost my interest in sport at school once we were made to do hockey. Hated it!" seethed Myra. "I used to throw my hockey boots in the waste bin and say they'd been stolen to get out of games lessons. I remember being freezing cold the moment I put on my PE kit. Exercising in a warm gym, with sunbeds and saunas nearby, would have been more to my liking."

Aware that her husband might be serious about this lifestyle change, her expression altered. She took a sip of her tea as she considered a new angle. With a glint in her eye, she put a novel proposition to him.

"If you become a member, I'll join too. I could do with losing at least a stone. We see less and less of each other these days. It would be good to do something new together."

He was not only relieved that she hadn't laughed his suggestion out of court, but also pleased that she'd be prepared to accept the same challenge. They must arrange to look around the two health clubs local to them. He hoped membership costs wouldn't be prohibitive.

"That's a great idea. I'll make appointments for us to check out our two local gyms."

"Could be that we'll be going out together on a regular basis. I like it."

****

All my love to a fine son and the best teacher in the world. Mum XX

His mother didn't hold back when it came to praising her children, and he wouldn't dream of questioning her judgement. In a world where one could fall out of favour with others, and even oneself, in a moment, he felt a sense of unqualified reassurance at his mother's unconditional love. But what of those who'd never known the guarantee of parental love? Life would be a far more precarious business for them.

Replacing the birthday card on the mantelpiece, he looked at his watch. Myra would be ready in fifteen minutes. She'd suggested all manner of exotic locations to celebrate, including expensive eateries in the West End, but he'd plumped for an evening out close to home at Bellini's. Twenty years ago, he'd have been in total support of a night out at a Soho brasserie for such an occasion, but not now.

It was January the 10th, the moody old Capricorn goat's fifty-first birthday. He hadn't forgotten his wife's description of him on their last day trip to Brighton. He didn't consider himself moody, just a little vacant on occasions. Myra had done well to tolerate him for three decades.

What sounded like a rhino charging across the veld preceded the appearance of his daughter before him.

"Wow, Dad! Why are you waiting for us in your best suit jacket and tie, no trousers and wearing those walking boots Mum bought for you?"

He smiled before answering.

"I have to break in Mum's present to me, to make sure they fit, before I wear them outside. We've got thirty days if I want to exchange them. Just thought I'd make use of the next quarter of an hour to put in a bit of daisy-root time."

"That makes sense," she chuckled.

"Mum and I are planning on doing some serious walks when the weather improves. She's already got a pair. That's why she bought me these for my birthday."

"Anyway, how do you think I look?" she appealed.

"We'll have to get in a structural engineer soon to check the soundness of those stairs. But, no, you look stunning, love."

She was wearing light blue jeans, a red woollen top and a styled blue jacket, all items she'd bought in the New Year sales.

"You've got to be the most affluent-looking sixth former in Twickenham, Ella."

"I suppose my financial situation will take a serious hit once I start uni, what with forking out for tuition fees. Got to enjoy myself while I can."

She was right. Best to put to one side all thoughts of future debt whilst she could. The idea that he hadn't been saddled with a burden of tens of thousands whilst studying at university brought on a bout of generational guilt. He'd lived for three years on a government grant. His daughter's generation had a much worse degree deal.

"Ready to leave in two minutes, you two?" Myra called from upstairs.

"Right, better get these off and my trousers on. Time to party."

****

"I can't help it, sir," Errol groaned.

Biggsy didn't need convincing of that fact.

"I start out concentratin' on the most important thing you told us to do – answer the question. I'm OK for about ten minutes, then I start retellin' the story."

28

The two of them were in the classroom. Errol Wickens' large frame was perched on a chair to the side of his teacher's table. There were ten minutes to spare before he went out on lunchtime patrol.

The student sounded desperate. Further remedial attention was required for Wickens to gain a respectable GCSE Literature grade.

"I know how well you're revising and that you have a detailed knowledge of the books we've studied, Errol. You're halfway there. You've just got to make the leap of faith and start offering your views and opinions in your answers. I know you have them."

"But I have trouble sayin' what they are in lessons. Everybody else says stuff and that's cool. I don't usually bother."

"Rather than think you're lacking in confidence, try to take the view that you're just modest. You get people who are like that. They're happy for others to take centre stage."

"You kiddin', sir? Me, modest?"

"Socially you're one of the most confident students I know, Errol. But when it comes to literature study, you hold yourself back."

"Yeah. Right, sir."

"And in your writing, you can't resist retelling large sections of a novel's storyline. That impulse arises from your belief that you must make the examiner aware of your detailed knowledge of the text. It's commendable, but it won't get you any marks."

"That's the whole point of doing literature, innit? To know books inside out. I remember everythin' about 'em."

"I know that, but our education system requires you to jump through hoops to pass the exam. In a sense, I can see the unfairness of the arrangement. You need to put together a series of arguments in response to a question about one aspect of your reading. What's your favourite film?"

"That's easy. 'The Shawshank Redemption'."

"OK. Great film! Now let's imagine I haven't seen it and I ask you a question about it. The question is: How does the film portray the extreme violence that goes on in Shawshank Prison?"

"Portray?"

"Show."

"Well, I suppose the first time is when…"

"That's it! You've got it," Biggsy enthused, raising his clenched fists in a victory gesture.

"What do you mean, sir? I haven't even started yet."

"Don't you see? Because you're relaxed and confident in your knowledge, you're going to answer my question by telling me about four or five different events from the whole film. You weren't going to give me a retelling of the whole film."

"No, sir," he conceded, as if surprised at his reply.

"You were focused on the question rather than the examiner. It's a trap examination candidates often fall into. I'm sure the things you remember from the film came to your mind pretty quickly, didn't they? Write them down quickly in note form now on this sheet of paper. No more than a line for each point."

He handed Wickens the sheet. The boy shifted his chair sideways, without standing up, so that he could rest the paper on the edge of the teacher's table. He began writing. Two minutes' later, he handed the sheet back. There were references to half a dozen incidents from the film, all of which Biggsy could recall.

"That's perfect. What you have here is a plan for an essay. Before you start writing any answer from now on, prepare something like this. That way you won't make the mistake of just telling the story."

"Easy as that?"

"Not quite, Errol. Once you've prepared a plan like this, you must write one or two paragraphs about each point you've made. Take this point here about the attack in the showers. You need to write a sentence or two explaining what is going on, who is involved, and what is said by those involved. Then you write a sentence or two about the effects of the violence on the audience – that's you as you watch each scene. By the time you've written about each of your six points, you'll have an answer of two or three sides of writing."

"Safe! Like it, sir."

"When you're writing about a book or a play, you should also think about including direct quotation from the text for each important point you make. Each of your sections will then include a quotation or two. These don't need to be long extracts or whole sentences; they could simply be short phrases. They'll be evidence for the examiner that you know the text inside out, as you call it."

"Why ain't nobody ever told me this before, sir?" an aggrieved Wickens demanded.

"The answer to that question may be that this is the first time you've ever had to write an essay of this kind. I want you to do something for homework that should only take you two minutes."

"That's the kind of homework I like."

"Prepare a plan, like the one you've just done, for a question on *Macbeth* that we're studying in class. Give me that piece of paper and I'll write it down."

He wrote quickly then returned the sheet to Wickens.

"Read the question aloud, please, Errol."

"How does Shakespeare portray the violent methods Macbeth is prepared to use in order to become King of Scotland?"

"Like I say, don't spend ages on your plan. Bring it to me here tomorrow after school, and I'll show you how to go about finding just the right quotation to include in each of your sections and making the kind of analytical comments the examiner will appreciate."

"Safe, sir. So, 'portray' means 'show'?"

"It does."

****

"I don't have enough copies of basic texts. I've a situation where GCSE students are sharing books during lessons and it's not working."

School was over for another week, and silence had descended over the building. Biggsy and Sarah were slumped in easy chairs sipping mugs of tea in the English office. She was the last person to complain about anything and was expressing a concern shared by everyone in the department. The situation had become serious.

"Been a problem since the introduction of LMS and nothing's changed over the past few decades. Subject areas constantly bleat about inadequate capitation allowances every year, but this year the complaints have been louder."

"It's going to get worse the way the national economy's going. Schools and hospitals will be run on a shoestring for the next five years, whatever the government says."

"I won't disagree with that. We've got a real challenge on our hands. I wish there were a way to print money in the AVA room."

Sarah extended her feet towards the single-bar radiator that provided warmth in the office after school once the heating was switched off.

"There must be ways to generate extra income. What have schools done in the past?"

"Jumble sales and school fetes. But they're whole-school events and one-off fund raisers. We need something in-house that provides us with a regular income."

"What about opening our own tuck shop?"

"A tuck shop? Selling what exactly?"

"Chocolate bars or yoghurt-covered grain bars if you want healthy. Protein drinks and things like liquorice. Liquorice is a health food too. That sort of thing."

"It's an interesting idea. But what objections would Fingleton make? He'd say a tuck shop would create a litter problem. There would be nowhere to set it up. Other departments would object."

"We needn't bother asking for his permission," Sarah stated. "We could just set up in a small way in my classroom at lunch times so that nobody notices, then expand slightly as word gets around. I could tell kids that they must eat what they buy in my room to contain any litter issues."

"But how do we get hold of stock to sell in the first place?"

"Dave Wheelhouse has the school's cash and carry card. We could borrow it once a week and nip into the warehouse in Sunbury to stock up. Even if we only got away with it for a month or so, we could easily make enough profit to buy a set of books or two."

"You've been thinking this over, haven't you? It could work, though there are risks attached. We'd need someone in your room to supervise every lunch time, and it would mean doing at least one shop a week at the cash and carry. I could help out there."

"No, you've enough to do. I'd do the weekly run on my way home. I'd just need people to help sell the stuff. Like I say, we could start small and, if there's no resistance to the project from any quarter, expand a little."

"Softly, softly, catchee monkey, eh?"

"We can only give it a go. We must get some more books somehow."

"You're right," he affirmed. "If a core subject area doesn't have enough books with which to teach, there's a major problem somewhere. I'll test the water by passing word on to everyone in the department that a potential money-spinner for us is in the offing."

"I had a word with Ella about the slight weight gain, love. Nothing to worry about, thank heavens."

Myra took off her dressing gown, hung it on the back of the bedroom door and climbed into bed. Giving her pillow a punch, she lay down and stared at the ceiling.

"What do you mean – nothing to worry about?" her husband asked, wobbling on one leg as he removed his trousers.

"You remember what we were talking about, don't you? I can confirm she hasn't got herself into any trouble."

"Oh, right. That must have been a tricky conversation. Hope you were your usual discreet self."

"Is that supposed to be a joke? I was discretion personified."

"So, how did you manage to get the 'p' word into your little chat?"

"Didn't need to. I just said that as she had a boyfriend now, I hoped she was being careful. She actually said herself that we had nothing to worry about as far as 'that' was concerned."

He could no longer dismiss from his mind the possibility of his daughter having a sex life. He knew he had much to be grateful for as far as Ella was concerned. Having reached her late teens without complicating life by attaching herself to a steady boyfriend, she'd so far avoided engaging in a relationship soon after puberty, a pressure to which so many young girls succumbed nowadays. Myra seemed very matter-of-fact in the way she was discussing the subject. He had to admit he'd always relied on her in every respect so far as keeping their daughter on the sexual straight and narrow was concerned. If Ella ever did find herself in trouble, her mother would know the best way forward. The facts of life were her domain.

The prospect of talking about the subject on any level with Ella terrified him. Any concerns on the topic would remain unspoken. But would obvious avoidance of that area of human relations make a difference to the way he and Ella interacted? Father and daughter had always been completely open with each other. But now there would be secrets he didn't want to know about.

"I didn't even know she had a boyfriend. Anyone we know?" he asked, trying to sound as level-headed as his wife.

"I assumed you already knew as he's one of your boys. His name's Neil Thompson and he's doing A-levels in your sixth form."

"Oh bugger! One of ours!"

He screwed up his face at the thought that his daughter had chosen to go out with a student at St Saviour's. He knew Neil, a quiet and mature member of the sixth form who was considered a high-flyer. This pedigree didn't detract from his concern that he would be bumping into the boy on a regular basis when he took up his position as head of sixth form in three months' time. He adjusted the waistband of his pyjama shorts and climbed into bed.

"He's a decent enough lad, but couldn't she have held fire on the boyfriend front until she started university?"

"Think yourself lucky that she's waited this long. Anyway, she thinks the weight gain may have something to do with being happy with her life."

He thought of Chris Colley's sister's acquaintance who was self-harming.

"In that case, we've a lot to be grateful for," he said. "It's going to take a bit of getting used to at school, though. I'll try to steer clear of him."

"What on earth are you on about? There's no reason to tiptoe around her beau. As it happens, he's coming around for tea at the weekend."

"Oh, my God! He's going to come into this house?"

"Yes. He may even see your threadbare worn-out armchair."

"It'll all get back to the kids at school. I can hear them now, whispering about me at the back of the classroom: 'Hey, sir's missus is a bit of all right.'"

"Don't be so alarmist. He's a very nice boy, by all accounts. You've nothing to worry about."

"Are you joking? Once Colley and Co. get stuck into him, he'll be putty in their hands. They'll get every tiny detail out of him about my home life."

"Well, Mr Melodrama, you'll just have to ride it out, for your daughter's sake."

Too agitated for bedtime reading, he put the copy of Brookner's *A Closed Eye* back on the bedside unit.

****

It had taken thirty hours out of his Christmas holiday to mark the year eleven mock English and English Literature papers. When the papers were handed back, most students looked straight at the mark awarded and no further. The detailed marking, on which he prided himself, was of little interest to the majority.

"I was pleased with your marks overall, guys. It was clear that you'd taken the two exams seriously. I've provided you all with pointers in my marking as to how you could pick up extra marks."

The quietest time in a classroom is when examination papers are returned to a class. It may only last thirty seconds, but no one speaks during that brief period of time. Students are totally absorbed as they assimilate percentages converted to grades and consider the likelihood of a decent pass at the end of the course.

"You really ought to look carefully at the areas where you lost marks, as well as those where you did particularly well, everybody."

"It's bad enough looking at the marks, sir," Tom Arnott moaned.

A student who constantly wore the expression of a wounded soul, the vagaries of comma use were currently a closed book to him.

"I spent hours marking those scripts over Christmas, so I'd be grateful if, in the future, you'd follow the tips I offer on your papers."

"OK, sir," Adrian Welby offered in support of the teacher.

Welby was a one-off. He was a capable student and openly proud of the fact. Biggsy valued this voice of reason in the mixed-ability class that was presenting serious behavioural challenges.

A trend was becoming evident at the school for more able boys to keep quiet during lessons, out of fear of being taunted as 'boffs'. Many of those able to offer mature responses to questions asked of the whole class now chose to keep their heads and hands down. Despite determined attempts to change the inhibiting mindset, he'd made only a limited impact in the face of the problem. The exclusive expression of reasonable and measured comments during class discussion was becoming a thing of the past. More and more topics of conversation were becoming no-go areas. One of his pupils had once attempted a defence of Curley's wife during a lesson on *Of Mice and Men*. However, he'd quickly been made aware of his 'error' by the spontaneous outburst from another quarter of, "Leave it out. She's just a slut, ain't she?" For the boy who'd uttered the statement, this viewpoint represented the only opinion that his classmates should adopt on that score. Biggsy had railed against the voicing of such an appalling sexist slur but had little confidence that his words would make an impression on every boy before him. Uninformed and ignorant prejudice was becoming an increasing threat to intelligent debate.

Online abuse, directed at the rational and well-meaning, was as commonplace a threat in school communities as it was in wider society. Freedom of speech was under serious threat from ignorant prejudice. It was at such times that Biggsy regretted teaching in a single-sex school. Attempts, in the past, to find employment in a co-educational environment had been unsuccessful. Girls would surely give short shrift to the sexist nonsense of which those in his charge could be capable.

"And what was your score then, Welby?" Arnott asked aloud.

"About thirty per cent more than yours," Welby declaimed, unabashed.

"OK, guys, let's not get personal about our performance, or lack of it. Please bear in mind that I desperately want you to do as well as you can in this subject area, particularly as it has such a bearing on university application when you're in the sixth form, as well as your own personal development."

Mention of the word 'university' had Arnott scowling in disgust and turning over the pages of his sorry script.

A hard-nosed approach to selling GCSE English couldn't do any harm.

"By the way, if any of you would like to discuss your papers with me in private, I'm available here in my room every afternoon after the final buzzer."

On cue, the buzzer sounded to end the lesson.

If he hurried, he could get to the AVA room to do the urgent photocopying for his lesson after break and get a cup of tea from the staff room. He locked the room as the last of the boys exited. Turning to make his way along the corridor, he saw Ms Toner, deputy head of curriculum, approaching him. However much he tried to avoid passing his nemesis in the corridor, there were occasions when it happened. Acknowledging her with any kind of greeting, however curt, was anathema to him, just as it must be for her.

"Good morning, Mr Biggs. I've sent an email around to all department heads about GCSE mock exam data. It's all very straightforward."

"Oh, thanks," he managed.

This was unbelievable. Not only had she greeted him by name, but she'd also made an innocuous remark about an email she'd sent him. This was a moment of note. Or was it a note of moment? It was generally accepted that her modus operandi with 'important' missives was to flood staff with emails in the hope that the important ones would be missed. The result: an enjoyable, for her, management bollocking to put the middle manager in his or her place.

The possibility occurred to him that Fingleton was very pleased with his acceptance of the head of sixth form offer, with subsequent promotion to the senior staff team. As a result, the head may have given Toner the word to go easy on him, a scenario that was disconcerting. There could be two possible consequences, a positive in the short term and a negative in the long. On the one hand, he would not be subject to her micro-analysis of his running of the English department for the remainder of his term of office. On the other, he was troubled by a feeling of foreboding that he had instigated the process of becoming 'one of them' – management. He would have to toe the line on enforcing school policy and initiatives which he'd have kicked against till now. He knew he could never become a Toner. Perhaps he could change the school's management ethos from within, using his pupil-centred philosophy to temper accountability and assessment excesses. Unlikely as that scenario seemed, he could at least put up a fight.

His professional world began to teeter on its axis once more.

Chapter 3

Myra observed the exaggerated muscular development of the specimens undertaking their sets in the free weights area of the gym. She'd never been this close to so much testosterone, and the experience wasn't fazing her. One tall, blond-haired male, his pectoral muscles stretching the material of his yellow T-shirt almost to ripping point, attracted her particular attention.

"How long would it take my husband to get a physique like that?" she asked the young gym-team member.

Looking a picture of fitness in a body-sculpted blue tracksuit top and white shorts, the young man responded with a polite smile. He assumed that the visitor was making a teasing remark at her husband's expense. Biggsy, standing by her side, knew that it was directed at the specimen of beefcake that had caught her eye.

He assumed a look of weary resignation for the instructor's benefit. He had no intention of taking physical fitness to such extreme lengths, and he knew his wife knew.

"It takes years of training to achieve that level of development. There are members here who train for body-building competitions, so don't be surprised at some of the sights you see here."

"I think I'll like it here," she smiled mischievously.

"Let me take you both upstairs to the aerobics theatre. It's the area where you'll spend a lot of your time if you decide to sign up with us."

They followed the young man up to a room filled with treadmills, rowing and cycle machines, and cross-trainers. Members of all ages toiled away, their eyes fixed either on the battery of televisions facing them or their own reflections in the mirrored wall below the screens. Dance music pounded from loudspeakers positioned at ceiling level in the four corners of the room. However, most of the members, wearing headphones attached to personal listening devices, were plugged into music suiting their own tastes.

"Good here, isn't it, love? It's nice and clean. There's every piece of equipment you could desire and tellies galore. What do you think?"

"What was that you said?" her husband mouthed, feigning sudden deafness.

Myra rolled her eyes, turned to her young escort and smiled an apology.

"I suppose it'll make a nice change from school. I'd probably pop in here a few times a week for an hour straight after work. I won't be wearing any of that tight-fitting gear, though, unless I managed to shift this."

Biggsy used both hands to grab hold of a portion of fatty tissue around his waist.

"Put it away, dear," she instructed. "I'll try and get here on the days you can make it. And we can also do a Saturday or Sunday morning."

"You've now seen all there is to see here at Platinum Fitness. I'll take you back downstairs to the office where I can explain membership terms."

"Oh, goody," Biggsy said under his breath.

"Don't be such a grouch!" Myra whispered, giving her husband a glacial smile. "Remember, this was your new year's resolution, not mine."

****

When the sound of the final buzzer signalling the end of the school day had ended, the hissing sound in his ears had continued. It usually took only ten to fifteen minutes to clear. But here he was in the Platinum Gym changing room, and the interference was still with him. Could it be the onset of tinnitus? Best not to mention it to Myra. He didn't want to give her another reason for labelling him a congenital hypochondriac.

"Haven't seen you here before. Just joined up?"

He'd thought he was the only person in the changing room. Looking up to see who'd addressed him in the pleasantly softened Liverpool accent, he saw the owner of a powerful physique, a towel around his waist, padding towards a locker on the other side of the changing room. The defined pectorals and solid biceps indicated a seasoned fitness devotee, not just a regular.

"Yes. First visit since signing up. Haven't exercised in years."

He approached awkwardly, extending a hand, and was relieved once able to withdraw it from the five-fingered vice. Tall and carrying not an ounce of superfluous fat, the new friend was in excellent shape for someone who looked to be in his early fifties.

"Right. How d'you do? I'm Steve. You do realise that this could be a life sentence you're starting."

"I'm Biggsy. What d'you mean exactly, Steve?"

"Biggsy? Interesting moniker. Once you get your body moving again, it won't give you any peace unless you keep it going. You'll find yourself zoned out watchin' TV, and your body will suddenly say 'Enough of this. Get yourself out of this chair and give me some action.'"

"Really? That bad?"

"That's why most people pack it in after a month. They realise what they may be lettin' themselves in for so jump ship before it's too late. An expensive lesson for the weak-willed!"

"My wife and I just thought we'd get ourselves into a routine of regular exercise."

"That's how it starts, mate, but your body starts taking control where it's never been allowed to do before."

"Glad you warned me. Thanks. I've never been to Liverpool, as it happens. What part are you from?"

"Croxteth. Not to be confused with Toxteth," Steve insisted.

"Must organise a weekend away with my wife. We've been saying for ages that it's a place we'd both like to visit, not just because of The Beatles."

"If you go, make sure you take in the cathedral and the docks. They've been turned into a leisure complex now. The area's worth a visit."

"We'll definitely do it one day. Any tips on working out here?"

"The secrets of working out?" Steve asked himself, raising his eyebrows. "The important one is variety. If you do the same things every time you come in, you'll be bored rigid. Vary what you do, and you should keep up the interest. If you ever need any help, just ask."

Biggsy tied up his trainers, padlocked his locker and set his teeth.

"Much appreciated, Steve. Well, here we go. Look forward to seeing you again. Wish me luck."

"And all who sail in her! Have a good one."

****

"Quick! Run across the school field and see if you can get the number of the blue Polo that you'll see going along the far road."

40

He had just given three loud blasts on his whistle, the signal for those brave enough to be outside in the January chill to go back inside for afternoon registration. Archie Matthews, the pastoral deputy head, had called out the instruction to him before hurriedly making his way to the rear car park.

Encumbered by his bulky outer jacket and slowed down by the muddy turf, he did his best to obey the command. The car appeared at the far end of the road. The driver was in a hurry, speeding dangerously down a road on which cars were parked on either side. He was twenty yards from the school railings when the vehicle swept by. It took a sharp left and was gone. He thought he'd been able to make out 'JB' as the first letters of the number plate but couldn't be certain.

A knot of boys, eager to discover what the emergency was, had followed him, rather than go to their form rooms.

"What's 'appening, sir?" one of them asked, his shirt hanging outside his trousers and the two ends of his school tie flapping in the breeze.

"Never you mind. You lot should be inside getting registered, not charging around like a herd of stampeding buffalo."

"Oh, Miss won't mind us bein' late. She can't stand us, sir."

"Well, I do mind. I can't go inside myself until the last of you lot are in."

"OK, sir. Just say the right words and we'll go in."

Fully comprehending what was required by the unkempt year nine pupil, Biggsy managed a smile before obeying the command.

"Get your arses to your classes!" he bellowed.

Snorting with laughter, the herd made its way towards the school building.

As he was shaking the excess mud off his shoes before entering the school building, a breathless and disgruntled Archie approached him.

"Sorry about that, but we think the drug-drop car put in an appearance."

"Drug-drop car?"

"Yes, there's reason to believe that a representative of the local dealer now visits the school periodically to do business just outside the back car park. Sixth formers have provided information anonymously. Must be doing a brisk trade to risk turning up here."

"That's unbelievable. I know there must be students who experiment with stimulants, but class 'A' deliveries for schoolkids is just brazen."

"Defies belief, doesn't it? Did you catch the number of the car? It pulled away before I could get close enough."

"I can't be sure, but I think the first two letters were 'JB'."

41

"That's a start, at least. I'll pass the information on to the head and Dave Wheelhouse. Sorry to be the reason for making you late for your form group. I'll chat to you further about the matter when I get a free moment."

"No problem. Just sorry I couldn't be more useful."

He inclined his head to one side in apology as Matthews nodded gratitude and set off for Fingleton's office.

****

Simon stared straight ahead, avoiding eye contact.

It was warm in the English office, thanks to the electric bar heater he plugged in when the school's ancient system went off. Housed in a dingy basement area on the way to the school gym, the boiler was temperamental in its operation. But it could always be relied upon to shut off at 4.00 p.m.

Seated in easy chairs, the sixth former and his A-level English teacher faced each other. He wasn't a psychotherapist and was uncertain how to deal with this situation, but he knew that the boy needed help and, for the past three months, he'd been doing his best to provide what support he could.

Simon Todd was an intelligent student who made no attempt to attract attention to himself. The fault for the constant psychological bullying to which he had been subjected was none of his making. The school had never been called upon by his parents or educational professionals to investigate the nature of his torment, or the identity of the many perpetrators, because he never made a fuss. Now into his sixth year at St Saviour's – the name of the school an irony in this young man's case – he had coped with the problem by focusing solely on his studies and withdrawing into himself.

Any personality he possessed was invisible to staff and fellow students alike. Thus, he made it easy for those with whom he came into daily contact to overlook his acute introversion. It was this conditioning against which Biggsy was battling. Slim and of medium height, Simon should have blended into the student body with no difficulty. The single detail of his appearance that did draw the constant attention of his peers was his auburn hair.

Possessing supreme academic prowess was the 'offence' he made every attempt to conceal, but he couldn't do the same for his hair colour. In class discussion, he never volunteered answers to questions or information on any topic. When pressed by any subject teacher to use his voice, he'd learnt to remain tight-lipped, the corners of his mouth revealing the merest hints of embarrassment and apology.

On any single day at school, Todd could reckon on the word 'Fire!' being bawled after him several dozen times. On most occasions, a member of staff would not be present to reprimand the culprits. They were devious in their name-calling, as practised adolescent psychological bullies have always been.

At university, the issue that was blighting Simon's secondary education would disappear. But the damage had been done, and he had yet to reach that haven. As far as his superlative academic record at the school was concerned, he was an ideal candidate for Oxford or Cambridge. There was no doubting his intellect for such a higher education placement. He would gain the examination grades required but would have to attend for interview before taking A-levels.

Simon had been schooled to silence. At this late stage, the silence would have to be conditioned out of him if he were to qualify for a place in the heady intellectual environment his intelligence deserved. He had agreed to his teacher's suggestion of aiming high, persuaded by the attractive picture that had been painted of the incomparable benefits available to gifted students like himself. Convincing Simon, in the first place, that he was exceptional had been a challenge.

The coaching sessions that had started the previous term were beginning to produce results.

"How has the past week been for you, Simon?"

He'd been tutoring his protégé to respond to even the most casual sounding of questions in detail. One-word answers or phrases were not permissible, whatever the prompt. Should he subsequently be called for interview, Simon was aware that he would be expected to take a fair degree of responsibility for the direction discussion took. He should be looking for opportunities to elaborate on topics of his own choice. Accessing the technique of wresting control of an interview from an Oxford don would be taxing for any student. For Simon, groomed to muteness by his peers, it would be particularly difficult.

"Um, well, I've been spending some time on…"

"Sorry to interrupt, Simon, but we did agree that verbal fillers such as 'um' and 'well' aren't allowed. I know they're difficult to resist."

Two months earlier, he wouldn't have dared to cut in once Simon had started speaking.

"I've done what you suggested and been reading broadsheet newspapers. I started off reading them in the school library. Now I buy *The Times* at least twice a week. I don't have time to read the whole newspaper, so I read sections that attract my interest."

"Do your parents read the newspapers?"

"They read the *Daily Mail*, but Dad has started reading my newspaper. He quite likes not having to read about the private lives of celebrities."

****

"I suppose I've always been aware of it. I should've acted to put a stop to it."

"What could you have done, though? This isn't a problem for one student. Name-calling is a problem of pandemic proportions."

He handed Myra a mug of tea. She'd switched off the evening news in disgust on hearing the details of yet another MP's fraudulent expenses claim. She adjusted her armchair cushion and wrapped her cardigan more tightly around her.

"As a teacher, I feel I should be coming down heavily on bullying. Poor old Simon's had over five years of grief and I've been instrumental in that process."

"You're taking all the blame for this on yourself, are you, love? It's a terrible fact of life that some people are targeted by bullies, but you can't challenge every boy with a predilection for teasing or tormenting the vulnerable. You'd never be doing anything else."

"But I should be. It's a devil of a job convincing him that the moment he goes to university all this taunting will stop. And how weird is that? I'm increasingly inclined to the view that schools are becoming unhealthy environments."

"How do you mean?"

"We herd all these young people together in vast institutions and, during breaks and lunchtimes, they're unsupervised. The moment children aren't being watched over, a significant minority identifies potential victims and subjects them to abuse. And what's the dominant motive? Fun."

"It is a sad state of affairs, I grant you."

"I've noticed a worrying trend. More of those who discover their clandestine bullying goes unpunished are becoming emboldened in the classroom. I've had to discipline kids for directing the insult 'boff' at those who simply put up their hands and answer a question correctly."

"I'm glad I'm not a teacher. I wouldn't want to be dealing with that," Myra sympathised.

"I could make lists of all the bright boys in each class I teach who have decided against speaking aloud during lessons. It's terrible. One of the problems of living in a democracy is that we constantly have to put up with sneering abuse issuing from the mouths of the ignorant. In fact, there have even been cases of teachers here resorting to that type of behaviour when dealing with difficult kids they teach."

"That's a coincidence. I was just watching the Commons in action on the news."

He couldn't laugh.

"Simon is opening up to me, though. He's agreed to make an Oxbridge application next year, which will involve him going to a college for a formal interview. I'm making progress in getting him accustomed to speaking at length in a one-to-one setting. We've progressed to literary theory. He's genuinely interested."

"That's great!"

"You won't believe it, but I gave him my Foucault book to read. He asked if he could borrow it for a while."

Another addition to his list of teaching tips occurred to him. Taking his notebook from his jacket pocket, he jotted down the latest addition: Top Tip No. 7 – Offer students suggestions for personal reading as a matter of course to develop individual interests and talents.

"Once a boy becomes accustomed to keeping his mouth shut during lessons, it's really difficult for him to get out of the habit, even when talking one-to-one to a teacher."

"A great shame," she concluded, picking up a newspaper.

Myra was tired of the conversation. He could understand why. There was so much he complained about regarding his job in particular and state education in general. Anybody would start to switch off in his company. His wife rarely railed on about problems in her job, though she had as much reason to.

"Fancy another cuppa, love?" he asked.

"So long as you're making it."

"Thanks for your help yesterday lunchtime. A student tipped me off recently about the drug deliveries and yesterday's events confirmed the truth of his information."

The deputy head had intercepted him in the car park as he was taking a pile of box files from the back seat of his Golf. It was a few minutes after eight o'clock.

"No problem, Archie. Just wish I could have been more help."

"Getting a bit of the car's registration will be very handy. We may be able to monitor any return visits. A student or two must have been on lookout duty for the driver to alert him so quickly to my presence."

If Matthews had been informed that the person with whom he was now conversing would be taking over as head of sixth form after Easter, he wasn't letting on. The likelihood was that the head would keep mum about the appointment before making a formal announcement to all staff.

"I heard tyres squealing soon after you spoke to me, so whoever it was must have been quick off the mark."

"Too bloody quick. This drug culture scares me. More and more of our kids are being stopped on the way home and robbed of their bikes, mobile phones, or money. Knives have even been in evidence. Something's got to be done."

Biggsy recalled a conversation he'd had with his wife a few weeks earlier, during which he'd put the case for moving house to the south coast, away from the London 'knifestyle'. Her reply was that serious crimes of violence have become a national problem, one from which it was impossible to run away. Thus, her reluctance to consider getting out of London was one of the main reasons for accepting the sixth-form leadership role. If he couldn't move away, he would move within the school. A new job could be a liberating experience.

"I'd guess the escalating drugs problem isn't solely a concern for our sixth form?" he queried.

"You're right. Years ten and eleven are also becoming a worry. Disaffection is hitting a sizeable minority. Some turn to artificial stimulants, perhaps to compensate for the stimulation lacking in the curriculum."

It came as a surprise to hear a senior member of staff criticising what was on offer to children in the classroom.

"Oh, I don't intend to be critical of St Saviour's here," Matthews qualified. "It's education nationally that I see going in the wrong direction. Teachers are becoming data analysts rather than educators these days."

"Older boys' awareness of the difficulties of finding employment in the long term doesn't help either," Biggsy pointed out. "A question that's regularly thrown at me during lessons when dealing with boys who've lost the will to work is: 'Why should I bother about passing exams when I'm never going to get a job, anyway?'"

"Yes, I've had to deal with that one. The job has changed out of all recognition. Teaching has become ultra-prescriptive, and that approach doesn't suit significant numbers of our school population. I can't understand how the profession has let it happen. Anyway, getting back to the immediate problem, Dave's fully aware of this worrying development and will be able to tell you more. Thanks again for your assistance."

Was he making a serious error? It might not be too late to reject the job. The frying pan of heading the English department suddenly appeared to be more bearable than the fire of taking responsibility for the sixth form. The only consolation he could come up with at this moment was considering the near-impossible challenge of being a school head teacher.

****

He sat up straight, pushed a hand through his hair then stretched his arms wide. It was five o' clock. The silence was broken by the sound of somebody in the corridor trying to open the English office door. As he got up to investigate, it opened. Sarah Clifton staggered into the room laden with two cardboard boxes.

"Mind if I make a space for these, boss? It's the only place I can think of to store them."

In the time it had taken him to mark 9A's homework, Sarah had been to the cash and carry warehouse in Sunbury and back. Instead of travelling on home, she'd decided to bring her purchases straight to school to unload her car in the dark, unobserved. She placed the boxes alongside a filing cabinet and took a reviving breath.

"Thought I'd empty the first load from the boot of my car while no one was around. No need to advertise that we're going into business."

"Blimey, you don't hang about, Sarah. Go ahead. I didn't realise you'd be making such an early start with your tuck shop project."

"Our tuck shop project," she reminded him. "We're desperate for books and, short of a lottery win, this is the only way I can see of getting them."

"How many more of those have you got?"

"Four – quite a selection of goodies. I'd appreciate a hand with the others if you're free."

He followed Sarah down the empty corridor. The idea of doing a first run with maximum discretion was a sensible one. Her hatchback was in the rear car park, close to the back entrance. She clicked open the boot and the two of them loaded themselves up. Then they stole away to the safety of the office. He imagined the pair of them being involved in a felony. Having stacked the haul next to a cupboard, he started wondering aloud about profit margins.

"Will you make much from what you've bought so far?" he asked. "Won't you have to do a mark up to make the project worthwhile?"

"I don't intend ripping the kids off. Selling the items at a little less than shop prices will still enable us to make a significant profit. I'd say we'll generate about fifteen to twenty pounds per box."

Although mental arithmetic wasn't Biggsy's strong suit, he ran through some mental calculations.

"So, to buy a set of thirty books at eight pounds a throw, you'd need to sell at least six more boxes like these? That's a tall order. You'll be up and down the Chertsey Road every day of the week."

"Not every day. I reckon on six boxes lasting three or four days. We may clear a weekly profit of eighty to a hundred pounds. In two and a half weeks, we could buy a set of books."

"That's incredible. But who paid for what you bought today?"

"Me. I'm happy making the initial outlay, on the assumption that I'll get that back. I won't be putting anything through the school bursar. Don't want to risk getting him involved. He could screw up our scheme before it's even off the ground. When I'm buying books, is it acceptable for me to put orders through the bookshop in Richmond that I use, rather than go through the school? They can deliver very quickly."

"Fine by me. You're in the wrong game," he laughed. "You should be going into business with Sir Alan."

"I'm not sure this enterprise will be allowed to last very long, so don't count our chickens. There'll be complaints from other departments that we have a money-making monopoly. There may also be criticism that we're selling unhealthy snacks to kids."

"The school hasn't complained yet about the huge profits the local newsagent down the road makes from our boys before and after school. What they buy there is mostly sugar-based. If we get into profit, as you're hoping, what shall we spend it on?"

"My suggestion is that we make sure every teacher has a full set of the GCSE set text first, and then we can discuss what additional material we should purchase at department meetings. This is all pie in the sky, of course. I certainly don't see it as a long-term proposition, so we must be as successful as possible during whatever time circumstances allow us to operate."

It was clear to him that Sarah had thought through the intricacies of this business venture in greater detail than he had. He foresaw complaints from other departments as an inevitability if the shop proved successful. The emphasis on national league tables had not only created enmity between schools but also between discrete subject areas within schools. The current educational ethos of divide and rule was setting teachers against each other, a situation with which the government was probably very happy. He was not troubled by the idea that this initiative would make him unpopular enough with management for Fingleton to think again about the wisdom of making him head of sixth form. That job was appearing less and less attractive by the day. However, he didn't want his hopes of promotion for Sarah within English to be affected by any confection fallout.

"Well, let's make hay while the sun shines. Where will you be setting up shop?"

"In my classroom, so there won't be any corridor congestion anyone can complain about. I'm hoping I'll have assistance from the rest of the department."

"Everyone's keen on the enterprise, so we shouldn't be short-handed. I'll pop in at regular intervals on my lunch duty patrols."

****

"All seems to be going along really well."

He gave Sarah a thumbs up as she took a proffered coin and handed the customer a yoghurt-covered protein bar. There was a steady stream of boys making purchases, but none of the wild excitement he'd feared of raucous hordes in the corridors.

"It's all down to teamwork," replied Sarah, acknowledging the efforts of Nick Devlin and Bridget Reynolds, standing either side of her behind three tables arranged to form a makeshift counter.

"My calculations of the amount of stock we'd need were pretty accurate. My only worry is that it all seems to be going too smoothly."

"Nick's discovered he's got a real flair for sales," laughed Bridget. "But he may be putting a bit of a dent in our profits."

By way of explanation, Nick bit into a liquorice stick.

"Haven't eaten this stuff since I was a kid," he spluttered.

"We're open for just twenty-five minutes each lunch hour, which means we still get time for a coffee," Sarah explained. "I'll put the takings in one of the lockable cupboards in the office each day. I'll have to get plastic money bags from the bank and exchange the coins for notes. Running a business takes more thought than I'd imagined."

"That seems to be the way schools are run in the twenty-first century – as businesses," mourned Biggsy. "Anyone applying for a headship these days needs an accountancy qualification. Sad, isn't it?"

"I agree," Sarah concurred. "As if teachers aren't burdened with enough responsibilities nowadays, we now have to resort to this in order to make sure we have enough teaching materials."

"A bar of that, please!"

The latest customer was Chris Colley. He stuffed his hand into his trouser pocket and produced a pound coin.

"You won't tell me to put this in the bin if I'm still eatin' it at registration will you, sir?"

"Not at all, Chris, especially as you were polite enough to say 'please'."

****

"Would you please remove your clothing in the cubicle and put on the gown provided?"

Biggsy had hoped that his afternoon hospital appointment would result in him getting home early, but there'd been a forty-five-minute delay. Seated at his desk, the urology consultant, Dr Bhattacharya, tight-lipped and humourless, added to his notes as his patient followed instructions.

Biggsy returned to the metal-framed chair next to the doctor's desk, sat down with a slap and winced. He hadn't reckoned on the plywood seat being so cold. He raised his buttocks slightly and pulled together the two halves of the thin smock behind him.

"It's all right to keep my socks on, is it?"

"That will be fine," the doctor reassured, adjusting his spectacles and standing up. "Would you now lie down on the bed so that I can carry out an examination of your abdomen?"

It hadn't been easy holding on to a full bladder, as per the notes he'd been sent. The doctor's cold fingers probed and prodded his skin below the waist. Relaxing his muscles, he worried that he might do something he hadn't done since childhood – wet the bed. Somehow, though, he managed to keep a clean sheet.

"That seems to be fine. Now I will need to make urodynamic measurements. I want you to return to your cubicle and urinate in this container. When you have done so, please bring the container back to me."

He examined the glass vessel that had been handed to him. It was big enough. Peeing into it would be the highlight of his day so far. He quickly padded back to his hidey hole and relieved himself. His whole body relaxed for the next fifty-eight seconds. Returning the container, after what he considered a lengthy passage of time, and urine, he was embarrassed by the bright daffodil yellow tint of the contents.

"Does it always take you that long to urinate, Mr Biggs?"

"These days it does, doctor. Everything changed after my prostatitis episode."

"How often do you urinate during the night?" asked the doctor as he manoeuvred his patient behind an X-ray machine.

"Twice is the usual, if I don't have any fluid after six in the evening. If I drink after that, it could be three."

By the time he'd finished his sentence, Bhattacharya was hidden from view behind a screen.

"Keep perfectly still for a few seconds, please."

There was the sound of an electrical discharge. The doctor returned.

"Thank you. You may put your clothes back on. I'll just complete my notes whilst you do so."

It didn't seem possible that very much could be discovered from such a brief examination. He dressed and was invited to sit down.

"Well, Mr Biggs, your GP informed me that your PSA result was all in order and that he suspects an over-large prostate gland is the cause of your micturition problems."

"Sorry, mick what?"

"Micturition – the medical term for the act of urinating. Many men of your age suffer from this condition which, although unsettling, does not in itself represent a serious health threat. I will compile a report and send it to your GP. He will contact you within a week or so to discuss my findings and any treatment I may be able to suggest. Is there anything you'd like to ask me?"

The fear of having contracted cancer somewhat allayed, he wanted an answer to the question concerning his future in teaching.

"Is it likely that this bladder problem could become worse, to the extent that I may be unable to remain in a classroom for two hours without a comfort break?"

"I understand your concern, Mr Biggs, but am unable to provide a categorical answer. The functioning of your bladder has been impaired, and that damage cannot be reversed. The condition will continue to deteriorate over the course of time, but the speed of that deterioration cannot be predicted. You may find that you are able to operate unhindered in the classroom for another five to ten years. On the other hand, there could be a more rapid decline in your bladder control."

The answer was, as he'd expected, not clear-cut. However, the prospect of continuing to teach until sixty-five was unlikely. No chance of ever attaining a full pension. Then again, he couldn't imagine having the energy to go on that long.

"Thank you for that, doctor. Much as I'd guessed, I suppose. Well, I'll be off then. Thank you very much."

"Indeed. You'll hear from your GP soon," Bhattacharya replied, inclining his head forward as the patient extended his arm and shook hands.

The news that he wasn't yet at death's door offered qualified relief. Making his way along the cream-coloured corridor, he reflected on what treatment or long-term medication might be in store.

****

"I can't believe Gloucester doesn't see through 'is tosser of an illegitimate son, sir."

The A-level class was discussing *King Lear*, and Colley's spontaneous interjection was just the sort of observation to initiate lively debate. The boy's sense of justice and fair play was clearly troubling him.

"It's because Gloucester's such a plonker that Edmund gets away with all 'is manipulation. How can he not see what's goin' on?"

Biggsy smiled at the inelegantly expressed but pithy summary. In an educational culture in which it was becoming increasingly difficult to develop students' powers of reflection, he was grateful to Colley for getting the ball rolling on such a thorny issue.

"There's a deal of unpicking to be done from those statements, Chris. What do the rest of you think?"

"Gloucester knows Edmund's a bastard, sir, but he should also realise 'is son really is a bastard," Colley persisted, by way of elucidation. "If you know what I mean?"

"Thanks, Chris. I think we can all see now where you're coming from."

Adopting the teacher's default position of devil's advocate, he decided to probe father/son relationships with the class. The idea of human blindness, metaphorical or literal, could come later.

"Do any of you think that your father knows exactly what sort of a son you are? It may not be as easy as you think for a parent to see into the mind's eye of his or her child."

Separate conversations broke out around the room, students eager to share strictly confidential admissions with each other before being brought back to order.

"He's got you there, Chris, mate," Bellchambers said aloud, quelling the rising volume of chatter. "There is no way my dad knows what I get up to twenty-four-seven. By the way, sir, this is a private conversation we're 'aving, isn't it?"

"Let's say we're just talking theory here, Belly. I do admire your honesty, though."

"My dad thinks I'm going into the brewery business to help him run his pub. Haven't had the heart yet to tell him there's no chance of that. Saving that one for later – say, three years' time," Dixon volunteered.

"That's not such an unusual thing to hear, Richard. My father died when I was quite young. We never really talked about my life – any ambitions or personal desires I may have had."

Richard Dixon, troubled by another aspect of the play, filled the silence that followed his teacher's remark.

"It's depressing to think of hating your own brother so much that you could think of killing him. I don't mind a fight, but I couldn't fight with my own brother, let alone want to kill him, whatever he'd done."

"Actually, I know your brother," Padfield interrupted. "A bit smaller, obviously, but he's almost as tough as you. I wouldn't advise taking him on."

Dixon flexed his pectorals and jutted his jaw to inform Padfield that he might be making an error of judgement.

"Edmund's completely evil," Jermaine Gibson stated. "Edgar has no choice but to get rid of him because no one else will."

"That's my point," Colley affirmed. "I can't understand 'ow Gloucester doesn't pick up on what Edmund's all about."

The concept of betrayal was raw with their teacher. One should never be surprised when somebody close and trusted commits an act of bad faith. He was not only thinking of Andy Orchard's Yuletide folly but also his own patronising behaviour towards Sarah Clifton when discussing her career. The faux pas is easily committed.

"I'm grateful to Chris for getting this discussion going. His comment invites the question: Discuss Gloucester's blindness to his illegitimate son's treachery."

******

Chapter 4

"It seems that appointing your successor in the English department will not be the straightforward task I'd hoped."

Fingleton's brow furrowed. Personnel changes should occur as seamlessly as possible. Going to the trouble of organising an interview for this post was not something he wanted.

Biggsy didn't like being taken unawares either. As he'd been making his way home, the head had ambushed him in the main corridor. Being unprepared for an impromptu interview with the top man was not to his liking.

"Is there a problem, headmaster?"

"I'm afraid so. I've had word from a certain quarter of the staff room that your second in department may be the person who anonymously sent Ms Toner the embarrassing gift at last term's staff Christmas lunch."

Fingleton was choosing his words carefully, but their full import was devastating. The 'quarter' had to be the PE area. Somehow, 'Doggy' Barker must have discovered that Andy Orchard was the Secret Santa, whose gift of a vibrator had so embarrassed Stephanie Toner. The only possibility was that Andy had admitted to the prank himself. Full of bravado and alcohol at the pub after the meal, he must have spilled the beans to someone in the PE department, having no idea that their youngest member, Aaron Aimes, was involved in a relationship with Toner. Biggsy had known about their romance, though only by chance. Had he told Andy about the passionate affair, of which few on the staff, if any, could have been aware, he might have thought twice about the wisdom of such a crudely provocative gesture.

He'd not even told his wife that he'd inadvertently witnessed the lovers carnally locked one dark evening after school in the old PE changing rooms. The pommel horse, put to energetic use in their coupling, had been the only other witness.

Barker must have planned the means to apprise the head of Andy's Christmas indiscretion. The thought that Toner now had the full force of the PE department behind her was troubling in the extreme.

"I'm assuming Mr Orchard's injudicious action was an entirely independent one. I can't imagine that anyone else in your department would have been party to such folly."

Much as these words annoyed him, he didn't respond to the remark. Confirmation of the assumption would have been fatuous. He looked into the head's eyes, waiting for the next thrust.

"Consequently, I have decided to advertise the vacancy for head of English. I'd rather not be doing so, but there is no alternative."

Fingleton shifted his focus to the wall behind the current head of English, fixing his attention on the framed photographs mounted there. His gaze caught a faded black and white print, taken half a century earlier of the then school staff. There were no female faces within the frame and the uniform expressions of male rectitude held a special appeal for him. Running a school with a male-only contingent in an age before rowdy staff Christmas lunches and electronic sex toys would never return.

Andy would grasp the enormity of this slight and surely have more than an inkling of the reason for the head's decision. He would approach his department head for an acceptable explanation, with the suspicion that his boss, and friend, may have provided information detrimental to his promotion prospects. Standing firm in the face of such unreasonable pressure was the only posture for Biggsy to adopt, whatever the additional harm to their already damaged friendship. Implicit trust was gone. Head of English applicants would, hopefully, include Sarah. Working under her would be preferable to having the new Andy at the helm.

****

"There was a bit of bother at the staff Christmas lunch."

He hadn't wanted to tell Myra about the incident. Now he had no choice. Negative knock-on effects would be felt in the school for months to come. Myra flicked the switch on the kettle she'd filled.

"Ooh! Did someone graffiti the door of Fingleton's office?" she asked.

"Bit more serious than that. Secret Santa exceeded his remit – big time."

"Sounds interesting. You kept this well and truly under your party hat."

"It was all very murky, and I really didn't want to give the episode another thought over Christmas. Andy decided that, having drawn Toner's name out of Santa's hat, he'd give her a gift to remember. He must have believed he'd been presented with the opportunity to repay her for all the daily management grief she dishes out to the rest of us."

"I'm guessing it must have been something spectacular."

"If a vibrator can be described in those terms, I suppose it was."

Myra laughed so loudly that the sound she produced developed into a scream. Her husband winced.

"Andy gave her a vibrator! How did she take it? Sorry, I shouldn't have used that expression."

Anxious she would be miffed that he hadn't confided the information weeks earlier, he retained his serious demeanour.

"Embarrassment initially, then anger. She walked straight out of the dining hall without a word. Then Fingleton's office had the red engaged light showing after the meal. They must have been in conference for half an hour. Nobody saw her again until the start of this term."

Wondering, indeed, why her husband had been so secretive about the incident, Myra composed herself and began her enquiries.

"Well, I do sympathise. I think I'm liberal-minded, but it's not the gift I would have appreciated from a colleague," she reflected. "If it were given anonymously, how did anyone find out that it came from Andy?"

"That's the problem. The head was informed."

"That's bad. Who told him? How did anyone find out?"

Steam billowed from the kettle as it came to the boil. Myra pushed the mug tree away from the spout and took from it the two damp Millennium mugs.

He wouldn't mention the detail that Andy, hoping to impress his line manager, had informed him of the stunt straight after the meal. Still troubled by the fact that his own open expressions of contempt for Toner had been responsible, in part, for the reckless act of his second in department, he would hold on to that information.

"My guess is that, in the pub afterwards, Andy's tongue loosened about his jolly jape to the wrong person – Doggy Barker, who must have gone to the head with the information."

"Why would Doggy do that? Surely, he's no fan of Toner."

"Seems that a member of his department is having a relationship with her."

"Seriously? This is getting genuinely interesting. I thought all teachers were like you – monkish. Go on then, which one?"

"Aaron Aimes," Biggsy stated, lacking the energy to counter Myra's disparaging epithet in reference to his own libido.

"He's only just out of university! Well, I'm knocked sideways but, then again, why shouldn't she have a toy boy if she wants one?"

"S'pose you're right. Don't get any ideas, though."

Myra shot him a questioning glance.

"I really can't understand why you've kept all this to yourself. I'm quite upset. Why didn't you tell me?"

"I'm depressed about Andy's behaviour and where all this leaves the department. I wanted to put it out of my mind over Christmas. Then I thought the matter had died a death, until today."

Myra didn't look convinced. She shook her head and smiled to herself. Filling the two mugs with hot water, a thought occurred to her.

"So, where do you think Andy bought it?"

He suppressed a smile and responded with the rueful look she was anticipating.

"I neither know nor care."

****

The clock in the English office showed a few minutes after three thirty. All was silent in the corridors.

"I've finished *The Quiet American*."

"Already? I only gave you the book a week ago."

"I'm quite a fast reader."

"Would I be making an assumption of immense proportions to think you enjoyed it?"

Simon's lower lip and eyebrows shifted upward half an inch.

"The politics and religion needed a bit of sorting out, but I did enjoy it. I found out about the background of the Vietnam War. The book showed it was a monumental mess."

Biggsy was pleased to hear the unprompted opinion.

"If you were to drop into an interview conversation with an Oxbridge don that you'd read that particular novel, you'd earn yourself a few brownie points, especially as it's a novel he or she would probably have read."

"Seems a bit childish to play games like that."

"There is something in what you're saying, but you only have a short time to show these people what's inside your head. You can't leave them guessing. You'll be applying to study an English degree, and they'll be looking for evidence that you've read widely outside of the A-level syllabus."

"I'm not into games – never have been."

This was a sign of progress. Simon had reached a point in their conversations where he was prepared to disclose personal preferences. He was an isolate at school, one who shunned casual acquaintance. The idea of participation in team sports was, to him, a ludicrous prospect. In PE lessons, he demonstrated only token involvement. Barker had once informed staff of an incident during a lesson focused on sprint time trials he'd organised with a Year 11 class. Simon had under-achieved magnificently. On being told that he was ten seconds slower over a hundred metres than anyone else in the class, he'd replied in a monotone, "You've broken my heart, sir." This, according to Barker, was the one and only time he'd ever heard the boy speak during a lesson.

"Yes, of course. I do understand the problem you're going to have with this Oxbridge interview. Try not to think of it as an exercise in which you'll be the only person jumping through hoops. Those interviewing you will also be doing the same, forced to ask the same questions of you that they've asked hundreds of times before of others. But I guarantee they will come up with some surprise questions, intended to allow you to show yourself to be the genius you are."

"I'm not a genius," Simon replied, with a shake of the head.

"I beg to differ. You are easily the most academically able student I've ever met. The enmity you experience from boys here is, to a certain extent, the result of jealousy, heightened to an exceptional degree because your peers secretly know that you're special. They're in awe of you, but they've a funny way of showing it."

"I thought it was just a case of them hating me."

"No, they can't hate someone about whom they know so little. Anyway, moving on, I've another suggestion for private reading. Have you ever read *Frankenstein?*"

"No, sir."

"It struck me as a must-read for a student like yourself who also gained high GCSE grades in the sciences. After all, we now live in an age where Mary Shelley's outrageous concept of humankind creating life in its own image is not the far-fetched one her readers imagined."

****

"I'm afraid it's not good news, Andy. The head of English post's going to be advertised."

He'd been dreading this conversation since Fingleton had spoken to him. Having lost a night's sleep trying to work out how to convey the salient details of his conversation with the head, he wasn't going to lose another. This had to be his worst professional duty yet. Whatever had become of their once-trusted relationship, he would be the one to explain why his second in department could not assume the job of leading English was his for the taking.

"The situation's not what I'd hoped. There'll be others applying along with you."

Andy closed the door behind him with a backheel. He would be seething inside but trying to cling to the remnants of their friendship. Biggsy found himself feeling sorry for the man. One act of madness looked set to screw up a promising career. He would maintain a sympathetic stance throughout the conversation that was about to take place but was no longer the undoubted professional ally he'd once been. He tried to look aggrieved, but his facial muscles were struggling to respond to commands. If Andy had thought his line manager would subsequently relent and find the sexist prank amusing, that was his problem.

"You must be joking, mate. There's no way anyone other than me can get the job."

He glared in disbelief at his boss. This was the first time he'd ever directed anger at his one-time partner and ally.

"I'd have said the same a month ago."

"What do you mean? Did you say something to the head to change his mind?"

The insult hurt more than Andy's undisguised anger.

"You shouldn't have asked that question. Somebody in the PE department went to the head and told him about your gift to Toner. Not me. You may have

60

got yourself hammered at the pub after the staff meal and let the cat out of the bag trying to impress the wrong person."

Andy looked into the distance, trying to recollect conversations from the night in question. He shook his head.

"I don't even remember getting home," he admitted, a calm settling over him. "Who knows what I might have said?"

After a moment's thought, an inconsistency occurred to him. "If that were the case, and I said something I shouldn't have, why would anyone in PE go to the head and tell him? Toner is nobody's friend in this school."

Biggsy knew about the deputy head's relationship with the youngest member of that department but had kept the information to himself. He'd confided in no one his chance discovery of their lovemaking. As far as he knew, nobody, other than the PE staff, could be aware of the affair. He would now have to disclose this fact to Andy and hope that he wouldn't question him further.

"Aaron Aimes is in a relationship with her."

"What!" Andy spluttered. "Those two! That's ridiculous. How do you know that?"

This further questioning was unfortunate. He couldn't lie.

"I'd picked up on their relationship from their behaviour towards each other. It became obvious to me."

That was as far as he would go.

"Why didn't you tell me? Why did you let me go ahead and do what I did?" Andy pleaded.

"Come off it. I had no idea that you were planning such an outrageous stunt. But, to answer your question, I didn't ever want to be identified as the source of such staffroom gossip."

"If I'd known, it would have made a difference to…"

Andy was looking for someone else to blame for his actions and the subsequent fallout. He would have to be disappointed. His line manager was bored and didn't want to continue this conversation. He wanted the old Andy back, not this mewling apology.

"Did you talk to Fingleton about me regarding this promotion?"

In other words, "Did you fight tooth and nail to get him to change his mind?"
He hadn't. But that wasn't the answer he could give.

"There was no changing the head's mind on his decision. He was adamant. You've no option but to put yourself forward for the post everyone still assumes will be yours."

****

"Oh, and there's been an interesting development which you should know about. Fingleton's had second thoughts about the head of English appointment, Sarah," he explained, trying to sound as phlegmatic as possible.

"Really? I assumed Andy's installation as English head would be automatic."

"It came as a surprise to me, just as it has to Andy. The head's advertising the position. He believes he should follow form over this one as it's a high-profile, core-subject post."

It was fortuitous that Sarah was still on site, a good two hours after the final buzzer. He hoped he'd be able to give the impression that he hadn't made a special point of seeking her out to discuss the matter. Walking along the corridor on his way out of school, he'd seen the light on in her classroom and had just looked in to say goodnight. He wasn't sure how convincingly he'd be able to maintain the pretence of just keeping her up to speed with events, his main intention being to talk her into applying for the post herself. Even if she weren't offered the job, the interview practice wouldn't do her any harm at all.

"Perhaps the governors suggested the wisdom of opening out the field to external candidates."

Sarah wrinkled her brow in thought, her pen suspended over the exercise book she was marking.

"Hmm. Andy's not going to be happy, though. And you say you've spoken to him?"

"I have, and you're right. Not at all what he was expecting. I'll probably be helping him out with interview preparation. I'm happy to do the same for you if you decide to apply."

"Me apply?" Sarah asked, surprised.

"I'd advise you to apply, whether or not you seriously want the position, one reason being that you'd benefit from the interview experience. Another is that your application would be perceived by management as evidence of your ambition. It's probably a while since you were last in the hot seat for a promotion."

The discovery that duplicity was a skill that didn't cause him great difficulty worried him. Deception for perceived good ends was still deception.

"I'm grateful for your advice, but I'm not so sure I want to put myself through an interview at this moment. Do you really think there's a chance he won't get the job? I suppose the fact that it's being advertised speaks for itself," she confirmed, in answer to her own question.

This was another conversation he wanted to end as quickly as possible, but this time the reason wasn't boredom. It was shame.

"He may find himself the strongest candidate but, as the old maxim goes, there's no such thing as a dead cert. At least, think about it. I'm sorry, but I've got to get off home. It's almost six o'clock and Myra's getting tired of me arriving home late every night. I'll see you tomorrow, Sarah."

"OK. I'll be away myself any minute. See you."

****

"Fukkem!"

Gales, blowing recycling bins along the pavement, caused the front door to slam behind him harder than he'd intended.

"The wanderer returns," called Myra from the kitchen. "Don't tell me what sort of time you call this because I already know, darling. The evening news has just finished. It's six thirty."

He detected a sarcasm rating of eleven on the one-to-ten scale.

"Yeah, I know. Sorry, I'm this late," he sighed, dumping as much of his school paraphernalia as he could on the hall floor. "I think I'm done as far as my relationship with long-time departmental buddy Andy is concerned."

"That sounds as serious as daily school shit can be," she commented, a note of sympathy creeping into her tone.

"It is," he replied flicking the switch on the kettle and arming himself with a mug.

Myra placed a plated-up meal in the microwave, turned the dial and switched on. He smiled his thanks then began an explanation. Gently massaging her forehead, she prepared herself for an extended account of her husband's school day.

"Following my chat with the head, during which he implied that he didn't think Andy was a fit candidate to take charge of English when I move on, I sought Andy out. I read his palm for him, and he was crestfallen, as expected. I could have said 'gutted' but I can't stand that expression."

"But you two are an institution at St Saviour's. Surely things can't be that bad."

The teabag he'd picked up split and the contents scattered all over the work top.

"Sod it!"

He snatched at the dish cloth and began wiping up. Having gathered the leaves into a small pile, he opened the waste bin, put it alongside the work surface and swept the leaves into it in one deft flick of the wrist.

"I can't believe that his ability to lead a department could be called into question simply because he gave somebody a naughty Secret Santa gift!"

"Unfortunately, in this instance, it was the only somebody who mattered."

"Is this promotion genuinely out of the question for him then?"

He took himself and his mug of tea on to the bar stool.

"Not entirely, I suppose. He'll apply along with whoever else wants the job and will have to be considered," he speculated.

"Can't imagine there'll be much competition out there. You've told me how hiring decent English teachers these days is almost as bad as getting Maths and Science staff."

"There is that, but Sarah Clifton may be up for it. She'd be excellent."

"If Andy doesn't get your job, it'll be criminal. He's been as good a second for you as you could have wished for."

"You're right," he affirmed, running a hand through his hair. "But he's compromised himself and the boss is likely to make him pay for the mistake."

The microwave pinged. Myra put on a floral oven glove and presented her husband with a steaming risotto. He raised his eyebrows and produced a pantomime grin as she placed the food in front of him.

"Switch your school brain off and get that down your clack before it gets cold," she instructed.

****

"I thought I'd better let you know that I won't be applying for head of English."

64

The final buzzer had sounded half an hour earlier. The school corridors were silent. Returning from the AVA room, he'd been surprised to find Sarah sitting in the office, doing nothing. He stood before her, disappointed by the decision.

"You've obviously thought this through, Sarah. What decided you against going for it?"

"Well, I gave you an idea that it might not be what I wanted. I enjoy teaching English, but I never saw myself as being a subject leader."

"Someone as exceptional as you could lead in so many areas. What's the issue with heading English?"

She reached out for the mug of tea on the low table beside her and took a sip. Her relaxed expression changed, taut features suggesting a distasteful preoccupation.

"I've seen what the job does to you. I don't intend to be rude, but you must be the person with the highest boredom threshold I know."

He didn't know whether to smile at this compliment of sorts or feel embarrassed at being recognised as possessing such dogged devotion to drudgery.

"I know that all schoolteachers these days have mountains of paperwork to scale, but subject heads' mountains seem to be of the Himalayan variety."

"I admit it's the biggest drawback of this job, but…"

"You protect the rest of the department by shouldering the bulk of all the admin that comes our way. Everybody knows that and we're eternally grateful. But I couldn't do it," she insisted. "And, anyway, I always saw myself in a pastoral leadership role."

"Yes, you explained that at the beginning of last term. It seems cruel that I'm the person who should now be thwarting you professionally."

"I don't hold anything against you. I obviously wasn't management's fit for head of sixth. Another position will come up here, or I can look out for openings elsewhere."

Hearing Sarah refer to the possibility of leaving St Saviour's raised his distress level further. He recalled the optimism of the department's mood at the start of the school year and the sense of unity that had got them through the Ofsted inspection. Things fall apart – starting with one's bladder.

"The most important teaching focus for me is student welfare, how students cope within the straitjacket of state education, as opposed to a career devoted to pupil performance and data management."

"That makes sense. I get hung up on those two in my role, as you've clearly witnessed," he admitted. "The paper trail never ends and I'm unable to stop chasing it. Doesn't make me feel good about myself."

"I'm not having a dig. I love teaching English, as I said, but my priorities as an educator naturally lead me in a pastoral direction."

"I can see that. I admire your conviction. The older I get, the more difficult I find it to hold on to convictions. Must be losing sight of what matters."

"There was another thing…" Sarah began.

The door opened and Andy walked in.

"Evening, you two. Bit chilly in here, isn't it?"

"Hi, Andy," replied Sarah, stirring herself in her chair. "We'll talk about this again later, Biggsy. No offence, but I really do have to get going."

She stood up, packed her things away, and put on her jacket.

"Right, Sarah. See you later."

"I sometimes forget I've a home, a husband, and a ten-year-old to see to. Catch you both tomorrow."

Sarah's coolness didn't seem to register with Andy. When she'd left, he delivered the breaking news he was itching to impart.

"Looks like I've done you a great favour, mate."

"How do you mean?"

"Toner's looking to get out. She's applying for a headship."

"Who told you that?"

"You know how the rumour mill works in this place. Nothing stays secret for very long."

Biggsy wondered if his second appreciated the irony of what he'd just said, having mistakenly assumed a month or so earlier that Secret Santa really did stay secret. If this announcement were true, Fingleton would not be pleased. He'd relinquished responsibility for all matters academic within the school to his deputy. His reliance on her to ensure sustained high levels of pupil performance across the board was absolute. Should she leave, he'd be stuffed.

"And…the word is that Aaron Aimes is also looking to jump ship."

Now who would have told him that? He wouldn't ask.

"Are you serious?"

****

"Absolutely," Bridget replied. "The History department's got agreement from the Head and cleared the trip with the LEA."

He knew that he would never want to travel to Krakow with the express intention of visiting Auschwitz and, under no circumstances, would he wish to take Myra and Ella there. He looked at Bridget's expressionless face, waiting for her to elaborate further.

"These sorts of trips are now being made available to sixth-formers, but I'm not a convert. It seems that the fad for atrocity tourism has become a favoured educational tool. Visiting the gas chambers of Birkenau is now an essential component of any Auschwitz programme. Cannot believe it!"

Having clarified her position, she shifted in her easy chair and assumed an air of bemusement. Taken aback not only by the news of the proposed trip but also by the bluntness of her language, he remained silent, deep in thought.

The school day had ended half an hour earlier, and there were only two other teachers chatting at the far end of the staff room. It was quiet enough for him to reflect on the issue. Whilst on a weekend break in Inverness, he'd taken Myra to Culloden to visit the site of the Jacobite slaughter in 1746. Children of all ages had been much in evidence on the day, roaming around the battlefield and viewing exhibits in the visitors' centre. Two thousand Highland clansmen, armed and prepared to do battle against superior numbers, had taken on the English. They had chosen conflict. But millions of passive civilian victims had perished two hundred years later at the hands of military monsters. The magnitude of this human barbarity was inconceivable. The idea of visiting an extermination site seemed akin to an obscenity.

The argument that teenagers must be informed of the dangers of fanatical ideologies by being shown their egregious consequences was a persuasive one. But there were also those who believed that the Holocaust was too recent a historical phenomenon for young people to be exposed to the minutiae of its horror. He tended towards the latter opinion in this case.

In a documentary he'd forced himself to watch, survivors of death camps had been absolute in their opinion that the proof of Nazi genocide should be preserved in perpetuity as a counter to Holocaust denial. He was in no doubt that humankind should never forget this darkest period of Europe's history and that students should be fully informed of the facts as part of the educational process. But he couldn't understand why anyone should want to take young people to explore gas chambers.

His heart was in accord with Bridget's viewpoint, but logic took a different course. He would have to be honest with her.

"I'm in turmoil here, Bridget. I really don't know that all teenagers would be emotionally equipped to grasp the enormity of six million innocent people being exterminated. As an educator, I'm caught between two imperatives. First, I've an obligation to protect children from exposure to experiences that could cause them lasting psychological damage. But, second, I'm committed to acquainting them with the full range of life's experiences, good and evil."

"Most people these days miss that first point. I struggle with the idea that tour companies are doing profitable business on the back of the most inhuman act in history," she continued. "I've been online and read promotional material put out by travel companies offering educational packages. For example, they blithely state that the gas chambers are 'just a short distance from the centre of Krakow'. Language of that kind is monstrous."

She was right. Were English teachers asked to write tour guides for such hideous excursions, what would they write? Auschwitz had been preserved as a museum, but it was one that he would never wish to see. This realisation was in direct opposition to his conviction that the site must remain as a terrible memorial to those who perished there, evidence that the impossible happened and could never be doubted.

"I must admit to being emotionally out of my depth here, Bridget. I'm entirely sympathetic to your viewpoint. I wouldn't be able to participate in this school venture. But a part of me feels guilty making that admission. I live with the shame that I'm a member of a species that could perpetrate such appalling acts. I feel ashamed that my nation gained huge profits from the slave trade. Perhaps my sense of shame is an obstacle to facing the harshness of reality, in this case a grotesque abomination to which young people should, perhaps, be introduced, at close quarters."

Bridget stood up, collected a selection of empty mugs from the coffee table at which they'd been sitting and carried them to the staff kitchen sink. She looked back over her shoulder at Biggsy as she rinsed them through under the hot water tap.

"I'll have to think that one through when I get home," she called back.

This conversation with Bridget put the internal problems of the English department in perspective. He now had deeper concerns, though: if his own sensibilities were an irrelevance, what worth his intellect? Beyond that, what worth the totality of human intellect when humankind was capable of atrocity beyond imagination?

****

He was agitated. He'd got ready before Myra, who was finishing her facial upstairs, and had laid the dining table as instructed. They probably wouldn't be here for half an hour at least, so he had time for music. What does one listen to whilst awaiting one's daughter bringing home her first boyfriend for a meal with the family?

He'd accumulated a large digital music collection, but he preferred the warmth of vinyl sound to that of CD. Recent recordings he wanted to buy, however, were not available in his preferred format. It would have to be an old vinyl this evening. He selected one of his Traffic albums and switched on the system.

The opening bass line of 'Walking in the Wind' soothed him as he relaxed in his armchair. In his early teens, his friends had thought him odd to be listening to older rock when he could have been enjoying their choice of current chart material.

Two minutes into the track the doorbell sounded. He leapt out of his chair and switched off the hi-fi. Hearing Myra hurrying down the stairs, he timed it so that he reached the front door seconds behind her.

"Come in, you two," she beamed, ushering Ella and Neil into the hall.

Biggsy extended a hand and worked his mouth into a smile. The boy's slim hand slipped gently into his.

Top Tip No. 8: As in the case of dealing with a vampire, avoid inviting a school student over the threshold of your dwelling. He'd have to write that down before bedtime.

He'd decided to present a formal front to the young visitor. His favourite jeans consigned to the wardrobe, he wore grey trousers and a white shirt.

Thank God he's not wearing a hoody!

"Hello, Neil. Haven't seen much of you at school lately. Been hiding from me?"

"Oh no, sir. I've erm…"

"Dad!" Ella interrupted, darting a reproachful look at her father.

"Just his little joke. Take your coats off both of you and come inside," Myra urged.

This is it. No going back. The school is finally invading my home. If Colley and his mates mention one detail of the interior of my home at school, you're for the high jump, young Neil.

The sixth former looked around him nervously, trying to retain his composure as he handed his anorak to Ella. She nudged him gently towards the living room.

"It's good to meet you at last, Neil. Ella's told us so much about you."

"Mum!"

It was Myra's turn to be scolded.

Neil was propelled onto the sofa. He settled himself, used both hands to push back the two halves of his centre-parted fair hair, and pursed his lips.

You can hold her hand in here, but that's as far as you're going, matey.

Myra hovered over the pair with a questioning look.

"What would you two like to drink before I dish up? Something hot or cold?"

Don't even think alcohol, son. It's not happening.

"Neil doesn't drink tea or coffee. I'll just come and see what we've got, Mum."

Left alone with the boyfriend, he wondered what subject matter might engage a seventeen-year-old who was probably too embarrassed to talk at length about anything. He opted for safety first.

"How's the sixth form going then, Neil?"

"It's great we don't have to wear school uniform anymore, but the work's a lot harder."

"Yes, quite a leap from GCSE to A-level. Are you enjoying it, though?"

"Yes," he replied, as though trying to convince himself. "I wasn't sure whether to go for sciences or the arts. But I really enjoyed reading so thought I'd give English Literature a try. My parents would have preferred me to study sciences, but they didn't interfere."

A good sign: a young man who knows his own mind.

"Being an all-rounder gives you the luxury of such a choice. Not many students are that fortunate. Any ideas what you'd like to do after university?"

"After the English degree, I'm not sure. My dad studied accountancy, but that would never have suited me. I'll think more about a possible career once I'm at university."

His sympathies were aroused. He'd had no firm idea about a career as a sixth former. Neil was fortunate in that he didn't have the sort of parents who insisted on reliving their lives vicariously through the achievements of their offspring.

"I worry about teenagers having to make important decisions at such a young age when many have little idea what they may want to do with the rest of their lives. I had no idea what I wanted to do when I was eighteen."

He resisted the impulse to tell Neil that he would soon be his pastoral leader. Taking up the post of head of sixth form, he would be expected to direct as many students as possible to higher education. In addition, he would be dealing with parental pressure. People could appear reasonable, but become obdurate when it came to directing the futures they'd set out for their children. Students' genuine freedom of choice would be a major issue for him in his new role. He understood more clearly Dave Wheelhouse's reasons for wanting to get out of the job as soon as possible.

Ella returned with two tumblers of Coke, a drink for which her father had never developed a taste in his youth. It had been the same with cigarettes. He'd wondered why anyone would want to indulge in a pastime akin to standing over a smouldering bonfire and inhaling as deeply and for as long as possible.

"Hope you weren't talking about school, you two. There are other things in life you know," she advised.

"Actually, you just interrupted a discussion we were having about the dwindling numbers of greater spotted flycatchers in the London area," her father replied.

Myra was standing in the doorway, drying her hands on a tea towel.

"Pay no attention to him, Neil," she said, darting a disdainful look at her husband. "He's just recovering from an acute thunderclap headache brought on

71

by three hours of book marking yesterday. An occupational risk of teaching, I'm afraid."

The teenagers exchanged puzzled looks. Biggsy rolled his eyes.

"Two minutes to mealtime, you lot."

******

Chapter 5

The waiting room at the surgery was packed. He could almost see the cloud of pestilential vapours suspended in the air above the sickly throng. Checking in at the front desk, he considered the possibility of contracting multiple viruses the moment he joined the mass of ailing patients. If he weren't ill now, he probably would be by the time he left. The receptionist provided the grim news he feared as she highlighted his name in pink on the sheet attached to her clipboard.

"Dr Panting's running twenty minutes late this morning, I'm afraid."

There were no free seats to be seen. He made the decision not to join the sick and weary beneath the fetid fug of the waiting room. There was a clear view of the illuminated board that also beeped to signal patients that it was their turn with the doctor, so he'd remain standing where he was until his appointment.

Before taking a section of the weekend newspaper he'd brought with him out of his pocket, he studied the faces of the forty or more people risking the menace of the waiting room. The efforts individuals made to ignore everyone about them amused him. A baby in a blue, hooded, all-weather suit struggled to free himself from his mother's grasp. She clutched the little one to her. Stretching himself forward, as he leaned over her shoulder, he extended an arm towards an elderly man in the row behind. The child made constant gurgling attempts to elicit a reaction from his aged playmate. An expression of stony gloom remained fixed on the old man's face. Locked in a silent world two generations away from the infant, he would be playing no games today.

Halfway through reading a review of the latest Spielberg film, the illuminated board sounded and gave him the instruction to proceed to Room 8. His left knee clicked as he strode off, causing him to list slightly to one side as he progressed along the corridor. He made a mental note to take it easier on the treadmill on his next gym visit. Two light taps on the door later, he was seated once again in the upholstered chair to the side of Paul's desk. Smiling as he studied the screen before him and typing out notes, the GP greeted his visitor.

"Morning, and how are we? You'll have to excuse me – I've got the sniffles today."

Just my luck: even the doctor's contagious.

"Sorry to hear that, Paul. Hope you're not feeling too unwell."

The doctor got up, walked to the sink behind him and laughed drily as he began washing his hands.

"I've a strange feeling our roles have suddenly become reversed. Shouldn't I be saying that?"

"My apologies. I was forgetting myself."

Panting took a paper towel from a dispenser, dried his hands, and returned to his chair. He concentrated for a moment on the computer screen then turned to face the patient, his manner businesslike.

"I'm sorry that your Christmas celebrations were interrupted by the sudden flare-up of your prostate condition. I've read the consultant's report. I should say at the outset that there are no immediate health concerns. However, although your most recent PSA was clear, your enlarged prostate is a problem. When it became inflamed to the point that you were unable to urinate, the excessive pressure you exerted on your urethra to empty your bladder will have caused a degree of permanent damage."

"I was told as much at the hospital appointment, so what you say isn't surprising. I'm taking even longer to pee these days because the speed of my flow has diminished noticeably and I'm going to the loo more often, day and night."

"Yes, your flow will be slower now, but you must avoid exerting pressure as you could do even further harm."

"I can't imagine being any slower. I suppose that puts an end to peeing-up-the-wall competitions with my old schoolmates."

Panting gave him a quizzical look, then smiled at the thought of such puerile games.

"There are surgical procedures available to sufferers like you, but there is a measure of risk involved. For example, possible erectile dysfunction and a reduction of sexual sensation to name but two."

"I've been online and read about that. I know a family friend who went ahead with surgery and now wishes he hadn't for the reasons you've just explained."

"There are likely to be less invasive treatments in the future, but prostate treatment is still in its infancy. If you're averse to surgery, you may find it preferable to nurse your condition along for the time being. If you're prone to sleep being interrupted by the urge to urinate, you could try double voiding last thing before you turn in."

"Sounds like a risky manoeuvre on the ski slopes?"

"Quite!" Paul exclaimed, with a chuckle. "Besides not drinking fluid after six in the evening, the procedure involves waiting a minute or so after you think you've finished urinating. A second flow is then likely to occur, helping you to empty your bladder."

Biggsy was worried and began massaging the back of his neck.

"If this is a condition I'm going to have to live with, it may affect how much longer I can continue teaching."

"That is, indeed, a worry. Your problem is, to some extent, a consequence of your career choice. You've previously told me you never hydrated regularly during the day because you feared having to go to the loo during a lesson. Prostates are temperamental little buggers."

"The thought of spending the next ten years worrying about having to make a hasty exit from the classroom is causing me some concern."

"Things may not be as difficult for you as you're imagining just at this moment," Panting reassured. "Men do cope successfully with the situation in which you find yourself. Let me take you through the various self-help procedures you can follow, as well as a look at palliative medication available."

****

"That was a smashing lamb joint, love. Having a roast again on Sunday is great."

"You can have a roast every Sunday if you'd like to cook it in future. I'd really enjoy that," came the tart reply.

"No, I mean, it was just like the old days when Ella was growing up and we'd eat traditional Sunday fare together every weekend."

"We can still have a roast every weekend without her. I'd appreciate it. You know where everything is in the kitchen."

There was no getting himself out of the hole he'd just dug for himself. He'd lost this one.

"I bloody hate roasts," he growled, trying hard to disguise the humour.

"Oh, and I was just getting excited about what you were going to surprise me with next week."

He stood up, took Myra's cutlery and plate, placed them on top of his and shuffled to the kitchen. The kettle filled and mugs primed with tea bags, he began filling the dishwasher. He wanted twenty minutes to complete the killer Sudoku in the newspaper before continuing his GCSE marking. Myra picked up the main section of the newspaper as he placed her tea on the Mrs Silly drinks coaster she treasured. He grabbed the review section before she could appropriate that, too.

"Look at this front page. Austerity continuing for us all, apparently. I can't believe we allow these public-school half-wits to run the bloody country!"

"Will you be changing your surname to Meldrew in the near future by any chance?" he asked as he flopped into his armchair alongside hers. "I preferred you when you were just passive-aggressive."

"It's obviously nonsensical to keep the whole country at a standstill, and for the foreseeable, even if the economy is in a mess."

"I knew that evening course on Keynesian Economics would be just the thing for you, love."

"All right, Mr Funnypants! Do you know that economics has been a closed shop to women since time immemorial? The renowned economists have all been bloody blokes. No wonder the world's in such a financial mess!"

"I think you're on the money there. Women run most home economies, so there's no reason why they shouldn't control the national economy."

"My father would disagree. He's always kept a tight grip on the purse strings."

"I think I'll keep out of that one. I don't want to spoil my evening by dwelling on your dad's Neanderthal leanings. That reminds me, Andy told me something today that pleased him no end."

He looked at Myra to see if her attention monitor would be receptive to his news. A frown began to form as she registered the change of mood from farce to sobriety.

"Hit me with it if you must."

"Don't worry. This won't take long. He told me that Toner's applied for a headship at a school out Reigate way. Fallout from the incident at the end of last term, I imagine."

Myra didn't respond immediately. She continued looking at the newspaper, but he could sense the wheels turning behind her eyes.

"Was that her own decision or one influenced by somebody or something else? I can't imagine someone as driven as she is feeling that she'd have to leave for that reason. It may just be a case of the right opening coming up for her."

"Aaron Aimes is also looking for another job elsewhere, if Andy is to be believed."

"That would definitely seem to be a consequence of the Christmas caper. I wonder if their liaison has come to an end. Then again, they may have decided it would be easier to continue their relationship beyond the reach of the St Saviour's gossips."

"I've seen no evidence that the relationship has ended. It would be ironic if she left the school just as I finish my stint as head of English. I haven't had an easy time with her on my back."

"You'd probably have had a tough time whoever was on your back. Core subjects in state schools are under the assessment microscope far more than other curricular areas."

He recalled how offended teachers of non-core subjects had felt when the national curriculum had first been introduced. Suddenly, humanities and foreign languages were reduced to second-class status in schools, and the arts to third. Educational crimes of monumental proportions.

"Nothing stays the same for long in schools these days, as you're always telling me. High staff turnover is the name of the game nowadays. Bet you're glad you're not a principal," Myra concluded.

He agreed, said nothing, and retreated into the comfort of his Sudoku.

****

Fingleton caught him as he was about to enter the staff room.

"How opportune! I know that you usually arrive early and have been looking out for you. Could you spare me a moment of your time? We don't need to go to my office. The corridor is private enough at this time of day."

The head's non-threatening confidential tone put him at ease.

"I've agreed with the governors about your move next term to head of sixth form. I'm pleased to say that they were unanimously in favour of my decision.

I've asked my secretary to type out a formal announcement of your new role, which will be posted on the staff notice board after lunch."

Conflicting thoughts occurred. Toner's sudden decision to seek a move away from St Saviour's might be her strategy to avoid working with him at management level next year. But Fingleton would never have risked appointing him to the senior team if he'd thought there was the risk that she would leave the school as a direct consequence. She may even have told the head previously that she intended to leave. He thought of the red light outside the head's office after the Christmas lunch. It had remained on for half an hour. Perhaps, rather than tearfully seeking the head's sympathy after her embarrassment, Toner had informed him, in no uncertain terms, that the time had come for her to leave St Saviour's.

"I then discussed with them my recommendation that you join the management team from the start of the next academic year. They were also happy to ratify that promotion. There will, of course, be no reference to that when I make the official statement this afternoon to the staff."

This was the way Fingleton liked to work. It was generally accepted by staff that they were given information about any important school matter on a need-to-know basis. It troubled Biggsy being the main protagonist in this latest episode of management secrecy, trivial as the matter might seem to be for the head.

****

"I hope they let us in. You look significantly shadier in civvies than I'd expected."

The students had been told to look respectable for their evening trip to the West End. Arctic weather had gripped the capital for the past three days, conditions that militated against the smart/casual dress code stipulated for the theatre trip. He studied the group clothed in furry parkas, luminous puffer jackets and bulky sheepskin coats. Colley, who'd already annoyed him by turning up ten minutes' late at Osterley tube station, was wearing Scandinavian winter headgear, complete with dangling woolly plaits.

After handing out the tickets he'd collected from the box office, he consulted Bridget, the teacher with whom he shared the teaching of the upper-sixth Literature group.

"I'll sit at one end of the row of boys, and you sit at the other. It'll be easier to keep an eye on them if we pen them in. We may have to split up at the interval, one of us staying with those who are happy to remain in their seats and the other tailing those going off for comfort breaks and refreshments."

He recalled the joyless task of completing the health and safety forms. The logic of taking every possible precaution when supervising boys off-site was understandable, but he rued the consequence of fewer and fewer out-of-school activities being organised at St Saviour's. Yet another admin layer was too much of a discouragement for some colleagues.

"Do we really need to bother about that kind of thing with sixth-formers?" Bridget asked.

"Don't you believe it! Years ago, I accompanied an A-level group up town and two of them disappeared at the break. They took themselves off to the shadier evening haunts of the West End and eventually arrived home, totally inebriated, in the early hours. I hasten to add that I wasn't in charge of that trip."

"Point taken."

"Listen, guys. This production of *King Lear* is a sell-out, so we're privileged to be here. Try to forget that we've been studying the play word by word and view it simply as a piece of theatre, not a study text."

Richard Dixon and Ian Padfield exchanged dubious looks.

"If you've all got your chocolate and liquorice allsorts, we'll go and find our seats."

The two teachers followed the party upstairs to the balcony. Nobody would be offered any opportunity for absconding at this early stage.

The thick red stair carpet deadened the sound of footfalls as they ascended. Old timbers beneath their feet creaked politely. A lean and officious university undergraduate directed them to their row of seats. Biggsy noticed the young man's black trousers were frayed at both heels as he scooted off back to his post. Jermaine Gibson, in the seat next to his, looked up and smiled as he lowered his teacher's seat.

"I've brought some matchsticks, sir, if you have trouble staying awake."

"It may be a long play, Jermaine, but I'm up to it, despite my advancing years."

The seating wasn't that uncomfortable, with just enough legroom for him. Whenever he took a seat on a flight, in the cinema or at the theatre, he was grateful that he was of only medium height. Long-legged theatre buffs, male and female alike, must suffer terribly. He made minor adjustments to the position of his legs and elbows then placed his coat over his knees. Beginning to feel warmer here at the top of the auditorium, he was now ready to relax into the performance.

With time to scan the stage and audience before the curtain rose, he became unsettled as he concentrated on the row of students directly in front of him. Teenage girls occupied every seat. He glanced along his line to discover that his charges were way ahead of him. Colley was offering a jelly baby to a girl with long blonde hair. She put an index finger to her lips before refusing with a coy smile and turning back to face the stage. The girl beside her leaned over and whispered in her friend's ear. The two looked at each other and then down into their laps. He winced.

Voluptuous sirens represented the most serious distraction possible on occasions such as this. Crossing his fingers, he hoped that his boys would be able to devote a modicum of attention to the play over the next three hours.

****

Checking that the padlock key was in the pocket of his shorts and not still in the locker, he made his way downstairs. This was his first time at the gym on his own as Myra had an appointment with her hairdresser. He took several feet of paper towel off the roll provided in the gym, in anticipation of breaking out into a sweat.

Having made a speedy exit straight after the school buzzer, he'd arrived at the gym before the evening rush. His preference was to start each session with twenty minutes on a treadmill machine. Turning into the aerobics area, he was pleased to see that only one of the six machines available was in use. He took the spot furthest away from the young man whose emaciated frame suggested that he ran marathon distances daily. Getting fit surely shouldn't be taken to such extremes.

He studied his reflection in the wall mirror facing him. By contrast with the youth loping easily on his merry way three machines away, he looked gargantuan. Alarmed at the sight of his muscle-free physique, he took consolation in the fact that, late in life as it was, he had signed up to arrest further physical deterioration. All he had to do now was visit Platinum Fitness regularly.

Programming completed, he set off at an easy trot. Watching the calorie counter clock up the energy he was expending spurred him on. In truth, he considered jogging to be an enjoyable pastime. He regularly found himself thinking through school problems, quite forgetting that he was exercising. Professional cares seemed less pressing when his body was aerobically engaged. He'd been told to expect the sensation of floating over the revolving rubber mat beneath his feet in the course of time. That would probably take several months to achieve. But no worry. Jogging on rubber was not only less stressful to knee and ankle joints, he'd been advised, but also an alternative means of relieving emotional stress. He had a way to go to reach that state.

"Looking good. Didn't know you'd signed up for this year's London Marathon."

He turned to see Croxteth Steve taking up position on the treadmill alongside him.

"That's something that'll never happen, Steve," he replied, trying for the first time to talk whilst running. "If I can get along with this, I'll be pleased."

"You're off to a good start, anyway, because you've got a good running action."

"I imagine you clock up hours on here by the look of you," he replied, returning the compliment.

"I do a fair bit. Don't want to risk having chicken legs like the top-heavy meatheads here."

"I think I've got hippo legs."

"No, you're doing fine. Good pronation by the looks of you. You'll be surprised how quickly you'll pick up speed and distance if you stick at it."

"Never heard of pronation. What does it mean?"

"Just a running term for the slight inward movement of your foot as it rolls to absorb impact. Yours looks spot on, but you may need to get yourself a better pair of trainers than those old things if you're going to be a regular at this."

"Thanks for the technical advice. I struck lucky meeting you here."

"No problem. Right, better get started."

Steve switched on his MP3, inserted his headphones, and entered the desired treadmill settings. He was soon jogging along at almost twice the speed of the machine next to him.

Biggsy wondered what type of music he would listen to if he had an MP3. He made a point of googling 'pronation' when he got home.

******

81

"Every subject area will have responsibility for organising a programme of extra-curricular GCSE revision sessions for the second half of the Spring Term."

Toner's statement at the Monday morning staff meeting held the attention of every teacher present. All eyes were fixed on her, standing at the lectern before them. Quizzical expressions replaced the customary bored indifference of those readjusting to professional responsibilities after their weekend respite.

"This is gonna hurt," whispered Andy to his department head.

Where he might have responded three months earlier with a knowing nod and chuckle, now he didn't react. If Andy were in charge of the department, it would be his responsibility to implement all the unpopular management diktats, the worst part of the job. Although he didn't relish the prospect of his second taking charge of English, he felt that Andy should start paying penance for the damage he'd caused to their relationship.

Fingleton had taken him aside and confided that the applications to date for the post of head of English were not promising. There were no external applicants he was prepared to call for interview. As there were no other contenders from within the department, it looked as though the head would have no alternative but to appoint the candidate he'd previously considered to be unfit for the job. The prospect of undeserved good fortune brought on a wry smile.

Misinterpreting his boss's change of expression, Andy continued.

"She's back on form, mate. She loves dishing out extra work to keep us all under the cosh."

"Please discuss this initiative at your next faculty meetings. I'll email a pro forma to all subject heads, outlining details to be entered of those sessions departments agree to implement. Please ensure that this document is completed and returned to me by the end of the week. I do understand the additional burden we're putting on everybody's workload, but we must do everything we can to boost our boys' examination results. Thank you."

She wouldn't have added her thanks last term, he told himself.

He looked along the row at the other members of the English department. Varying degrees of consternation were written on their faces at this latest news. Beth's Mona-Lisa expression betrayed nothing. She seemed as aloof from the tribulations of teaching as ever. Sarah pouted in annoyance. He understood she'd be feeling offended that anyone should think her students were not already being prepared to the nth degree for examination.

There were already mutterings from the staff as Fingleton closed the meeting. Biggsy understood, along with everybody else present, why this latest request was unpopular. School leadership teams still relied heavily on goodwill when it came to imposing additional responsibilities. However, the issue of mounting teacher workload, a constant professional grievance over the three decades he'd been teaching, had seen a decline in teachers' willingness to burden themselves with further 'voluntary' duties. Trust in the DfE had broken down. The causes, too numerous now for most managers in schools to remember, included: the imposition of the heavily prescriptive national curriculum, masquerading as an 'entitlement curriculum'; the perceived insult of 1,265 hours directed time per year; 'Baker Days'; school playing fields being sold off to raise funds for educational essentials; and the paper mountains Ofsted inspections generated.

He reflected on times past when inter-school sport had been a regular feature of children's state-school experience. He'd been one of those who'd volunteered to train and supervise cricket, football, and rugby teams in the early years of his career. Those days of after-school and Saturday morning competitive sport were now long gone in all but a very few state schools.

In his opinion, teaching itself now seemed more akin to training, the focus on pupils learning key points taking precedence over reflection and independent learning. He and his department were subject to the most stringent controls on what was expected of them in the classroom, but they were not provided with the necessary materials to do this job. Hence, the maverick decision to open an English tuck shop to buy essential textbooks. Hypocrisy figured strongly in the way state schools were funded and run. But central government was in the enviable position of being blameless, whatever the colour of government, because school failings had to be the responsibility of local government.

He walked to the staff room, his spirits low, telling himself that his days as a teacher were numbered. An educational imposter, he was complicit in the crime of cheating children of an authentic education. Another voice told him that he had a family to support and should not jeopardise their financial wellbeing.

"By the way, mate," came a voice behind him, "I'm being interviewed next week. Can you spare an hour before then to give me a few pointers? I need to make sure I don't fluff my lines."

****

83

Noah Mintern and Tony Tranter, sitting beside each other on the far side of the room, were not having a good lesson. Whilst the rest of the class were beavering away at the written work he'd set, the two boys were thrusting elbows at each other. He walked in their direction. They stopped arm wrestling as soon as they realised they'd attracted the teacher's attention and carried on with their work. Disciplinary action had been pre-empted.

Standing behind the two boys, he looked down to see what progress each had made. Before focusing his gaze on their books, he noticed a dark mark on the back of Tony's neck. It looked to be what his mother had referred to in his childhood as a 'tide mark'.

He recalled the importance she'd always attached to personal hygiene. High on her list of maternal priorities was the requirement that her son wash himself thoroughly twice a day, before breakfast and going to bed. Even if it weren't a bath night, he'd be expected to scrub his armpits and neck, as well as face and hands. She'd make a point of inspecting his neck for the fabled 'tide mark', a clear indication of gross uncleanliness. The origin of the strange term was never explained. They didn't live close to the sea, so he assumed there was no possibility, anyway, of him ever becoming a victim of the condition. Regular reminders were issued that, if hygiene standards were allowed to slip, he would end up looking like one of the Newman urchins a few doors away. That warning kept him on his toes throughout childhood. Myra had once informed him that his clean habits had been an important factor in her decision to accept him as a lifelong mate.

Tony had been the culprit when Noah's fountain pen had gone missing the previous term. Fortunately, the plan hatched to get the boy to return the stolen item without the risk of him falling under suspicion of being a thief had been successful. Tony had kept his nose clean since that incident, although he'd not been so particular, it seemed, about his neck. A closer look revealed that the collar of his white shirt was also grubby.

His mother's awareness of the effects of child neglect had stayed with him, but he hadn't inherited her labelling tendency. The Newmans had been the scruffiest and dirtiest children in the street, but they were harmless and good-natured, like their parents. Mr and Mrs Newman, bedraggled in appearance and oblivious to the true nature of the squalor in which they were raising their four children, knew no better. Some had said it was criminal they'd been allowed to procreate.

Child neglect had proved to be a less straightforward concept for him once he'd started teaching. He believed, for example, that parents who allowed their children to watch hour after hour of television were unwittingly guilty of the crime. The worst case of neglect he'd known involved a boy at the onset of puberty who came to school smelling of excrement. He sat alone in the corner of the classroom, friendless and taciturn. When social services were alerted to the case, they visited his home, the source of the offensive smell. The parents, both unemployed and the owners of half a dozen dogs, were as foul-smelling as their son. On being presented with evidence that they were guilty of child neglect, they were bewildered. This experience forced Biggsy to discard his assumption that all adults must be conscious of their actions when negligent of their children's general good health.

Trained to be aware of changing circumstances in the behaviour, appearance and general demeanour of children, he was concerned. Tony had been growing increasingly sullen since the start of the spring term. He was also showing signs of becoming unmanageable with certain members of staff who lacked a sympathetic disposition towards children. Problems in the child's home life could be the cause. Any one of myriad possible parental problems from drug addiction to divorce would have a profoundly unsettling effect on a child.

Other than his responsibility of being in loco parentis for every boy he taught, he liked Tony and was worried for him. The thought occurred of keeping the child behind after the lesson and questioning him, but he decided against this course. Archie Matthews, who had responsibility for safeguarding, would be the first person to approach. His patient manner with children would get to the root of any troubling domestic issues. A visit to his office, as soon as possible, was in order.

****

Myra was stretched full length on the sofa, gripping a mug of tea to her chest. He sensed all was not well: she hadn't even taken off her anorak. He leaned down and kissed her on the cheek.

"You OK, love?"

"Nothing wrong with me. But my line manager could do with a poke in the eye with a blunt stick. You should see the new performance targets we've got to meet. They're impossible."

"Oh, bugger!" her husband sympathised. "Surplus management personnel trying to justify their existence again?"

Although performance targets were now all the rage in the public sector, there was a flaw in their application. Those fortunate enough to meet them, in any walk of life, would find themselves burdened with even stiffer targets year on year. He was reaching the point where the performance bar had been raised to a point, in his particular role at St Saviour's, that was unattainable. Faced with the impossible, one could either fail, but retain a degree of sanity, or succeed until professional burnout took its inevitable toll. He had no intention of becoming such a casualty.

Myra took a deep breath, pouted expansively and began speaking with eyes closed.

"I'm sure Doreen is a wonderful wife and mother, but at work she's an arsehole. She gives everyone earache, except her favourites who get away with murder."

"Yes, I'm sure bureaucracy's a great thing in the right hands. Unfortunately, it's often in the hands of jobsworths."

"She was lording it over Eileen today, who's a lovely woman. Keeps herself to herself. Gave her a right mouthful in front of all the girls. Eileen went home in tears."

"That's terrible. Sounds like an example of 'Stenders Impulse."

"And what, may I ask, is the 'Stenders Impulse?" Myra asked.

"You can be excused for not knowing because you don't watch soaps. I'm referring to the emotional reflex of creating high drama out of sweet FA and I'm not talking football. I'm sure one's promotion chances these days are enhanced immeasurably if one has the temperament of a bullying shit."

Did he believe what he was saying or thinking? He'd read of the workplace phenomenon of women holding themselves back from career advancement out of fear of being disliked. Perhaps things were changing in that respect if Doreen and Toner were anything to go by. Possibly a good thing too in terms of female equality. The thought occurred that his daughter might one day lack the confidence to promote herself in her chosen career. But what sane person nowadays would want to climb the greasy pole? This twenty-first-century career quandary was insoluble. He blocked any further confusion in his thinking by reassuring himself that Ella could never become a Toner.

"Oh, I see. Another of your oblique television references."

"It's not oblique to me. I've always made my feelings clear about the programme. Why give characters lines reflecting any degree of emotional intelligence to deliver if it's more entertaining to see them spitting a volley of verbal vitriol or punching somebody's lights out?"

"That's a bit extreme, love. Have you had a bad day too?"

"Let's just say that my educational perspective is diametrically opposed to that of the Deputy Head Curriculum."

"Right. I guess another storyline about she-who-must-not-be-named is coming up."

He knew well enough to limit his criticism this evening. Myra's workaday problems must not play second fiddle to his grievances.

"I've got to organise a departmental programme of voluntary after-school and Saturday morning GCSE revision sessions, to start after half-term. As is customary these days with top-down information about teachers' additional responsibilities, management's use of the word 'voluntary' is euphemistic."

"I suppose she's only protecting her back. You have to consider that her position in the school is dependent upon continuing academic success."

"By that token, you should be more sympathetic to Doreen's situation. The trouble is, she and Toner really seem to enjoy the browbeating aspect of their jobs. I'll bet a pound to a penny they were the playground bullies when they were schoolchildren."

"Well, good luck with that one, love. Don't pencil yourself in for any Saturday morning slots though, because that's when you do our weekly Sainsbury's shop."

"Oh no! I'd forgotten that."

Myra's thinking was rarely short of stiletto sharp.

****

"Thanks for this, mate. I know you're busy."

The term of familiarity had become an irritant. He no longer felt he merited the appellation and didn't consider Andy to be a 'mate'. Nobody in the department, to his knowledge, was aware of any change in his attitude. That must remain the case. The professional axis the two of them had forged should never be perceived as anything but unbreakable.

They sat side by side in easy chairs. Biggsy thought about switching on the light to dispel the gloom but didn't bother.

"I don't think anyone will ask anything in the interview that'll take you by surprise. You know as much about the running of the department as anyone. The same applies to the latest DfE initiatives. You've got all that covered."

"Thanks for the reassurance."

"You'll have to suggest new directions for the department so that you come across to the governors present as a leader with vision. Mind you, what chance vision in these educationally prescriptive times!"

"A fair point. Do you think Fingleton will have said anything to them beforehand to stymie my chances of getting the job? You know…the end of last term?"

"Wouldn't have thought so. I don't think he'd dare. He knows how difficult it is to get capable middle managers these days. Apparently, there isn't too much material out there with genuine leadership qualities."

His use of the derogatory term 'material' was intentional.

"No. He wouldn't want to cut off his nose to spite his face. The main problem for you, I suppose, will be trying to sound excited about all the crap going on here that drives us insane. Assessment procedures, lesson observation programmes, differentiation by task."

"I see what you mean."

"I think that last one, something we've not been keen on, is an area that may well come up. You might be able to seal the Faustian pact by expounding ad nauseam on that topic."

"Don't fancy that, but I see where you're coming from. I'll try to put some ideas together."

"I suppose it would be worth giving assessment a battering too. Parents and governors love tests. The media has brainwashed the nation into believing it's the raison d'être for state schools' existence."

"I can see I'll have to resign myself to being a hypocrite for an hour."

Perhaps longer than that, Biggsy thought, reflecting on the misgivings he was experiencing about his own career.

"Yes, an hour of torment is the price you'll have to pay to land the big one. To get anywhere in teaching nowadays, you learn to 'smile, and smile, and be a villain' as the Danish prince says."

"Strange isn't it, that teaching has become such a duplicitous business. Officially we espouse all the educational psychobabble we're supposed to believe but, privately, we're constantly working against it."

There was a moment's silence whilst the two assessed their roles as fifth columnists within St Saviour's. In the department head's case, he felt his days of outlawry had taken their toll on him.

"What if I'm asked about departmental funding?" Andy asked. "They may try to test my loyalty – find out if I have any grievances about our faculty allocation."

"Best to give short shrift to any discussion of that sort if it comes up. And, if I were you, say you had no involvement in the setting up of the tuck shop. We've not made ourselves popular by organising that little sideline. It's likely to be shut down soon by management, anyway."

"How do you mean – shut down?"

"I've a feeling in my water that we'll be undone by the jealousy of other departments. I can see their point, I suppose. Sarah and I started out thinking that we'd only get away with this money-spinner for a couple of months."

"That's a shame. Still, the department's done well so far. Every GCSE student will soon have a copy of the syllabus text. No sharing anymore."

"Yes. No mean feat as they're the most expensive books we have to buy. Anyway, let's spend half an hour going through the English handbook to see what else needs firming up for your interview."

****

Chapter 6

Benito, bubbling with bonhomie, showed them to their favourite table in a cosy corner of the restaurant.

"You choose a bad night to come out," their diminutive host laughed as he took their wet coats. "This rain is weather like we never see in Italy."

"I don't know how you put up with it, Benito," Myra said, shivering. "It's lovely and warm in here, though."

"The main thing is it's Friday night," Biggsy said, pulling Myra's chair back for her. "For a few hours, we can relax."

The thought of this evening treat with his wife had made this last, most tiring, day of the school week bearable. Throughout the day, he'd anticipated the welcoming atmosphere of subdued lighting, the aroma of garlic, flickering candles, and sweet-smelling sprays of freesias on red starched tablecloths.

"We don't do this nearly often enough, love. The way things are at the hospital these days, I could come here every night. It's the perfect way to relax."

"True but coming here that often would be the perfect way to go bankrupt," he replied, perusing the menu. "Now, will I be able to resist the spaghetti carbonara?"

"Before you concentrate on your stomach, have you noticed what earrings I'm wearing?"

Not wanting to be caught out, he quickly looked up. Small red stones in silver settings. *Garnets or rubies,* he thought. Myra waited, impressed that he'd interrupted his study of the menu. Just as she was growing irritated at her husband's complete lack of jewellery-awareness, he surprised her.

"The anniversary arm-and-a-leg ruby earrings I bought you two years ago. They look lovely, darling. Weren't expecting that, were you?"

"And I was only telling the postie this morning you didn't have a romantic bone in your body. How wrong could I have been!"

"He must know more about our love life than your mother. Seriously, you really do look fabulous, as ever."

"I suppose that'll have to do."

"May I take your drinks order?" Benito asked, returning to their table.

"Yes, please. What are we drinking tonight then? I think we'll splash out and have a bottle of the house red."

"Very good, sir."

With a flick of pen on pad and a polite bow, the waiter bustled off.

"By the way, Andy's going to get the head of English job. There's no competition. Fingleton'll have no choice."

"So, that's your idea of an affectionate opener for our first evening out together since well before last Christmas, is it? Please, can we have one meal out where you don't bore me to death with school stuff?"

"Just thought I'd put you in the picture. Get it out of the way early, so to speak."

"Do you ever think of anything else besides that bloody place? Does it ever occur to you that, on certain special occasions, I don't want to know the latest from St Saviour's?"

"Sorry, love. Matter closed."

"What I do want to talk to you about is where you plan to take me for our summer holiday," she purred, softening in a moment.

Taken aback at the speed with which she was able to change tack, he worked at adjusting his brain to summer mode.

"You know that's your domain, Myra. Wherever you choose to go, I'm up and ready to follow."

"I've got ideas of my own, but I'd like a little input from you for a change. It's not just me I'm thinking about for a holiday, you need to switch off from that damned school at least once a year or you'll crack up."

She was right, of course. His career consumed him. He was grateful that his wife wasn't also a teacher, or their marriage would have been at risk. She was the outsider, in terms of all things educational, that he needed to survive. He put out a hand across the table and placed it over hers.

"Greece gets my vote. An island or the mainland. Don't mind which."

"Blimey, I could almost believe you'd thought that one through. As it happens, Greece was top of my list. We've never been to Athens. From there, we could cruise the capital, take in a tour, and do a spot of island hopping."

He was interested. Delphi could be incorporated into a tour programme. Whilst in his first year at university, he'd been fired up with the idea of spending the summer holiday travelling around Greece, with the express intention of seeking out the site of the Delphic oracle. An idea it had remained. The practicalities of supporting himself had meant finding paid employment instead of doing the tour. Joining a student acquaintance who'd found labouring work, he'd spent the summer months in Kingston digging out a cellar in a sprawling detached property belonging to a film actor. The celebrity had been well known for playing plummy-voiced politicians from a public school background. The work hadn't been fun, but his body had never been in better shape.

"Sounds exciting. Any chance we could do a trip inland and visit Delphi? Always had a fancy to go there. The site of Apollo's temple is halfway up a mountain. The whole complex there is supposed to be amazing."

"Why not?" Myra replied, seizing on her husband's sudden animation. "Wherever we go, I'd like to think there'd be itinerary input from both of us, not just me as is normally the case."

"No problem there, then. This sounds exciting. Let's raise a toast to adventures in Greece."

Myra made no pretence of trying to conceal an expression of relief as she chinked glasses.

"Well, that was painless. Thought I was going to have a battle on there. So, what has Andy done to deserve getting your job?"

****

The temporary spell of calm was broken. It had been a blustery day, one guaranteed to make the boys excitable. Classroom control had been more difficult than usual, and his throat felt sore. Being alone in the English office, marking a pile of books after school in total silence, was a welcome relief.

A light tapping on the door was followed by the entry of Archie Matthews. He wore the expression of one reluctantly delivering unwelcome information as he stood hunch-shouldered in the open doorway.

"I'm sorry to interrupt you, Biggsy, but I've been sent on an errand by the headmaster."

"Hello, Archie. Come in and sit down. I think I can guess the purpose of your visit."

Matthews seated himself, extended his legs and began scratching the back of his neck.

"If that's the case, I don't feel quite so bad about bringing the bad news. I've been told to let you know there's been a complaint about your tuck shop from another department."

Although the message wasn't unexpected, he was surprised that Archie Matthews, the deputy head pastoral, had been earmarked to deliver it. A look of apology was fixed on his face, indicating how unhappy he was about this latest task he'd been assigned. Biggsy knew that an unavoidable confrontation with Fingleton was in the offing.

This first shot across the English department's commercial bows meant that the tuck shop could, perhaps, continue for another week or so before closure. During this period, the department might have time to make enough to buy another set of books.

He tried his best to look dismayed.

"Really, Archie?" he laughed softly. "Where did the complaint come from?"

"Can't tell you that, but you may be able to guess if I say that the department in question is concerned about the health aspect of children eating sweets. Various arguments were put to the head, such as extra sugar being no good for children's teeth and making some of them hyper during afternoon lessons. He took the view that they were justified."

"No mention of jealousy that we're making enough money to equip our students with basic reading material?"

"Funnily enough, that objection didn't get a mention."

The science department's stated complaints weren't unreasonable. The health aspect was the one game changer he'd envisaged. But he knew the real motive: jealousy. Nobody had said anything to his face, but there had been mutterings abroad. It had taken a full half-term for the opposition to organise itself. It would be best to put up token resistance, he decided, before accepting defeat.

"As it happens, the snacks the department sells are mainly health foods, with minimal sugar content. But let's not waste time on that score. There were no complaints about the liquid fizzies available from the soft drinks' machines in the dining hall as well, I suppose. There are also E-numbers aplenty in most of those."

He knew his rebuttals were futile, but he felt compelled to air them.

"I'll pass the word on about that, mate, but the writing's on the wall. The head has no real problem himself with your venture, but he can't make a stand on this one against the rest of the staff."

"Our customers won't be happy. It's so much easier for them to get their nibbles at school, rather than having to queue up after school at the corner shop down the road."

"Fair point, but I suppose schools aren't corner shops, are they?"

Biggsy grinned at the retort but was a little disappointed that Archie was warming to his task.

"We've a department meeting coming up. I'll let everyone know about the rest of the staff's sweety concerns and report back to the head, if that's fine with you?"

"Fine by me. Sorry to be the bearer of bad tidings. Nothing personal, you know that."

"Of course, Archie. It's just business."

****

"My English teacher's crap, sir. You're much better than him."

Him? Had to be Andy or Nick. More likely to be Nick as Andy was Mr Popularity with the students at St Saviour's.

"Sorry, I don't know your name?"

This was one of the problems with revision sessions for groups of students on the C/D grade borderline for GCSE English. Subject teachers who'd 'volunteered' for the extra-curricular programme found themselves teaching boys they'd never met before. With reams of helpful worksheets to flog through, there was limited time to get to know this moody brood, who'd rather be spending their Saturday morning salivating at displays of the latest trainers in the local mall.

Somebody would always try to employ this work-evasion chestnut. He'd learnt, however, that receipt of such an accolade should be met with caution. Being nominated a favoured teacher offered the inexperienced member of staff, momentarily overcome with apparent praise, the opportunity to take the bait and make unguarded comments about colleagues. Older children with a mischievous bent found this game endlessly entertaining. He wondered when this teacher-dissing tendency had started. The choicest terms were used to denigrate colleagues, colourful language and television soap epithets issuing from adolescents' mouths as though the practice were a school norm.

Perhaps the fault was in him. His pedagogical style was firm but fair, as recommended by most professionals, even those with half a brain, and he was a keen advocate of open expression amongst the young. The approach of fairness was beset with issues, the most important of which was that most teenagers are not equipped with the linguistic nuances to express controversial opinions with a measure of decorum. Thus, the acceptable and preferred statement, 'I consider you to be a slightly more skilled exponent of language teaching than my current teacher who, for the moment, shall remain nameless,' became a character assassination of monumental proportions: 'My teacher's crap!' And all with a smile thrown in. Such was a liberal teacher's life. He supposed he should accept it as a compliment that this newcomer felt relaxed enough to 'large it', as he had just done.

"Baines, sir. Steven Baines."

"Is that with a 'ph' or a 'v'?"

"A 'v', sir."

"I guessed as much," muttered Biggsy to himself, making a pertinent note on the register Toner had given him.

"Ah, I see from my list that you're one of Mr Devlin's students. I don't imagine he'd be pleased to hear the remark you just made about him. To clarify things for you, Mr Devlin's examination results are consistently on a par with every other member of the English department. Therefore, I consider your opinion not only disrespectful but also inaccurate. I'm sure you'd be a little upset if you were to hear that he described you to every other teacher on the staff as a bad lot."

He looked at Steven to check whether he'd fallen asleep yet. Unfortunately, he was still prepared to stand his ground on the issue.

"I'm just saying that he…"

"No need to say any more, Steven. Mr Devlin believes that, with a bit of fine-tuning, you can achieve the high grade of which you are capable. He deserves your gratitude for the faith he has in you."

"He doesn't like me, though, sir."

"I'm sure that's not true, Steven. We don't have time to dislike the pupils we teach. But one thing is certain, he does like your ability in this subject."

"Give it a rest, Steve! We want to get this over with and get off home," came a cry from the back of the room.

"Fair point, whoever said that. Now, if you'll look at the first sheet I handed out, you'll see a summary of the section in your textbooks that deals with the differences between emotive and objective language. Do you remember what emotive language is, Steven?"

****

"I've received an offer from Southampton, sir."

The first to appear for registration on Monday morning, Jermaine Gibson delivered the news before anybody else had arrived. Students only risked expressions of undisguised delight when there was no threat of sarcastic commentary from envious peers.

"Well done, Jermaine. That's fantastic. What did Mum and Dad say?"

"They're really pleased. Relieved too after me going off the idea of uni for a while last term."

"I can imagine. It's great that you're now determined to continue studying. So many go to university these days thinking that's what they ought to do."

"What grades do you need to get?"

"Two A grades and a B. Just got to get my head down for the next five months. Can't wait."

"I think you've got everything in hand, but, if you need any extra help, let me know."

"Thanks, sir."

"I should soon be finding myself in a situation where I can provide more assistance than you may think. The head boy should hear this news first, straight from the horse's mouth. From next term, I'll be switching to a new role in the school, from head of English to head of sixth form."

Jermaine took one step backwards, raised his eyebrows and grinned.

"Wow, sir! That's amazing. I never imagined you taking over from Mr Wheelhouse."

He fussed over papers on the table, for a moment wondering why he had agreed to accept Fingleton's offer. Jermaine stood before him, awaiting further details.

"Nor did I, but the opportunity came up, and I thought a change of air might be rejuvenating. Keep all this to yourself for now – being head boy should bring its privileges. Nothing's been announced by the head yet."

"When will we all be told?"

"Any day now, I reckon. I'll be relying on you to keep me up to speed with sixth-form mutterings. There'll be so much that I'll be clueless about."

"You won't have any problems, sir. The rest of the students will be really happy to hear this. I'll have trouble holding on to it without spilling the beans. It's brilliant, sir."

"What's brilliant?" Christopher Colley asked, sauntering into the room, Richard Dixon in tow.

"Jermaine's been giving me the good news of his university offer," came the swift reply.

"What offer 'ave you got, mate?" Colley asked.

"The one I wanted from Southampton."

"Result!" Colley exclaimed. "You must be made up. I fancy getting away too but need to be somewhere down this way so that I'm not far from the Bridge. The Blues need me. I'm bankin' on an offer from St Mary's, same as Banger."

"Fingers crossed, Chris. I imagine your rugby prowess alone will make you a certainty for St Mary's, Richard, besides the fantastic supporting statement I wrote for you."

Richard shrugged his shoulders and assumed a clueless expression.

"Hope so, sir," he sighed, now gazing at the ceiling.

"You'll save a fortune in accommodation expenses, too, by living at home while you're studying for a degree."

The words were out before he could check himself. Gibson, desperate to get away from London after coming so close to losing his life following the knifing incident, did not believe he had that option.

"True! We're not all minted, sir. Like I said, the idea of going away to uni appeals, but Chelsea need me," Colley added in a tone of mock melodrama.

The sound of more students arriving for registration ended the conversation. Biggsy plugged in his laptop and switched on, hoping he hadn't unintentionally upset Gibson.

******

A hurried visit to John Vernon's domain was necessary before his lunch duty on the school field. The *Of Mice and Men* support materials for his GCSE class after registration were essential. Arriving at the AVA room, he was relieved to find John alone, finishing a doughnut as he sat before his PC.

"Thank God you're alone, John," he declared in a theatrical tone.

"Just the way I like it."

"Wish I had a job where I could play Space Invaders all day."

John didn't take the bait, remaining hunched over his keyboard and squinting at the screen. A long arm reached out towards the white paper bag on a table to his side and, without interrupting his concentration, he withdrew another doughnut.

"Glad to see you're sticking to your high-carb diet. There's far too much talk of healthy eating nowadays. You need to build yourself up."

John was at least six and a half feet tall, but he'd never been anything other than whippet-thin since starting at the school six years earlier. Those wanting to thank him for a last-minute photocopying run need only provide him with a bag of his favourite iced doughnuts. The requirement was to buy five. On finishing the contents of the bag, he could announce, with total conviction, that he'd had his 'five-a-day', a carbohydrate alternative to the usual fruit and vegetable recommendation for the health-conscious.

"I'm sorry to interrupt your lunch, John, but would you be kind enough to run off thirty stapled copies of these GCSE study notes before the afternoon buzzer?"

He finished his request in a rush, wincing at the audacity of his plea.

"I should have known you were only after one thing. Thought for a minute you'd come to get the benefit of my scintillating personality," John replied in a deflated monotone.

"That's taken as read, John, of course. But I thought you might be able to help me out whilst I was enjoying your colourful repartee."

"See what I can do after I've knocked out a hundred and eighty copies of this letter to parents. I've got to put thirty into each register before the buzzer goes."

"Sounds important. What's it about?"

John squinted at the sheet and then grinned.

"Oh dear. Says here the school's starting a cross-curricular literacy initiative. Looks like you're all volunteering for more hard work. Didn't you know about it?"

Biggsy recalled an email he'd received a week or so ago on the subject from Toner. He'd given it a cursory glance and forgotten about it. You had to give Toner credit: she knew every trick when it came to bumping up a CV. She really was going all out for a headship.

"Bugger! Good job I've got a sense of humour."

"You've not had it easy lately. I see you drew the short straw for your department's Saturday morning revision slots. Didn't you get the chance to delegate that to someone else?"

"You don't miss much. I suppose I could have done, but it was that or the week's supermarket shop. My wife loves to get me in there when it's busiest. Come to think of it, her sense of humour is even sharper than yours. Anyway, we need to get the weekly shop delivered like most sensible people."

"By the way, word is that you may be taking on new responsibilities sometime soon?"

"You're well informed. Don't know which little bird told you, but whatever you have heard may be true. I'm switching from English to heading the sixth form. Mum's the word, though, for the time being. Fingleton will probably make a formal announcement soon."

"Good luck with that one. I'll keep it under my hat."

He had no qualms about one of his favourite people on the school staff knowing about the job switch and wasn't in the least interested in finding out who had given him the information.

****

There was a mark on Tony Tranter's face. One cheek was a vivid red with a bluish hue, and Biggsy wanted to know the cause. It could be the result of a squabble at school or, what he feared, a case of domestic abuse.

"Could I have a quick word with you, Tony, before you go off for your next lesson? Won't keep you a moment."

As the rest of the class filed out, the boy lingered at his table.

"Thanks, Tony. I couldn't help but notice you seem to have been in the wars. What happened to your cheek?"

The boy put a hand straight to his face, fully aware of the blemish to which his teacher was referring.

"Um, I had a fight with another boy, sir. He punched me."

"When did this happen?"

Every teacher knows that, when trying to get the truth out of a minor, a series of quick questions can catch a child off guard. It's much the same technique as that used by the police when questioning suspects. He knew teachers who enjoyed playing the role of an officer of the law trying to winkle information out of a criminal, but he didn't.

"On the way home from school yesterday, sir."

"Well, if you tell me the boy's name or give me a description, I'll find him now and sort this out."

"Oh no, sir. We were only messin' around. It was nuffin'."

"Was he in your year or an older boy?"

"He was older than me, but I don't know him."

"Did you tell your mum and dad about it, Tony?"

Much of what goes on in schools, according to children, is 'nothing'. A teacher becomes suspicious the moment he hears utterance of that word from a pupil. The other student cliché that is overlooked at professionals' peril is 'We were just messing around.' He'd witnessed all kinds of facial disfigurements and body damage that had been dismissed by juvenile casualties as a consequence of messing around. Parents didn't know the half of it.

Childhood victims write off various personal mishaps, from stealing to bullying, as 'nuffin'. Most don't want to make a fuss. He thought of Simon Todd who was resigned to suffering. A minority becomes conditioned to accept suffering as an everyday aspect of school life. Tony must not become one of that number.

The boy's eyes welled up. He brushed a hand across them and looked down at his feet.

"My dad doesn't live with us anymore. I didn't tell my mum."

More bells started to ring. He didn't want to probe any further yet, but he had to ascertain one final detail at this stage.

"So, you and your mum are all on your own now?"

"No, Uncle Vince came to live with us," the boy replied, trying to disguise his agitation.

He folded his arms and looked down at his feet.

There was more to be found out about Uncle Vince, but now wasn't the time. Biggsy knew nothing about this man, but he already felt antagonism towards him. Tony was a lightweight for his age, but he had a reputation for being a bit of a rascal who could take care of himself. For the first time in his life, it looked as though the little lad might have met his match. Enquiries would need to be made before this situation got out of hand.

"We'll leave it for now, Tony, but look after yourself. Nobody should be hitting you for any reason whatsoever. It's against the law. If it happens again, come and see me."

"Yes, sir."

A teacher's life is a busy one, a hundred new children's narratives coming one's way daily. None of them can be ignored. Top Tip No. 9: If a student replies, "It's nothing," to the question "What's wrong?" then it's something.

****

Despite the absence of any proof, he visualised Tony receiving a painful blow to the head from Uncle Vince. The little boy's plight would have to be dealt with immediately. He was certain the child had become a victim of physical and, more than likely, emotional abuse. Standing outside the office of Archie Matthews, the pastoral deputy head, he put his ear to the door. Archie was on the phone. He decided to wait until the call ended before knocking.

As the deputy head was also the school's Safeguarding Lead, he dealt with cases of child abuse, a responsibility that required discretion and tact. Biggsy's anger at the violence to which Tony was probably being subjected was such that he wanted swift intervention to put an immediate end to the boy's suffering. But he realised that nothing could be done until social services were certain of the claims of cruelty he was about to make.

Hearing the phone being replaced on its base, he knocked. The green light illuminated. Archie spent a great deal of his time taking calls when he wasn't dealing with visitors to his office. He was the most patient of men when dealing with child protection matters.

"Morning. You're lucky to get me. I've just come off the line after a very lengthy call."

"That's fortunate, Archie. I've come directly to see you because I'm concerned about one of my pupils in year seven."

"I see. I'll put the red light up again outside. This could take a while."

"Thanks. Tony Tranter, you may know him, has already developed a reputation as a bit of a scallywag, but he's essentially a good sort. Anyway, I noticed discoloration on his face this morning and questioned him about it after the lesson. He says he had a fight with an older boy, but I think otherwise."

Archie leaned back in his chair and reached into a drawer at the side of his desk. He took out a wad of papers, laid them out before him and smoothed them flat.

"What do you suspect?"

"When I questioned him about the mark, he clammed up. In my opinion, he plucked answers out of the air that he thought I'd accept. He referred to an older boy hitting him. Said it was somebody he'd never seen before and didn't seem at all sure when or where the supposed fight took place."

"Is this the first time you've seen him with an injury of this sort?"

"Yes, but he's been looking more dishevelled and grubbier lately. He let slip that his father has left home, and his mum has taken in an 'Uncle Vince'. When he gave me that name, he looked anxious. What with cases I've read about in the press, where stepdads and boyfriends inflict violence on the children of new partners, I want to be sure that Tony gets protection, if he needs it."

"Have you noticed any changes in his general demeanour recently?"

"More withdrawn, most definitely, over the last few weeks. Something's burst his bubble. I'm genuinely worried."

"Quite so. I think in all the time I've been doing this job, this is the first time you've ever come to me with such an issue. It must be serious. I'm glad you've reported it straight away because the boy will still be marked, and we can get school welfare on to it. We don't want to alarm him, but we need to come up with a pretext to get him examined. He's unlikely to come out with the true cause of his injury but, ideally, we need a photograph to get us started. There are so many protocols to follow in these situations."

"How long before we see any real progress as regards getting Tony protection from his 'uncle'?"

"The problem is that, without a disclosure from Tony, any action will be delayed. We'll need to monitor him closely. Could be talking about weeks in the worst case."

"That's a concern."

"Social services will be alerted the moment we have the evidence we need. They can't risk making accusations that can't be substantiated."

"I guessed it wouldn't be easy."

"If you'll bear with me, I'll need to get all the details from you down on paper. Then we can consider the possibility of arranging a welfare visit."

****

There it was, at long last, on the staffroom notice board. A signed letter from Fingleton on school-headed paper pinned prominently in the 'Headmaster's Notices' section. There was a brief paragraph explaining that he was pleased to announce that Mr Biggs would be taking on the role of sixth-form head, with effect from Monday, May 2nd. As expected, no mention was made of the promise of promotion to the leadership team the following September. Deceit or caution on the head's part? It didn't matter now. If anyone asked him about a salary increase, he'd play dumb. The only person who would dare ask him would be Barker, the head of PE.

The only other person in the staff room at this early hour was Helen Staddon, head of modern languages. She gave him a minute to read the posting before commenting.

"I would never have imagined you taking on a pastoral role in the school," she called out to him.

"Desperate times, Helen," he joked. "The head asked me to do the school a favour, so there it is. For how long, I'm not sure."

"Other irons in the fire?" she asked.

"I don't know about that, but I'm open-minded about the change. This job could turn out to offer exciting new challenges that keep me going for years. If it doesn't, then I'll reassess."

"You sound a little uncertain, if you don't mind me saying so."

"Not a problem, Helen. At this stage in my life, I'm no more certain about anything career-wise than I was thirty years ago. I still haven't ruled out a media job in animation before I pop my clogs."

"That's about as far away from teaching as one could imagine," she smiled. "How on earth did you end up in the classroom?"

"Why does anyone do anything in life?"

"Well, I'm impressed at how relaxed you are about everything."

"Don't be fooled. I'm never relaxed about work, however much I might give that impression."

"Morning, folks!" Chris Barker greeted, bustling through the door. "Hope I'm interrupting."

Throwing his kit bag on the floor, Chris removed his heavy jacket, hung it over the back of a chair and made a beeline for the kitchen.

"Hope you put plenty of water in the kettle, mate. What are you two hatching then?"

"We were just discussing the head's latest appointment," Helen answered.

"Oh yeah. What's that then?"

He looked a question from one to the other. Raising his eyebrows, Biggsy jerked his head in the direction of the noticeboard. His curiosity aroused, Barker interrupted the tea preparations to take a look. As he read, he began to smirk with pleasure.

"It's not April the first, is it? You must be kidding, mate. Have you suffered a bang on the head?"

"I'm sure I don't know what you mean," the answer came. There was no chance he'd allow the head of PE to wind him up on this occasion.

"How the hell did you let yourself walk into that one?" he laughed aloud.

"You're only jealous you didn't come into the reckoning?"

"You've gotta be joking! Have you noticed what effect the job's had on Wheelhouse? And who's going to get yours? Andy? Could be a problem there."

Realising that the conversation had descended into testosterone sparring, Helen lost interest in the two men and returned to her marking.

Male teachers could be just as immature as mischievous children when it came to 'just messing around'. Noting Helen's withdrawal from further involvement in the frank exchange of views, Biggsy decided that it was also time for him to disappear.

"If you're going to descend to making disparaging comments about Andy, I'll be off. See you both later."

He shot a smile at Barker that could be interpreted as playful and left.

He couldn't give the head of PE a serious response to the questions he'd posed with such sarcasm: they were all questions he was asking himself.

****

Chapter 7

Pat Jenkins, the school nurse, never had a quiet day. Any member of staff calling in at welfare would find her in the company of a large group of boys, usually younger ones. Most would have been placed in her 'waiting' room by teachers. There would be those suffering from headaches, some with stomach upsets, and others with minor grazes causing the most intense pain. She also had her regular clients, malingerers and the work-shy, avoiding lessons or teachers they disliked. No pupil was allowed to turn up at her door without the express permission of a member of staff, but many tried it on independently.

Whilst Pat did her best to cater for those genuinely in need of her welfare expertise, she patiently dealt with those who didn't. Her ability to maintain a level head and calm manner was mythic. When the head of English arrived to speak to her about Tony Tranter, it was business as normal. He waited for her to solve an urgent case of rising damp before announcing his arrival.

"But, miss, my trousers are soaking wet. I can't go to lessons," a tiny boy groaned in a puddle of water.

"And how did they get wet, Bevan? Have you been standing in a bucket of water?"

He recognised the pupil who had been assaulted by Bulmer, the school caretaker sacked the previous term.

"No, I was playing football, miss. It was pouring with rain."

"You know very well you shouldn't be outside in this weather. I've told you before. You'll catch your death."

"We play football every lunchtime, miss."

"Don't I know it! Whatever does your mother say when you get home in this state!"

She instructed the boy to remove his wet trousers behind a curtained partition and wait, whilst she went to a cupboard and rummaged through a box of clothing cast-offs. Finding a pair of voluminous rugby shorts, she held them up by the waistband and gave them a dubious look. They were long enough to double up as a spare pair of trousers for the diminutive footballer.

The temporary solution to the boy's problem in hand, she passed them to Bevan behind the screen.

"Put these on. They'll see you through the afternoon. I'll dry your trousers and you can come back after school to collect them."

"But, miss!" he cried in alarm.

"Now come along, Bevan," she insisted. "I have this pantomime with you every time it rains. Put them on then hurry off to registration. The buzzer will be going soon."

"I can't wear these, miss," he wailed, reappearing for inspection. "They're too long."

To make his point, he emerged from the changing area performing a kind of jig, shifting his weight from one foot to the other. His tiny feet, protruding from the bottoms of the shorts, emphasised his point.

"That's all I can manage, I'm afraid. Anyway, they'll keep you nice and warm during the afternoon. Be sure to see me again straight after school."

"Thanks, miss," Bevan scowled, exiting as slowly as possible.

This was the moment to intervene.

"Hi, Pat. Sorry to bother you when you've got your hands full."

"Hello. You don't need a change of trousers as well, I hope."

"As it happens, I don't. Just popped in to see if there were any developments regarding that case of facial bruising we asked you to investigate?"

She ushered him into her small office space.

"Sorry about that. Yes, I did check him over. I have to admit, Tony must have been struck very hard for that sort of mark to appear. I'd say a blow must have been delivered by an adult rather than a pupil."

"I thought as much. Did he give anything away?"

"No, he said very little. He seemed worried and uncertain when I asked him for information about the injury. Stuck to his story that it was a big boy he didn't know."

"Yes, Uncle Vince must be a big boy all right."

"Archie mentioned that name. I managed to stand behind Tony at one point as I was talking to him. While he sat there quietly, I quickly took out my phone and got a photograph of his profile without him realising. I'll just show you what I managed to get."

She unlocked a filing cabinet, reached for her handbag in the top drawer, pulled out her mobile phone and searched through her gallery. Finding the image, she presented it for inspection.

"What do you think?"

"That's pretty clear, Pat. It does look like a very serious injury from that angle. You've done well there. This is going to be serious. Could you send a copy of the image to Archie?"

"I will, of course. Poor Tony. It's difficult to believe any adult could do that to a child."

"I'm genuinely worried you may be seeing more of the same in the future, unless we can put a stop to it. I'll get back to Archie. This photo will be the first step in nailing Uncle Vince."

****

"This *King Lear* is a bit confusing, sir," Colley complained. "If you ask me, the plot's all over the place. I can't keep track 'alf the time."

The *King Lear* revision session had been progressing without alarm. And now this. Biggsy wondered why this attack on his favourite Shakespeare play had suddenly surfaced. He stood up and walked to the student's table. So far, Colley had seemed to be enjoying it as much as could be expected.

"I thought you'd been enjoying this play, Chris. Can you be more specific as to what you mean by 'all over the place'?"

"Well, now that I've seen the whole play at one sitting up in town, it all seems a bit chaotic, if you know what I mean, sir. There are nutters everywhere. There's the old loony, King Lear, the king's personal loony, the Fool, and the young loony, Edgar. Know what I mean?"

Something was going on. Colley's outburst had the flavour of mischief.

"I sometimes wonder if I've got Shakespeare all wrong, but my mate, Neil Thompson, reckons all of his plays are a bit off the wall. S'pose I just have to accept it."

The penny dropped. An exquisite piece of tangential flannel. Ella's relationship with the lower-sixth former had, at last, become common knowledge. There was no possibility that Neil, a year younger than Colley and an innocent by comparison, could be his 'mate'. Even now, the boy could be coming under immense pressure to tell all about the home life of the head of

107

English. He began to imagine all kinds of lurid gossip about his private life flying around social networking sites. Then again, Colley could be bluffing. Perhaps nobody had approached his daughter's first boyfriend so far, and nothing whatsoever had been revealed to the inquisitive student body.

"Ah, I see now where you're coming from, Chris," he said, leaning forward to give the discomfited student a closer view of his rictus grin and the glittering eyes that now saw everything clearly.

"Just thinking aloud, sir. Could be wrong."

"Your assessment that *King Lear* is full of 'nutters' could possibly be a reflection of the world in general, one that has been the case down through the ages. Just look at the student population of this school. You could also say St Saviour's is full of nutters, and I've got the nutter-in-chief in my English Literature class."

He laughed quietly to himself, shaking his head from side to side.

"You are such a tonic, Chris. I'm laughing because you're genuinely amusing. Whatever you choose to do with your life, make sure you opt for a career working with people, one that enables you to use your wit to best advantage to cheer people up."

Colley turned in his seat and bowed three times to each area of the class behind him.

"You heard that, the rest of you. I'm a tonic."

"Anyway, it may come as a surprise to you all to hear that my daughter also knows young Neil."

"What a coincidence!" Bellchambers called out in mock surprise.

"Yes, isn't it? On a serious note, what worries me about your generation is that you have no privacy. Everything you do is out there for all the world to see, whether you want that or not."

Adopting the viewpoint that Colley had intended no malice by his lesson interruption, he assumed he was simply dealing with a case of a student being playful. He tried to look matter of fact to conceal his genuine fears for the personal privacy of these young men, as well as his own. Securing and maintaining one's own private space in life would be difficult for this new generation.

It also wouldn't do to disclose any anxiety he was experiencing about his daughter's romantic liaisons becoming of interest to the whole sixth-form body, especially as he was about to take up residency with them.

He decided that this unexpected break presented an opportunity to inform the class of his new school role.

"By the way, there's something else that everyone here should know, before anyone else in years twelve and thirteen is informed."

The only person not appearing to pay particular attention to what he was about to say was Gibson. Sitting in the corner, his gaze was taking in every student in the room.

"What's that then, sir?" Padfield asked, alive with curiosity.

"Now seems a good time to tell you that, from next term, I'll be the new head of sixth form."

The surprised class expressed its approval en masse with a mixed chorus of hoots and cheers. Gibson, smiling broadly, turned to look at the teacher and nodded his approval.

"Yes, I thought you'd be upset. I have to say I'm glad I'll be seeing friendly faces every day in the new job. It'll make the move so much easier for me."

"Nice one, sir!" Dixon complimented.

"Now we've wasted too much lesson time and need to get on. Before we start, copy this homework question into your diaries. You've a week to complete the assignment."

Picking up a felt marker, he wrote the essay title on the whiteboard.

The plot of 'King Lear' is all over the place, and the play is full of nutters. Discuss.

As soon as he'd finished writing, he picked up the eraser and wiped the board clean with a single stroke.

"Only joking!" he exclaimed, turning to face the students busily scribbling away.

"Oh, sir! I could've done that," Colley moaned.

****

He'd not yet talked to Sarah about Angela and Nick. If they were romantically linked, he'd seen little evidence. That fact didn't surprise him because, as Myra often pointed out, he would always finish last in the courtship-spotting stakes. Bearing her sentiment in mind, he was unprepared when Angela arrived at the English office after school and requested a confidential chat.

"I'm sorry to interrupt you when you're busy, Biggsy, but I need advice on a personal matter. I've thought long and hard, but I don't really know anybody else I'd be prepared to talk to about it."

This was serious. He'd never been approached by a female colleague before on this basis. He prided himself on being able to think on his feet, but there were certain subjects about which, he'd freely admit, he was ignorant. He'd never seen himself as an agony uncle. Then again, he'd managed to box his way out of the occasional tight corner in delicate conversations with Ella. His stomach muscles tightened.

"I'm gratified to think you have that opinion of me, Angela. Of course, I'll do my best to help in any way I can. Sit yourself down."

Angela sat in the easy chair alongside him and sighed the sigh of one with much on her mind.

"Take your time. There's no hurry."

But she couldn't help herself and, in a rush, provided a summary of her life so far.

"I come from an ordinary background. Dad worked in a shoe factory and Mum was a cleaner. Money was always short at home, and there were regular arguments. I've never got on particularly well with them. I've never confided in my parents, and my father's a bit of a tyrant. I've always found it difficult to make friends."

Taken aback by the flood of information, he did his best to assimilate the details of Angela's past, none of which he would have guessed. But the realisation dawned on him that there was a parallel with his own past: she was struggling against the tendency to be a loner.

"I need some advice, and I thought I'd ask you."

Just as he was trying to imagine the sort of man her father could be, a cross between Alex Ferguson and Attila the Hun, an obvious question dropped into his frontal lobe.

"Before you continue, are you certain a female member of the department wouldn't be more useful to you with what's on your mind?"

The previous term, he'd dealt with the delicate issue of Angela's teenage social-networking stalkers. He'd wondered if the majority of those populating such online sites were misfits and isolates, unable to form attachments outside of their virtual world. That matter had been his responsibility as her line manager. He couldn't help but think that a woman would be a preferable choice as confidant in a matter of the heart.

"I don't really want women knowing about my personal life. I've had unfortunate experiences in that respect. You're the most dependable person I know as regards discretion."

Her compliment brought to mind his Literature group and the brief reference he'd made to them about the absence of privacy in their lives. Angela could be right about him. If that were the case, that quality had landed him in this tight spot. Myra's opinion that he was totally out of his depth in the love stakes was probably an accurate one.

"If you think I could be helpful…"

"The thing is, I had a brother…"

For a second time, he found himself taken by surprise. This wasn't merely a chat about a romance.

"Had?"

She paused, took a breath and continued.

"Richard was two years older than me. He was the odd one out in the family – outgoing and full of energy. He and Dad never got on, but he was Mum's favourite. A real party animal, unlike me."

She laughed to herself as she took out her mobile phone. When she'd accessed what she was searching for, she handed it over.

"This is Richard at sixteen. He was so good-looking."

He took the phone and studied it. The smiling face reminded him of the boy who'd played the adolescent Tadzio in *Death in Venice*. Richard had been strikingly handsome.

"He could have done well at school, but he was too much of a rebel. He got into taking drugs when he was doing his A-levels. He didn't last long in the sixth form. Dad was disgusted and threw him out."

Biggsy sensed where this was going. It was clear that Angela still struggled with the loss of her brother. He wanted to speak, if only to give her a few seconds' relief from her narrative, but couldn't.

"I'd finished my post-grad and was looking for a teaching job when he died. He'd been in a terrible state for a few years. The transformation in him was horrendous. I used to see him from time to time, but nothing I said could make him see sense. Richard dossed down with acquaintances when he could. Didn't have a place of his own. He was found dead from an overdose one morning in the back of a friend's car. It was terrible."

"I can't imagine living through that kind of emotional trauma," he reflected aloud, trying to imagine how he would feel if something that awful happened to Ella.

"Mum blames Dad to this day. I can see why. But Richard always enjoyed living on the edge. I seemed to be constantly fearful for him for as long as I can remember."

"So, this awful event happened not very long ago?"

"Last June. Seems like only last week."

"I could never have imagined you've been going through such distress, Angela. What you're telling me is so difficult to grasp because you seem to have limitless energy and such an appetite for hard work."

"Throwing myself heart and soul into teaching has been wonderful therapy. Being busy helps me to cope with the loss of Richard. And now, I don't know if you're aware, there's Nick. We get on so well, but I don't know if I'm being fair with him. That's why I needed to talk to you."

"What exactly do you mean?"

Angela paused again before disclosing her anxieties. He wondered how he could have been unaware, for so long, of what lay behind her mask of bubbly enthusiasm. A wave of guilt washed over him as he recalled ticking her off for her insouciance when engaging online with students the previous term. He reminded himself that what we think we know about everyone with whom we come into contact is often a fraction of what there is to know.

"We've become closer at school since the start of term, although we haven't actually begun dating or anything. I had no intention of becoming involved in a relationship, particularly one at my place of work. I've never even had a boyfriend. Always been more of a solitary individual, content in the security of my own space. But I find I enjoy his company and wonder if there could be a future for us as a couple."

"That can only be a good thing, can't it, Angela?"

"That may be the way it seems. I think I first became interested in him as a person, and not just a colleague, at the parents' evening last term when he spoke up in defence of the woman whose husband was so abusive to her. I was stunned that he was so principled, even at the risk of putting his job in jeopardy."

"You're right. Not many teachers would have done that. Why do you say it 'seems' to be a good thing?"

"Our backgrounds are so different. He's from a well-to-do family and I'm from nowhere, or somewhere near there. There's so much about my past and my family that I would never want to tell anyone. I don't know if I could ever open up to anybody on any level other than friendship."

"You must doubt what you're saying or you wouldn't be talking to me now. And if you have doubts, you're on the way to doing what people most desire in life – creating a strong and lasting emotional bond with one special person."

"Perhaps that's true."

"The thing you may not know, and I do from personal experience, is that this special person is not hamstrung by your past in the way that you may think you are. This person is interested in you, as you are now."

"But Nick would have to meet my parents. That would be unbearable. And he'd find out that my father disowned Richard and how that contributed to…"

She didn't finish the sentence. The phrasing of his next statement came easily to him.

"To a greater or lesser extent, everyone gets the heebie-jeebies going through the rituals of starting a serious relationship. They can be a trial, a torment, or a thrill. But, if you're mutually compatible, you soon find that you can relax in each other's company. More to the point, the tragic aspects of anyone's personal life shouldn't influence whether they enter a loving relationship with another person. That would be irrational."

"I've always feared that I'm irrational at times," she reflected, brightening.

"Don't get me on that one, Angela. I've a pet theory that we're all touched by a degree of insanity. Concealing it can be an issue for us at times. Just thinking of unguarded comments I find myself making in certain company confirms my theory. My own hypocrisy often appals me. What we think about people and situations is often far darker and more insidious than anything we allow ourselves to say about them. Bugger me! I'm raving. I've got to shut up."

He began laughing aloud and was relieved to see Angela joining in.

"With Nick, just try to give in to your hopeful impulses. Try not to allow extraneous considerations to spoil them. I wouldn't wish to downplay the ghastliness of what happened to your brother, but terrible things happen in life. It's the wonderful things that keep us going."

"Then I should enjoy a bit of wonder?"

"I'd support that. I hope I've been helpful. Sorry if my ramblings have been confusing, but life is a struggle to find a course through the confusion. Ever read *The Pilgrim's Progress*?"

****

"You can help me with this stupid newspaper crossword. It'll make a change for us to do something together besides sleep."

Myra was agitated, so it was best to do as requested in this instance. Whenever he sensed he may have irritated her, he took the view that whatever reason she had for being annoyed was a good one. She wasn't an unreasonable woman, and marriage to a teacher tests anyone's patience. Top Tip No. 10: Take the flak with good grace when being married to a teacher gets under your partner's skin.

"Try this one: 'Fastener used on clothing' – four, three and four?"

"How would I know that?" Biggsy queried.

"Oh, I see. That's something only a woman would know, is it? Think!"

"Um. Hole and peg? You get that on a duffel coat. Clip and pin?"

"You'd go into a menswear shop and say, 'I'd like a jacket with a clip and pin fastener,' would you?"

"Perhaps not."

When Myra did the Saturday morning quick crossword, it had to be quick. She did occasionally ask her husband to join in the fun. Two problems presented themselves when she made him this unrefusable offer. First, he wasn't a crossword fan. Second, Myra could become impatient if she didn't believe her husband was taking the joint activity seriously.

"It's 'hook and eye', for heaven's sake."

"Never heard of it."

"Well, give this one a go. 'Repair', three letters? I've already written it in."

"I can manage that – 'sew'," he volunteered mischievously.

"No, it's not. You're not concentrating, and you're still locked into clothing. It's 'fix'. If you repair something, it would be highly unlikely you'd sew it. If the door fell off the shed, you wouldn't try to sew it back on. Anyway, the next clue is 'Extravagant', and it's eleven letters. What about 'spendthrift'?"

"Yes – definitely that."

"Thank you. Try this one – you may have to use your feminine side. The clue is 'Gemstones', eight letters and it begins with an 'e'."

"You two having an argument?"

Ella shuffled into the kitchen in her dressing gown and eased herself onto a stool.

"Morning, love. Of course not. Your father and I were just doing the crossword."

"I can see why they're called crosswords," she chuckled.

"What a coincidence! I'd just thought…"

"You just thought what, darling?" Myra interrupted, with a warning look.

"Emeralds!" he shouted, saving himself with a light-bulb moment.

"Well, if you're offering, we could take a walk to the high street later."

"No, that last clue – 'Gemstones', eight letters and it begins with an 'e'."

"I know. Only joking," Myra reassured him. "You can put your wallet away."

"Have you two ever thought of doing a double act at the Comedy Club? Neil and I would come along for moral support."

"You're quite the comedian yourself, girl," came her mother's swift rejoinder. "Anyway, what are you two up to today? I take it you'll be seeing him later?"

"Ah, now I'm glad you asked that, Mum. How would you and Dad feel about meeting Neil's parents? A nice meal together at a local restaurant?"

"That's a sweet idea, Ella. It's the sort of thing that's not so common nowadays. Your father's parents and mine did it. It could become a family custom."

"Your mum's right, love. This was a joint idea, was it? Yours and Neil's?"

"Absolutely, Dad. He's a real fan of yours, though you probably wouldn't know it. He's so glad now that he chose to study literature."

"Yes, he told me. That's one of the problems with being multi-talented in our education system: you have to specialise too early."

"When did you have in mind for the powwow then?" Myra asked, pleased at the prospect of a meal out.

"What on earth's that, Mum? Sounds like a rendezvous at Battersea Dogs' Home."

"A word we used that came from watching too many western films. It just means a ceremonial meeting of Native American Indians. I take it the dress code won't include war bonnets."

"You've lost me, Dad. What about midweek? Wednesday evening?"

"All clear as far as I can see here," Myra answered, studying the kitchen calendar. "Hope your dad's not about to put the mockers on it?"

"I wouldn't dare."

"That's a relief. Looking forward to it already. Right, darling, let's get back to this crossword."

****

Cover lessons were the bane of his life. Just as he'd planned the shedload of work to get through during his first non-contact lesson for three days, he read the dreaded notice on the staff cover board. Alan Baker, his least favourite teacher at St Saviour's, was down as absent for the day, and he'd been pencilled in as the stand-in with a year nine group just before the lunch break.

Year nine was also the year group with which secondary teachers were more likely to encounter an increased incidence of behavioural difficulties, particularly with groups one had never met before. The conduct of boys struggling with the physical and emotional torments of puberty, he found, could vary in extremity from the unpredictable to the manic. Consequently, he was on his guard whenever he had dealings with this cohort. Nothing personal, he just had an aversion to offers of fisticuffs from minors. This undignified proposal he had, indeed, had to face down once in his career, all because the pupil in question had taken offence at being asked to pull his trousers up from his thighs and tuck his shirt into them. Miscalculating the seriousness which boys attach to aping the appearance of prisoners on death row in the States was a mistake he never made again. Maths was also the subject he'd struggled with during his time as a scholar. The omens were not favourable.

He decided not to adopt Baker's practice of making the boys line up in silence outside the classroom before allowing them to enter. This deviation from standard procedure might, he hoped, earn him brownie points that could prove valuable.

Those who'd already arrived, he ushered into the room and followed after. Latecomers took their places as and when they arrived. The novelty of the arrangement seemed to go down well with everybody. One stolid character, grinning malevolence in the corner, seemed less than happy with the change of routine.

"What's wrong with old Baker, sir?" he called out.

Deciding to overlook the negligence with which the strapping lad had posed the question, he offered a polite response.

"Unfortunately, he's been taken ill, so you've got me to put up with today."

"Baker is scared of us, sir," came the follow-up.

If it is the case that Baker is scared, he thought, *you're definitely the one who scares him.* Proceeding with caution was required.

"I'm sure Mr Baker is genuinely unwell. By the way, what is your name?"

"Me? I'm Alan Treadway. 'Ave you 'eard of me already, sir?" he answered with an intended hint of menace.

Whenever a pupil addressed him with such casual indifference, his reaction was to consider the possibility that the boy was taking artificial stimulants, anything from glue to grass. This individual showed no symptoms of any kind of addiction.

Alan was known to him, although he had never taught the pupil. His was one of the names that cropped up in staffroom conversation whenever discussion focused on behavioural problems. A week earlier, 'Doggy' Barker had made a telling contribution about this very boy during an informal after-school debate on the head's mooting of a zero-tolerance approach to classroom misconduct. He'd earwigged on the PE head's comments to his colleagues whilst pretending to read yet another 'key' assessment and testing document on the notice board. On no account did he wish to be a participant in consideration of this topic at any level. At one point, Barker had made an incisive contribution, cutting through the exchanges of psychobabble and producing a few moments' silent consideration: "Take Treadway in year nine, for example. He's a complete shit!"

"Now that I come to think of it, I have heard mention of you."

Nothing produced absolute silence during a lesson more effectively than the anticipation of a serious set-to between teacher and student. Young boys, he was convinced, could smell testosterone. Its odour had the effect of temporarily anaesthetising them. That was until the scent was replaced by the smell of blood. At which point, any teacher should watch his or her back. All eyes were back on Treadway.

"I bet you've 'eard a few good stories, sir."

"As it happens, the teacher who mentioned your name was very complimentary about you," Biggsy lied. "He was talking about your excellent physique and hoped you might turn out for the school rugby team."

Treadway's malevolent sneer changed to a broad smile. He leaned back in his chair and stretched his legs out, kicking those of the chair in front of him and jerking a classmate out of his daydream.

"I bet I know who said that. I know everythin' that goes on in this place. Anyway, rugby's a stupid game. I go boxing at the boys' club. I'm gonna be a pro boxer."

"Well, I'm sure if what I've heard is true, you'll make an excellent boxer. Incidentally, what you said a moment ago interests me. Can I ask you to step outside the room for a moment to check something with you?"

Treadway was unused to this kind of attention. Pursing his lips in thought, he nodded, stood up and followed the teacher.

The class, taken off guard by the unique developments at the start of the lesson, was guaranteed to remain silent whilst the two talked outside. If Treadway suspected he was the victim of a ploy to get him out of the room for the purpose of being punished, he gave nothing away.

"You mentioned just now that you know everything that goes on in this school. If that's true, would you consider helping me out with a situation?"

"Depends what it is, sir."

The 'sir' was appreciated.

"There's been talk of a suspicious vehicle turning up at the school occasionally during lunch times. I've been asked to keep an eye out for it. I was wondering if you could help me by letting me know if you spot anything unusual going on?"

"Don't see why not. What sort of vehicle is it?"

"A blue Volkswagen Polo. You don't need to do anything yourself. Just tell me if ever you see it around. Keep this between ourselves. No one else is to know I've spoken to you about it."

He understood that he'd made an unusual request of the boy, one that could expose any other boy to danger. But he was certain that Treadway was not a run-of-the-mill pupil. He was unique. No risk at all. Alan wanted to be noticed and had, indeed, been duly noticed. His special talents had been registered and would, hopefully, be put to good use.

The cover lesson passed off with no further interruptions.

****

"You did what?"

"I just asked him to keep an eye out for the car."

"You mean you asked a little boy to become your spy, watch out for the car of the local drug-running gang? Whatever possessed you?"

Myra was so incensed she began gagging on her muesli. He realised now that he should have kept his pact with the don of year nine to himself. He'd only told her about the incident at the start of the cover lesson because he thought she'd be amused.

"You don't know him. He's not a 'little boy'. He's the head honcho of his year group. He's got bigger biceps than me – and a moustache."

"He could be Popeye's son, for all I care. He's a minor and minors shouldn't be asked to do that sort of thing."

"If you spent more time at our place, you'd discover that Fingleton has a host of snitches in every year group. He'd never be able to keep a tight rein on the place if he didn't. If any serious disciplinary matter occurs, the head rounds up the relevant informants tout de suite. As the saying goes, a snitch in time saves nine."

"But they're only school matters, not criminal activities carried out by gangs with heavies on every street corner."

"All Alan will be doing is keeping an eagle eye open for one vehicle and telling me about it. I haven't provided him with a Heckler and Koch to wreak carnage amongst the west London drugs cartel."

"I hope, for your sake, that's all it comes down to. I wouldn't have dreamed of approaching a boy to do something like this."

"I've given him specific instructions and made it clear I trust him to do nothing more."

"You shouldn't even be getting involved in this yourself. It's a matter for the police, not Mr Chips. Who knows what sort of trouble you could be getting into?"

"The police can't do anything, Myra, unless they have evidence to work with. The school needs to provide it."

"Well, on your head be it. The whole drug culture of involving children in trafficking terrifies me."

"It is terrifying. Schools are a soft touch, offering rich pickings to criminals without conscience. Dealers are now diversifying into schools because they're ready marketplaces of a thousand or more children just waiting to be exploited. We can't just sit and watch it happen."

Imagining the scale of potential corruption, Myra became subdued and said nothing more.

"I'll play everything low-key and simply pass details of any sightings to Fingleton. He'll deal with the police himself. There'll be no risk to anyone at school."

Despite the reassurance he'd provided, he couldn't deny now having a misgiving or two about the wisdom of recruiting young Alan as his lookout.

****

Chapter 8

This was another occasion for the new blue suit. He'd bought it last term, coincidentally just before an Ofsted. It would be his 'new suit' for a year or so yet. Putting it on, he realised he'd have to polish his shoes. Wearing smart clothes was such a chore.

That job done, he went upstairs to see how Myra was getting on with her preparations for the evening out. Glaring at herself in the mirror of her dressing table, she stretched her mouth wide after applying strokes of lip gloss. Lipstick was anathema to her. She saw herself as a natural girl, not madly keen on covering her face with layers of make-up. Her final job was 'doing something with my hair'.

"Be right with you, love. Just putting the finishing touches to the war paint."

He sat on the end of the bed.

"You know you don't do war paint."

"I know. Just a smidgen of blusher here and there. Be right down."

"My lot had a good laugh at my expense a few days ago," he called up to the bedroom.

"Who do you mean by 'my lot', love?" Myra asked, snapping her handbag shut. She knew who he meant, but still asked the question.

Her foundation work completed, she made her way downstairs.

"My A-level group. Chris Colley started talking nonsense about *King Lear* and, by a deviously circuitous route, made it clear he knew the identity of Ella's boyfriend. Chris is such a great lad. I'll miss him when he leaves at the end of the year. Obviously, I'll miss them all. I've been their form tutor for seven years."

"I envy you that aspect of your job. Having the kind of rapport you have with those boys is a unique workplace experience."

"Just hope they all get the exam grades they need. Jermaine needs two A grades and a B for Southampton."

"How's he doing after almost losing his life last term? You were so badly affected by it all I was so worried about you as well as that poor boy."

"Physically he's doing well, although he's no longer the star of the first fifteen. Such a loss to the school! If he'd been available for the semi-final of the County Cup, who knows what the team could have done!"

"There are more important things in life than rugby, though," Myra cautioned. "How's he doing otherwise?"

"That scare's transformed him. He's of a sombre temperament now, whereas he had been such a livewire. His mind is all on schoolwork. The emotional consequences of a brush with death must be unimaginable."

"He's a lovely boy. I don't understand how anybody could want to end Jermaine's life."

"His mates have been great with him. They know he's changed but don't make a fuss about it."

"What sort of people are Neil's parents? Have you met them?"

"No. I've never taught him so haven't met them. Only know what Ella's told us. Mum works in advertising and David's a finance manager. Neil gave me the impression that his parents would have preferred he specialise in the sciences at A-level, but they didn't interfere when he plumped for English Literature and humanities subjects."

"They sound very reasonable people to me. You wouldn't have stood in Ella's way if she'd wanted to do sciences, would you?"

"Certainly not, but that wasn't a problem because she's always been so keen on reading."

"Well, the likelihood is that you'll get on well with his dad. Don't be your usual hyper-critical self with him. I know what you're like."

"And what's that?" he smiled.

"A closet misanthropist," she replied playfully. "I know you get on well with children, but you have a problem with adults."

"You know me so well. Nothing I can do about it though. I'm a lost cause," he added, grimacing. "Anyway, looking on the bright side, a financial expert could be useful if we ever come into money."

"Indeed. Could be useful if we want a sound investment opportunity or need to go on a spending spree."

"We're never likely to be that fortunate. Public servants like us will always have to watch the pennies. Ella says they're nice people who have a lovely house in Teddington. I got the impression she wished we lived over that way."

"So, Twickenham's not good enough for the little madam now she's moving into money."

"Don't jump the gun by getting those two married off. They haven't done their A-levels yet."

Her eyes narrowed and a thin smile appeared. He could tell she was going into devious-thinking mode.

"Well, now that you'll be Neil's pastoral leader, perhaps there may be ways that you could grease the academic wheels a little to ensure that he gets blinding exam results, and the family will be forever in our debt."

"I think I'll be more worried that he doesn't screw up with me in charge, and that I end up taking the hit for his failure."

Examination success was taken as read by many parents sending their children to state schools. The new educational realpolitik, with its emphasis on assessment, testing, league tables and cramming had resulted in one unintended consequence: academic success for offspring was assumed as a legally binding right. Litigation was no longer beyond the realms of possibility as a course of action for those wishing to punish schools for 'failing' their children. Fortunately, it was still the case that courts almost always threw out such lawsuits against schools. But that could change.

"Don't let me down, love. Could be on to a winner here."

The glint in his wife's eye had him worrying that she might be serious. Just in case, he decided to lay down a friendly marker.

"I just hope that Neil's parents aren't as mercenary as you and think that I can work a few fiddles on their son's behalf."

"Don't be a spoilsport. If they are fortune-hunters, no harm in doing yourself a favour."

She laughed a little too loudly, offering reassurance that she was, indeed, only being her usual mischievous self. Myra stood up, added a few make-up items to her handbag and adjusted the collar of her blouse.

"Right, I've finished here. Let's get going and meet the Fockers."

******

"I feel a bit more relaxed about meeting Neil's parents on our turf," Myra said in an undertone. "Just hope Benito's is in their league."

He pushed open the door of the restaurant for her. There were no more than half a dozen customers, Wednesday evening not being the busiest of times for dining out. The owner himself approached them with outstretched arms and a hearty laugh. Pleased at the prospect of a party of six arriving, he was bonhomie personified.

"Good evening. Good evening. So pleased to see you both again. You look so lovely, Mrs Biggs."

"Hello, Benito," she smiled. "You're the first man to say that to me this year."

Her eye-rolling husband ignored her sidelong glance in his direction. He could always rely on Benito to be gushing in his compliments to the ladies. But where was the proprietor's praise for her husband, looking equally the part with his new suit, polished shoes and combed hair? Restaurant business etiquette could be so sexist, he concluded.

"Managed to get my husband away from his books this evening. Are we the first?"

"Yes, you arrive first. The others are on their way, yes?"

They were shown to a circular table by the corner window, giving them a full view of the high street.

"Would you like drinks while you wait for everybody?"

"Could we just have a jug of tap water for now, please?"

"I'll also have a gin and tonic with lemon, but no ice," Myra added, directing an extravagant smile at her husband.

"Such a lovely man!" she enthused as she perused the menu. "I don't need to read this. I've already chosen from the menu online. Prosciutto di Parma to start; porchetta with a seasonal veg side order as my main; and panna cotta for dessert. What are you having, darling?"

"Bruschetta, carbonara and sticky toffee."

"Your usual, I see. You should be more adventurous when eating out."

"I'm not keen on any dish with an adventurous price, so I'm a bit limited."

"I don't understand why you feel the need to watch the pennies when we eat out so infrequently."

"After living from hand to mouth in London for so many years, it's a habit I can't shake off."

"Look! Ella and Neil are just crossing the road. You'd better shake yourself out of this stuffy mood of yours or the whole meal's going to be a fiasco."

He knew she was right. He could feel what personality he had tightening the moment he was placed in a formal setting. He wished he could be as relaxed and spontaneous as his wife. It must feel wonderful.

When the youngsters arrived, she launched herself at the pair. Her husband followed Myra's lead, but with less effusion, offering a hug and kiss for Ella and a handshake for Neil. Benito, flashing eyes and teeth, fussed around collecting coats.

"Your dad and I have only been here five minutes. I hope you've both got an appetite. The food here is lovely, Neil."

"I'll say. I was telling Neil about our meal with Nan and Grandad the last time we were here."

Ella sat to the left of her mother and pulled her beau down beside her. To her parents, he seemed completely relaxed with their daughter. Any nerves he may have been experiencing were not in evidence.

"Mum and Dad should be here any time," he announced. "Mum sent a text just now saying they were parking up."

Meeting a woman for the first time wasn't a problem for Biggsy, but meeting a man was. From his standpoint, the absence of testosterone and higher levels of emotional intelligence made women far more agreeable company than men. In his book, prey to a tendency to generalise, there were two male types. There were the horn-lockers who were impelled to assert a show of masculine ascendancy over any other male on first meeting. That crude impulse told him all he wanted to know. He had no truck with buttheads, despite the fact that they were the people who ruled the world. He didn't fear them. Endlessly fascinating to themselves, they were a tiresome breed, and he would wish to be anywhere else but in their company. Then there were men like himself, tagger-alongers, who subscribed to the belief that those wishing to take centre stage socially were welcome to the limelight. If Neil's father were predisposed to dominant stag status, the evening could be a trial.

The restaurant door opened. A slim woman in tight blue jeans and a dark brown suede jacket entered. Dark-haired, and like Myra, not heavily made up, she spotted Neil and her mouth formed an 'O'. Her husband, a hand around his wife's waist, narrowed his eyes as he peered over her head to scan the room.

"There you all are. Sorry we're a little late. David had to take a call as we were about to leave."

"Yes, I do apologise. I'm very sorry. I've switched my mobile off now."

The sincerity of the apology didn't go unnoticed. Benito reappeared and hovered whilst further greetings were completed.

"We're here now, thankfully. We're Jan and David. So pleased to meet you both."

"Lovely to meet you, too," Myra replied. "I'm Myra and this is…"

"Biggsy," came the interruption. "It's what everyone calls me, including most of the boys at school, behind my back that is."

Jan offered a diffident smile as she wondered how she'd feel about using the term.

David's handshake was firm, without being knuckle-crunching. He looked down at his son and Ella, both observing the proceedings in silence.

"These two really seem to have hit it off," he said.

"We feel the same way, David. We've been so looking forward to meeting you both," Myra gushed.

"I can't believe our little boy has suddenly grown up," Jan confided. "I can still recall every detail of bringing Neil into the world, and now look at him."

"Mum, you don't need to go all gooey," her son protested meekly. "Time has moved on, you know."

"Mum's just the same," Ella laughed. "Wait till she gets started. You'll even find out what baby milk she gave me."

"No, I won't. She does exaggerate."

"The two of them thought it would be a good idea for us all to get together, and David and I were only too pleased."

Biggsy observed the exchanges with interest, secure in the knowledge that he needn't speak whilst everyone else was bubbling with excitement. Then he noticed David doing the same thing, and it struck him what an agreeable chap he seemed.

****

"What lovely people! I could have talked to them for hours. I can't believe Ella has found herself such a lovely boyfriend. When I think of the hours I've fretted, worrying that she'd one day bring home some caveman. He's just the sort of boy I'd have wished for her."

"I gather from that eulogy you think highly of the Thompsons. I must admit that I also enjoyed their company."

"I couldn't believe it. Jan was lovely and I found myself mistaking David for you, though a slightly taller version. He's just as difficult to draw out as you are."

"Harsh, but fair, Myra. He strikes me to be a genuinely unassuming person. I found myself talking at times and being listened to. It was a bit unnerving."

"Jan more than makes up for his quiet disposition. She's really good company. The stories she told me about the advertising business! Made my hair curl."

"I don't know about you, but I didn't drink a huge amount. Didn't seem to need it."

"No. They're not heavy drinkers either. That's why David was able to drive over. I noticed he only had one glass of wine. Jan and I had a couple and no more."

"Talking to them, I didn't feel like the poor relations, even when the subject of their villa in Menorca came up."

"Exactly. When she said it could be available to us for a free holiday there over Easter, I thought she was joking. We've only just met them."

"You really must have a sixth sense. All that talk about them being useful people to know. Did Ella tell you about this villa beforehand?"

"It may have come up," Myra answered, with an arch smile.

"I was taken aback. It seemed to be a genuine offer. Still can't get a handle on that myself. How could they know to trust people they'd never met before to share a property they own?"

"I told you we might be on to a good thing with Neil's well-to-do parents."

"A very generous offer, but we could never take them up on it. I'll be Neil's year head soon. I couldn't be seen to accept gifts from parents. Could be perceived in a questionable light. And, anyway, I need those two weeks to tie up all my examination admin."

"Be serious. He'll be leaving the school in June of next year. And I'm tired of your job dictating how we live our lives. There's more to life than St Saviour's," was his wife's swift reply.

She'd already thought this through. There were occasions when he couldn't be sure what schemes his wife had in mind. He gave her a quizzical look and rubbed his chin. She responded, all innocence, with the expression of a small child who'd just been told she was going to the seaside. He half-filled a glass with water from the tap.

A rumble on the stairs preceded Ella's appearance in the kitchen. She pulled her dressing gown tightly around her.

"So, what did you think of them, then?"

"Can't believe how well we all got on. Really lovely people. I've never seen your dad talk so much outside of the classroom."

"That's good. Jan's something else, isn't she? Can't believe she's forty-six. Seems much younger, don't you think?"

"Yes, a very attractive woman. Looks good for her age, but she could do with putting on a bit of weight."

"I think she's got a great figure. I might need to lose a bit of surplus midriff."

"Don't get ideas like that into your head, my girl. You're perfect as you are. Don't want a bulimic on my hands at this stage. I'm more in need of losing weight than you," she stated, looking at her husband.

"Don't get me involved in a conversation on women's weight. It's become a national media obsession and I refuse to be involved in any debate on the subject."

"But don't you think I should lose a little off here, love?" she asked, tugging at her hips. "It's not my fault. It's what comes of having a job where I'm sitting down all day."

"You're perfect as you are. Don't give it another thought. Come on, both of you. Off to bed."

"Looks like we'd better make a date for the gym tomorrow evening if that's how you feel."

****

"That wasn't nice."

"I'd been expecting Fingleton to get Biddlecombe in on the interview to give you a hard time. A real grilling was on the cards, wasn't it?"

Tom Biddlecombe, one of the school governors, was a local councillor who didn't mince words in any company. He had the physique of an all-in wrestler and the face of someone you'd expect to see playing a hoodlum in a gangster film. Biggsy wouldn't know if the burly governor had been primed to make the head of English interview as gruelling as possible, but he suspected it. The head would possibly want word to get back to Toner that the man it pained him to put up for interview had suffered in the hot seat.

What dish of revenge she'd be plotting, if she were still at the school next term with Andy in her sights, was not on his mind at this precise moment. Biggsy stood gazing out of the office window, his focus on the tall trees wailing and wavering in the wind.

"I had no trouble with the interview until he got started on me. I feel as though I've been roughed up in a pub brawl. I don't even know if I want the job now."

You better had after all the trouble you've given me.

"By coincidence, I've been saying that to myself for the past few years. At least you didn't have Toner gunning for you in there. That would have been worse."

"I haven't been appointed yet. Who knows what they'll decide!"

Andy may have avoided her on this particular day, but she could soon be in his face, putting as much pointless paperwork his way as possible. If she were intent on leaving St Saviour's at the earliest opportunity, she wouldn't have long to avenge herself. There wouldn't be enough time to get rid of him, as she'd reportedly done with previous members of staff who'd upset her.

Andy was liked and respected in the staff room and could rely on the support of colleagues. The PE department excepted, he was as popular with them as he was with the boys. Those teachers who'd discovered that he was the donor of Toner's sex appliance believed his jest was well-targeted. Biggsy wondered again if he had made too much of the incident, but not for long. He knew he hadn't.

"Biddlecombe must have picked the school prospectus to pieces to try nailing me. He's not nearly as stupid as he looks."

"Well, you did a good job of keeping him at bay and not losing the plot."

"Thanks for your list of likely questions. I boned up on assessment last night, so that gave me the chance to prattle on quite happily."

"You've had the grilling I'd expected, but there's no chance they won't give you the job. I don't see why they're wasting their time now. Could just be trying to keep your anxiety levels raised for as long as possible."

The office phone rang.

"That'll be them calling you back."

****

"We haven't got time for you here."

Simon sat before him, his expressionless face a rebuff to the harm state education had done to him. The search for a personality behind the mask of emotional isolation was yielding results. The student cooperated with every request made of him, the fixed expression of indifference beginning to fall away. In the past, he had responded to all academic success that regularly came his way with the same reaction he might demonstrate on being given a new exercise book.

"State schools simply aren't equipped to cater for unique individuals like yourself. I'm as guilty as every other teacher in that respect. I spend an inordinate amount of my time dealing with petty paperwork out of the classroom and, during lessons, my attention tends to be monopolised by boys with behavioural difficulties."

The hint of a smile and the nodding of Simon's head indicated understanding. But he remained icily composed, now concentrating on his hands clasped before him.

"It's likely that, during your school career, you could count the occasions on one hand that a subject teacher has spoken to you at length about yourself and your own interests. There's also the issue that your intelligence is intimidating. Adults may not wish to address your ability too deeply out of a sense of professional inferiority. I've admitted to you before that your intellectual potential far outstrips my capabilities at your age, but very few other teachers would, I imagine."

He caught a twitch of Simon's mouth as he looked up.

"I can't begin to tell you how different from this place an Oxbridge university environment will be. There you will regularly be tutored on a one-to-one basis by someone genuinely interested in the unique quality of your mind. Here, your academic ability is respected, but the main focus is on the exam results that you'll gain to boost the school's league table position."

The apparent unresponsiveness of his listener presented no difficulties for Biggsy. He was fired with a determination to explain, in the clearest terms, how

Simon's life would come into its own in higher education. The boy must be persuaded to welcome and anticipate the magnitude of that transformation.

"But I'm jumping the gun here. These meetings are intended to prepare you for the interview you have to get through before you can be offered a place. Your abilities will come under scrutiny, and that doesn't mean the interviewers will simply be trying to find out how much you can remember of all the texts you've studied. State schools tend to play safe by specialising in getting you to regurgitate key points and relevant backup information, but higher education is about more than that."

Simon put a hand to his face and stroked his chin. Energised by this gesture, his tutor continued.

"You'll be required to demonstrate how you engage with literature whilst discussing your favourite novels and authors. For example, you could be asked to present a case for naming one novel you think everybody should read. In this example, you'd be expected to state your views succinctly and respond, on the hoof, to university lecturers who may question your choice. That scenario wouldn't throw you at all, would it?"

"No, sir. I might choose *The Quiet American* if I were asked something like that. Although it was written over fifty years ago, it's still considered influential. An English writer dared to publish a book in the 1950s, not that long after the Second World War, that he knew would be viewed by many as anti-American. That was quite something. There'd be plenty to talk about there."

"Yes. Now we are talking. Do you realise that most people of your age would struggle to produce a spontaneous response of that coherence? You didn't miss a beat there."

"Thank you, sir."

"I'd encourage you to continue researching the books you've tackled in the private reading programme I suggested you undertake. I can see, though, that you're already doing that fairly thoroughly."

"There's more to reading books than simply understanding what's going on in them. It's interesting trying to analyse each writer's fix on life and the world."

This wasn't academic arrogance, merely the statement of facts.

"Excellent, that's exactly what the panel would expect from a genuine applicant: a student who researches beyond the A-level syllabus, out of a sense of personal curiosity and inquiry. Many will do it because their teachers say it's something they must do, and it's merely a chore. Interviewers will be able to tell the difference between one who talks knowledgeably about a book or a writer, and another who's spouting the key points of literature they've been set as a compulsory extra-curricular study."

Simon smiled, in recognition of the transparent trickery schools were apt to employ.

"I'm aware that much of what I tell you in these sessions has already occurred to you, Simon. I apologise for that now. I would guess that one of the reasons you hold yourself back in classroom talk is that your conversation entry level is much higher than the norm. For example, I can't imagine you getting excited by chatter about last night's football on the TV or where to buy the cheapest trainers. This is why I'm so determined to convince you that you need the best higher education environment available, where you will come into regular contact with like minds."

The pomposity of his expression was of no consequence. A young man's psychological wellbeing was at stake.

"You make me sound like a freak, sir."

"Very astute of you. I was waiting for you to say that as soon as I'd finished speaking. We regularly turn out boys who are high-class rugby players and direct them to clubs and facilities where their exceptional ability is developed to the highest level. If you consider they're freaks, so be it. More freaks, please!" he said, raising his voice in excitement.

This time Simon laughed.

"Your intellect operates at a high level. It can't help it. It demands stimulation. That's you. You understand that most of your peers can accept the physical excellence of a gifted footballer, but not the mental excellence of a gifted mind. I don't know what it is about children in this country. The word 'boff' trips off their tongues at the merest opportunity. You've been a victim of that. You'll be leaving that intellectual envy behind you in a year and a half's time, thank God!"

He paused for breath. Simon looked him in the eye, registering the force of his teacher's words.

"I'm starting to become tired of the sound of my own voice again. I very quickly do once I start sounding off. Let's change tack. You've outgrown this school, but you still have time to put in here. Try not to let the hamstrung way we members of staff teach affect your enjoyment of literature. We flog set texts to death out of fear that students will fail their examinations. You aren't going to fail, so you can afford to use the books we have to cover as starting points for further reading. For example, there's a novel called *A Thousand Acres* by Jane Smiley that will strike a chord with you. Give it a try."

****

"Can't believe I'm saying this, but you've excelled yourself, love."

Myra sat on the bed and gave it the bounce test.

"Well, I thought a little half-term break would do us both good. This hotel is very homely, isn't it?" he replied, pushing aside a floral drape and peering out of the window of their room on the first floor.

Looking beyond the narrow cobbled street, he saw a bowling green. Beyond that, flat open countryside beckoned. He'd booked a stay of two nights in the middle of the half-term week. Temperatures during their stay were predicted to reach double figures, the forecast promising blue skies and no rain.

Their hotel, The Castle, was situated just up the hill from the Landgate arch, one of two gateways built centuries earlier to defend Rye from invaders. He'd struck lucky with the room, the last one available in this busy February week.

"You're right. Smashing place. I love the king-size bed. This all seems too good to be true. Actually, let me just check something."

Myra frowned, went to his weekend case and began unpacking the contents with customs-officer concentration. As she placed his pyjamas and underwear on the bed, he looked on in amusement.

"What are you up to?" he asked. "Checking whether I've forgotten anything?"

"No, I'm checking you haven't smuggled exercise books down here to mark. Remember, you've got form."

He laughed aloud.

"You don't seriously think for one minute I'd…"

"Why not? This area is renowned for smugglers, as you well know."

Satisfied that his suitcase was clean, she returned the items she'd so urgently removed.

"Now that you've satisfied yourself I'm not related to Captain Kidd, what do you say we get straight out and look for an eatery to have some lunch?"

Feeling more relaxed after her precautionary check, she settled herself in the room's one wing-backed chair and perused the welcome pack, whilst Biggsy picked up the TV remote and began scrolling the channels.

"Nice picture, and a good six inches bigger than what you'd expect to find in a four-star hotel."

"You won't be watching any television tonight, my love," Myra purred.

He looked away from the set to his wife. She looked up from the guide with half-lidded eyes and smiled.

"Anyway, getting back to Rye, there are plenty of little places to choose from according to this. After lunch, we could take a stroll along the high street, head up to Mermaid Street, then visit St Mary's church. If our legs are aching after that, there's a selection of tea rooms where we could have afternoon tiffin."

Evening tiffin's more on your mind, he thought.

"Hasn't taken you long to sort today out. I'd like to take a drive to Winchelsea tomorrow and then drop down for a walk along the coastline."

"Sounds lovely. Right, I'll just go for a tinkle, then we can go out and see what Rye has to offer."

Minutes later, they were descending the flight of thickly-carpeted stairs. With a polite nod to the young receptionist in the entrance area, he followed his wife out into the street.

"Let's turn right and see what we find, shall we?"

Her suggestion was perfect. He pulled up his jacket zipper a little and they set off. It dawned on him that he felt happy, and the awareness warmed him to the core.

"Oh, look at that delightful little sweet shop! Will you buy me a bag of lemon bonbons?"

"My pleasure."

****

Capitalising on the success of the Rye visit, he'd decided on a final half-term excursion before returning to the chalk face the following day. They were on the road by 10.18. Myra had brought all they would need: two bottles of water in her daysack and the small tin she kept in her handbag topped up with a fresh supply of aniseed balls – ideal for car journeys. In competitions to see whose aniseed ball lasted longer, Myra always won. Just as he'd reached the point where he was

134

nursing a tiny pearl on the tip of his tongue, he would lose concentration and start crunching.

Mid-February was not the ideal time for taking a trip to the seaside, but there was again the promise of bright, though chilly, weather. They looked forward to wrapping up in quilted anoraks and braving the winds as they trudged through pebbles along the beach from Bracklesham Bay towards West Wittering. A pub lunch would set them up for the return journey, this time with the wind at their backs.

"Maureen, as usual, wants us to do almost a hundred miles, going down the M3 and back along the M27 to get to Bracklesham."

He'd given the name Maureen to the car's satnav. Maureen Chapman, the next-door neighbour who would waylay his mother whenever she appeared in the back garden to hang out the washing, was a gossip whose yarns about local news tended to be unreliable. His mother subsequently informed him, years later, how ironic it was that she believed she knew everyone else's business but never found out about her husband's affair with the wife of the publican at The Red Lion. An inveterate inebriate, he'd also been unaware of the liaison.

They must get down to Bath again soon to visit his mother. He phoned a few times a week, but she found it difficult to speak naturally into a mouthpiece and was ever anxious to get off the line.

"I'll programme it for Petworth and adjust the destination setting when we get there."

"I'm thinking it's a roast-beef day today, with a vegetarian starter. You can only watch your waistline for so long. What will you be going for?"

"Need you ask? Steak and ale pie for me."

"So predictable. Here, have an aniseed ball to keep you going."

Once the car had wound its way through Petworth, the countryside opened out. The run to Chichester was one of his favourites.

The wind threatened to take Myra's door off its hinges as she opened it forty minutes later. But she was standing no nonsense from the elements and kept a firm hold of the handle. There were half a dozen other vehicles in the car park, indicating that they weren't the only hardy souls drawn to the sea. Within minutes of arriving, they'd fed the parking meter and were off.

They decided to walk along the top of the ridge of shingle, the crunch of the pebbles beneath their feet preferable to wet sand.

"If you can't afford February in Fuerteventura, blustery Bracklesham comes a close second," he enthused.

"Who needs to slum it in thirty degrees of sunshine when we've got this almost on our doorstep?" Myra questioned with a sweep of her arm. "Race you to the next groyne!"

She bent her back into the wind and lengthened her pace. He trotted up alongside her and took her hand.

******

Chapter 9

It would be interpreted as a magnanimous gesture but wasn't intended as such. He hadn't imagined that handing over the reins of power would be so dispiriting. The two of them were getting along well enough, but more now went unsaid between them. The implicit trust that had existed between them, forming the basis of their professional relationship had, possibly, been illusory all along. Top Tip No. 11: Be realistic about the strength of workplace relationships, particularly in schools.

A tide of weariness and self-doubt swept over him. He wondered how long he'd be able to tolerate life as a sixth-form leader. The fear within him grew that he'd reached the point where the pleasure of working with children could no longer sustain him in his career. He smiled as it occurred to him that he should have chosen anything other than *Hard Times* as the final set text for his A-level class.

Although Andy wouldn't be taking over the running of the English department until after Easter, he'd jumped at the offer to take the next department meeting. That would involve speaking individually to colleagues in advance to prepare an agenda, chairing the meeting, typing up the minutes, and sending copies to everyone in the department, and Toner, within twenty-four hours. The sooner Andy got stuck into the nitty-gritty of the job, the better. There were countless other daily responsibilities, over and above teaching a full timetable that he may not have bargained for. He was welcome to them.

The moment the appointment had been made, Biggsy no longer felt that it was his department. He wondered how it would fare under its new boss. Leadership was a collegiate can of worms. The main task of a middle manager, as he saw it, was one of protecting those in his team from the bureaucratic nonsense that could be binned the moment it came spewing down from management. If Andy saw it that way, he'd be fine.

"Thanks a lot for trying to bed me in gently to the new job."

"Don't thank me yet. I just hope that you continue to find your classroom teaching rewarding with all the additional nonsense you'll have on your plate. Whatever the volume of grief you find yourself dealing with, try not to let it affect the enjoyment you get from teaching."

"You seem to have managed that one well enough."

He didn't feel in the mood to pick up on that comment. Children would always be more important than data, but he was aware that an increasing number of his lessons didn't do justice to the boys. Fatigue eventually gets to a teacher in his fifties who's been in the job for three decades. He'd become only too aware of his own reduced physical and emotional stamina. Taking out a gym membership had been a good idea, he reminded himself. He'd go there after school to clear his head. Myra might also be able to make it. He'd give her a call.

"If there's anything else you feel you'd like to take over from me, Andy, feel free to ask."

****

"It's not fair. This is better than anything I can get in the canteen. Why are you closing down?"

The disgruntled year nine pupil gave Sarah a level stare. She returned him a sympathetic look and a lie.

"Sorry, Jamie, but we don't have enough free time to keep the shop going. The last few months have been so hectic that the English department can't manage teaching and running the shop any longer."

Jamie sauntered off, grumbling. Biggsy watched him leave in silence and closed the door behind him. The final lunchtime session of the tuck shop had been busy. Sarah tipped the coins from her biscuit tin into a small canvas sack which she tucked away at the bottom of her school bag.

"Must be over fifty pounds there. Not a bad final haul."

"May I have the honour of being your very last customer?"

"You certainly may."

"I'll take one of those banana energy bar thingies."

"You can have that as a freebie as you've already spent so much here," Sarah declared.

"Well, it was a good thing while it lasted, a very good thing. Thank you for raising a huge amount for the department in such a short space of time. We're indebted to you for providing us with books we'd otherwise be without."

"That's kind of you to say so, considering the bad feeling we've generated from staff members over the past few months. I'll be diplomatic and won't mention the science department."

"Not a problem. Our students were in desperate need of the books your enterprise provided. Jamie's not the only aggrieved customer, by the way. Archie Matthews runs the school council, and the closure of our tuck shop came up as an agenda item. The boys smell a rat that we had to shut up shop only a couple of months after opening. There was talk of them organising a petition."

"Good for them."

"The thing is, if they put forward a petition and it was successful, any future tuck shop would be school-run. It would have to be for the benefit of every department, not just English."

"I see. We dream up the initiative and a school monopoly takeover quickly follows. Ain't capitalism great!"

Her mimicry of a Stateside tycoon almost had him choking with laughter on his banana bar. He put a hand to his mouth as he started coughing.

"I see you've given Andy the chair for our next department meeting."

His laughter stopped.

"I thought I'd give him his first chance to start bedding himself into the new role, and he was happy to take it on."

"I thought he was lucky to get the job after what happened at the staff Christmas meal."

"Fair point, Sarah."

She was the first member of his department to reveal to him that she knew what Andy had done. How long had she known? He'd hung on to the hope that nobody else knew anything, but realised he was being naïve. Sarah could also know, from staffroom gossip, that there had been resistance from on high to the appointment. She must have wondered why her line manager hadn't confided his thoughts to her on the folly of Andy's behaviour. He and Sarah were as close as work colleagues could get, after all. The only card he could play to her was that he was not one to gossip to anyone about any matter, even one as close to home as this. She would discover, should she care to find out, that he'd spoken to no one whatsoever about the embarrassing business.

"Andy thought I would approve of the stunt to ridicule Toner and be pleased when he told me he was the architect of her public humiliation. I didn't and I wasn't. I found the episode appalling. Don't get me wrong, I am antipathetic to everything she stands for professionally, but I couldn't condone his conduct. I haven't spoken to anybody here about it, other than Fingleton. That was only because I had to. His intention to make Andy a shoo-in for the head of English post came close to foundering."

"Is that why you suggested I apply for the job?"

This crippling question required an honest answer.

"Not quite, Sarah. There was a strong part of me that wanted to work in your department, not Andy's."

"I started trying to get to the bottom of the business when you spoke to me that evening after school a while back. It seemed obvious you were up to something."

The impulse to tell her how disillusioned he'd become with Andy was difficult to resist.

"Did it? I should have come clean with you then. My relationship with him is changed…damaged. I'm still struggling with it all. Nobody should be subjected to ridicule and humiliation in the workplace, whatever anyone else on the staff believes."

"It must have been difficult for you, witnessing what he did."

"I can't begin to tell you. I bear a portion of guilt myself for what happened. He and I often exchanged vitriolic observations about Toner. He must have felt that he was only doing something of which I'd heartily approve."

"I'll tell you what, I'll do you a favour and take the second-in-department job, that you know I never really wanted, just to keep an eye on him. How does that suit?"

"I would consider that very magnanimous of you, for all manner of reasons."

He wanted to give her a hug of gratitude but resisted the impulse.

****

"Where's that bloody list?" Myra asked, opening her jacket and plunging one hand down the 'V' of her cashmere top.

"You what?" Biggsy asked, aghast. "You can't adjust your bra in the high street. You'll get arrested."

"Can't find my shopping list," she gasped, struggling with her left 'D' cup. "I definitely tucked it into this one."

"If you insist on writing lists on tiny pieces of paper, it's small wonder you can't find them once they go in there. Just accept that it's lost and forget about it."

Myra manoeuvred herself to the side of a pillar box, yanking her husband back by his shoulder to stand in front of her.

"Just stay there one moment and shield me."

"I don't believe you're doing this. I'm getting a You've-Been-Framed anxiety attack. Where are the cameras?"

"Wardrobe malfunction, Mum?"

Ella and Neil appeared from nowhere. Neil pretended to check out a motorbike revving in the high street.

"Got it! All under control, my love. I mislaid my shopping list, and I've just retrieved it. What are you two doing in the high street?"

"Well, apart from watching my mother having a senior moment in a very public place, Neil and I are just popping down to the retro-sweet shop in Church Street. They do the most brilliant nut cluster."

"Your dad and I are just doing a bit of shopping together."

"Not like Dad to be out doing local shopping with you, Mum?"

"There's some truth in that," her father replied. "After her performance of the last few minutes, you can guess why."

"I managed to drag him away from the telly. He spent the morning marking books so I thought we ought to spend a little time together. It makes a nice change for us to have half an hour in the high street. He'd only be spending two hours following sports results. Complete waste of time."

"I'm sure Neil isn't at all interested in how I spend my Saturdays, darling."

He shot his wife a cautioning look, but she wasn't looking at him. *Colley had better not get to hear of this.*

"Just popping into Boots before they close, then into the shoe shop to look for winter shoes for your dad. He's so heavy on footwear; he gets through a pair in no time."

He was sure he saw a smile beginning to form on Neil's face before a hand went to his mouth. Giving in to Myra's protestations and accompanying her to the high street had been a bad move.

141

"See you later this evening, both of you. Neil and I are going back to his for a while."

"OK, you guys. You can microwave what's left of our chicken casserole when you get home if you're peckish. See you later."

Ella pulled Neil away in the direction of the sweet shop.

"Bye!" the young man called back, smiling as he was led away.

"You didn't have to talk about me as if I weren't there, you know."

"Sorry, love. I'm so used to you not being there that I forgot you were. Come on. Everything will be closing soon. Now, what did I do with that list?"

"Oh, for heaven's sake!"

****

"I can't imagine you know anything about it, but I thought I'd approach you first."

Gibson shook his head slowly from side to side. He'd assumed that his tutor wanted to talk about the latest developments regarding his university application. When it became clear that the purpose of the after-school chat was to discuss recreational drug use in the sixth form, he'd become guarded. He'd never been tempted in that direction, just as he'd never had any interest in alcohol. His initial reaction was one of surprise that his tutor should raise the subject with him.

"I couldn't think who else to ask, Jermaine. I thought that you, in your capacity as head boy, might be a good starting point. Dealers target adolescents to create a market for their goods, and where better to find young customers than in schools."

Realising that his tutor wasn't expecting him to provide names and character details, Gibson relaxed visibly in the office chair.

"There may be boys who are at risk here, and I'll be expected to do something to protect them from next term when I'm in charge along the corridor. I see it, potentially, as one of the biggest problems I'll have to face in the new job."

"There's nobody I know who's taking stuff. Anybody who does is keeping quiet about it."

"That's comforting to know. As yet, we don't have a situation here where anybody's talking openly about drug abuse in the school."

"If there's anything going on, there can't be many involved."

"I'd hope it stays that way, if that's the case. But I've been receiving information to the contrary recently. I've had reports that the occupants of a blue VW Polo may have started dropping substances off here. If that's the case, I'm going to need eyes and ears about the place."

He could tell that, despite being uncomfortable with the subject, Gibson was anxious to treat the matter seriously. Had he been tight-lipped, there may have been something to worry about.

"If I notice anything I'll let you know, sir."

"Thanks for that. Those involved in last week's sightings may have been warned off after Mr Matthews gave them a scare by running after their vehicle when it appeared at the back of the school."

"I usually make a point of closing my eyes and ears whenever I get wind of anything to do with drugs where I live, sir. But I'll watch out for anything suspicious here. Myself, I can't see what could make anyone start an expensive habit that's likely to kill them."

"I was the same at your age. I never started smoking for exactly that reason. I suppose nicotine was my first exposure to drug abuse, albeit a common habit in those days."

"I don't know many people my age who smoke cigarettes."

"I only know one or two. Anyway, you know how much I respect your integrity, Jermaine. There's no reason why someone of your good character should be approached on the subject, and I can understand that you may feel offended. On the other hand, you could take it as a compliment that I feel you're the only boy in the school I feel I can trust to ask about this business."

The flash of a smile from Jermaine reassured him that the head boy hadn't been offended by the request.

"If you're unable to tell me anything because you simply know nothing, I understand and accept that. To be honest, it's helpful simply unloading my anxiety onto someone I know I can trust. There were drugs around when I was young and, like you, I was determined to have nothing to do with them. But the scale of this social problem has escalated. Intelligent people everywhere need to discuss it. The thought terrifies me that there are those under the influence who may be behind the wheel of a car."

******

Hazel Frears remained in her seat at the conclusion of the department meeting. She took her time returning papers and books to her bag, watching Biggsy as she did so. As soon as he entered the office, she stood up and followed him.

"Can I have a quick word, Biggsy?"

He turned quickly, surprised to discover that he wasn't alone.

"Didn't realise you were behind me there, Hazel."

"Sorry. I wanted to catch you on your own for a confidential chat."

"Oh, right. Must be something serious. What have you got on your mind?"

"Something nasty's going on that you should know about."

Hazel wasn't one to waste words on matters she considered important. She went about her work with a quiet assurance that he sometimes felt he took for granted. Recognised as the staff's leading bibliophile, she would regularly advise him on holiday reading. Aware that she was not one to make a fuss about molehills, he prepared himself for the bad news.

"It seems that Toner is gunning for Nick for some reason. I overheard him talking to Angela. She was doing her best to reassure him about something, but he struck me as being very upset, angry even. I heard him mention Toner by name before they moved out of hearing."

"That does sound as though something nasty is going on. Thanks for coming to me with it, Hazel. If Toner is on his case, he does have a problem. Come to think of it, he was subdued during the meeting. Angela too, for that matter."

"I noticed it. That's why I decided to speak to you straight afterwards."

"I don't suppose you managed to catch anything more that was said?"

"I can't be sure, but I think I may have heard mention of a parent's complaint. But whatever Toner may be up to, he seemed more angry than worried."

"Toner's got form when it comes to getting at members of staff. There's no way I want Nick being given a hard time. I'll have to get on to this directly. Do you mind if I mention to him that you came to me with this concern?"

"Not at all, but make a point of saying that I'm only too well aware of Toner's capacity for upsetting staff. There's not much I'd be able to do, but you may. I don't want him thinking I'm being a busybody."

"There's no chance anyone would ever think that of you, Hazel."

"I don't know if there's any connection, but something else is also going on with another young male teacher."

His ears pricked up. He guessed that Aimes would be mentioned. Whatever Hazel was about to report, there had to be a connection with Toner's treatment of Nick.

"I don't like to pass on gossip, but in this case I feel justified. She and Aaron Aimes have been an item since last term, but they aren't any longer."

Hazel was justified. He gave a moment's thought to the fact that the deputy head's relationship with the young PE teacher must have become common knowledge but had no interest in asking Hazel for the source of this latest development. She wouldn't wish to go into those details.

"The plot thickens. I'm going to have to work out how to play this one. Can I ask that you tell no one you've spoken to me about this relationship, Hazel? I think it best that our conversation remains entirely confidential."

"Right. Sorry to be the bearer of bad tidings."

"I'm glad you did, so very glad."

He'd never been one for professional confrontation. The job was stressful enough. But events over the past term and a half had caused him to reassess this impulse. Nick must be protected at whatever cost.

****

"I've been thinking you haven't been your usual contented self lately, Nick, and what Hazel told me yesterday explains why."

Nick was setting out books and papers on his table in preparation for the first lesson of the day.

"I didn't want to bother you with it, Biggsy. You've got more than enough on your plate. The deputy head has an issue with one aspect of my teaching and she's giving me a bit of a hard time. What did Hazel say?"

"That somebody on the management team is being less than supportive to you."

"She's sent me a couple of emails saying that I must mark boys' work regularly, calling my professionalism into question and querying whether I'm up to the teaching workload."

"If she were seriously concerned, she should have asked me to get involved. The fact that she hasn't suggests an ulterior motive."

"What do you mean? A vendetta against me?"

"That's an interesting word. Suggests hatred towards someone. If she does happen to have ideas in that direction, I need to see her pronto and advise her otherwise. How long's it been going on?"

"It started last week. She came into one of my lessons, saying she was doing random spot checks. I've had a couple of emails since."

"Could be nothing, but I have my doubts. I'd guess every member of staff here is guilty of not being able to keep up with marking, me included. Maintaining good classroom control and marking work regularly are the two biggest challenges for all of us."

"I've found that out. Marking takes me an age."

"If Toner does want to make an issue here, she has to take it to a full staff meeting. Singling out individuals for thumbscrew treatment is not the answer. We get a few free lessons a week to go over boys' written work but, more often than not, we lose those owing to covering lessons for staff on the sick."

"Like I said, I didn't want to trouble you with this. You put yourself in a difficult situation for me last term. I didn't want you doing it again."

"Protecting my staff is the most important part of my job, Nick. Exam results are important, but people are more important still. That includes the welfare of staff, as well as students."

At that moment, boys could be heard arriving for Nick's registration outside the classroom. There was a thud against the door.

"Sorry, just got to check what's happening outside."

He went to the door, opened it with a flourish, and a small boy tumbled into the room. Laughter from the corridor accompanied the proceedings.

"Are you all right, William? Up you get."

Nick helped the youngster to his feet, not an easy procedure as the rucksack on his back was so heavy he struggled to find his balance.

"Sorry, sir. I got pushed."

"From the state of you, somebody out there needs to be reminded that pushing others about is not the way to behave."

"Well, I'll get back to you on that one," said the department head, leaving the young teacher to manoeuvre William and his load into an upright position.

"Oh. Right. Thanks very much for that."

****

146

"Don't know for certain how I'm going to play this one."

The wind howled, blowing leaves and garden debris against the back door. He wondered what state the boys at school would be in if the wind kept up for the rest of the day.

"Like you always do, dear: professionally," Myra reminded him.

"I'm thinking I should tackle Toner full on at the earliest opportunity. I want to rule out any chance of whatever's going on becoming public knowledge."

"Nip the situation in the bud. Sounds like a good idea. What do you imagine is going on?"

"It seems to me as though the deputy head's personal and professional lives are getting confused. I suspect a spiteful motive on her part. Hazel must be thinking the same, or she wouldn't have mentioned to me that Toner's romance with Aimes seems to be over."

"What! That didn't last long. Wonder what happened there?"

"I'd guess that Aaron must have ended the relationship. My belief is that she's struggling to come to terms with rejection and is venting her spleen on an obvious target."

"What would make Nick Devlin an obvious target?"

Myra crammed a packet of herbal tea bags into her handbag and then struggled to close the zip.

"Well, he and Angela have become more than just good friends, which she must have found out about. I think she may be jealous of the pair. She could have gone for Angela or Nick. But my guess is that Nick got the nod because he's a man."

"Congratulations, my dear Holmes. Devastating logic."

"All too obvious, if you ask me."

"I was taking the piss, actually," Myra scoffed, with excessive emphasis on the adverb. "Come on, zip, I've got to get to work."

"Oh. Anyway, piss-taking apart, do you go along with the theory? And, if so, what do you think my strategy should be when I park myself on her office chair?"

"Close this bag for me and I'll give you thirty seconds of high-quality advice. Seems to me you've got nothing to lose if she's going to be leaving anyway. Just tell her what you know, but don't let on how you know, and tell her to lay off your man."

Having rearranged the contents of his wife's handbag and closed the zip, he returned it with a graceful nod.

"There you are, your ladyship."

"And if she gets the hump, tell her you'll take up the matter with Fingleton and your union representative. Bullying in the workplace is a serious matter."

"You must have read my mind, love. What a great team we make!"

"If that's it, I'm off. See you later, Sherlock."

"Bye, Watson."

****

"You know, your running action's excellent."

Steve approached him as he worked through his half-hour stint on the treadmill.

"Good of you to say so, Steve. How are you doing?"

"This'll be my last session here for a while. My wife and I are off to New Zealand for a month after the weekend."

"Tremendous! It's still their summer now, isn't it? What have you got planned?"

"Land in Auckland, stay there a few days, then take a campervan and do a tour of both islands."

"I envy you. I've never had an extended break of that sort. Must have taken a lot of planning?"

"It did. We found a travel agent locally that sorted the whole itinerary for us. Sorted us with a campervan company over there and booked the ferry connection to South Island."

Biggsy was finding it easier to run and converse at the same time. He briefly grabbed the handrails either side of him as he turned to face Steve.

"The end of our winter's certainly a great time to set off on the holiday of a lifetime."

"We've been planning this for a year. It'll be a pleasure to leave the UK gloom and rain behind for a whole four weeks, I can tell you."

"I won't be rude and ask how much it costs."

"Let's just say it'll cost as much as three or four of our usual summer holidays in Europe. Anyway, like I was saying, now you've trimmed down you make running look easy."

"Thanks for the compliment. I think not doing any exercise for thirty years must have preserved my joints because I'm finding running quite relaxing."

"Could be something in that. I used to jog regularly, and my knee joints are shot. How long d'you do on the runner now?"

"Thirty minutes. I've upped it quite a bit since I started. The aerobic stuff is my favourite form of exercise here."

"And what distance does the readout tell you you've completed in that time?"

"Six kilometres. Any good?"

Steve studied the figures on the display unit. He raised his eyebrows and looked up at the ceiling as he made a few mental calculations.

"I'll say! That's twelve an hour, well over seven miles an hour in old money. Keep that up and you'll finish a marathon in under four hours."

"Don't think I could keep this up for four hours."

"I bet you didn't think you'd be managing half an hour this soon. What are you thinking about when you're running?"

This question required serious consideration. He surprised himself when the answer came to him.

"Nothing. That could be why I enjoy this machine so much," he laughed.

The thought occurred that running, for him, was a variant of sleeping. He looked up from the small screen attached to the equipment as he needed no external distraction whilst running. Physical exercise was becoming pleasurable.

"You're a natural, mate. There'll be nothing left of you if you keep going at this rate."

He hadn't weighed himself in months but did feel less encumbered about the midriff. He realised he was also sleeping well.

"I'll leave you to it then, Lasse!"

"Who?"

"The Finnish long-distance runner, not the dog."

****

He was feeling guilty. He would admit to anyone, even Myra, that he was one who ploughed his own furrow in life. Capitalism went its way, for better or worse, and he went his. He acknowledged it was a flawed social model, but a constant focus on society's myriad problems was beyond him. Hamstrung freedom was a concept with which he had long ago come to terms. He occasionally found himself lying awake, fearing for the future of his daughter. But there was little he could do to improve the lot of those whose lives had become, often through no fault of their own, a burden to themselves. Myra had agreed when he'd suggested setting up a standing order to the Salvation Army, with its focus on aid for the homeless.

For all those fortunate enough to forge financial security in life, there were many who could not. The belief had stayed with him that, in life, good fortune and misfortune come one's way in equal measure. Sarah Clifton, he realised, felt the same way. Coming to terms with that existential statistic increased one's likelihood of surviving the slings and arrows intact. He'd also learnt the importance of curbing the appetite for the physical and sensual delights offered by capitalism. The philosophy came easily to him, and he considered it his responsibility to pass on the advice to students. They should avoid taking to excess any of the temptations coming their way. Young people were bombarded with seductive images enticing them into the pleasures of recreational drugs, pornography, violence, gambling, clothing fashions, computer gaming, and alcohol. Addiction, in all its forms, was, to his way of thinking, the great risk inherent in the twenty-first century's promise of limitless opportunity. Pinocchio escaped the sinister threat posed by The Land of Toys, but his students mightn't.

He consciously eschewed dwelling at length on the multiplicity of the world's social problems, for which he had no answer, fully aware that he could be accused of being heartless. There was one aspect of being a teacher that he chose to ignore because, had he embraced it, he might have found himself overwhelmed with the feeling of helplessness. He worked at the social interface between wealth and poverty. The majority of children he taught were healthy, well-balanced individuals whose parents had successfully negotiated the procedural intricacies involved in being financially stable. They understood how to pursue a career, remain employed, manage their incomes, and pass on these life strategies to their children.

At the other end of the wealth spectrum, significant numbers of children he taught came from backgrounds where their parents led lives of personal and bureaucratic bewilderment. They struggled to grasp the procedures and tricks of providing for themselves and their families and, it seemed, always would.

Coping with his own domestic economy had become an ingrained priority for him. The filing cabinet at home bulged with every aspect of the family's documentation, from council tax to birth certificates. How did people cope without one?

He recalled a concern about letter writing he'd experienced as a young child. Observing his father sending and receiving letters on a daily basis, he'd asked him the reason for this regular activity. The explanation had been given that grown-ups had to write letters to pay all the bills for the house they lived in, the coal to keep warm, the clothes they wore and the food on the table. He'd worried that, by the time he was a grown-up, he might not have learnt how to write letters and have nowhere to live. Without clothes and food, he would die. Silly as this childhood anxiety now seemed to him, he was convinced that there were people unable to cope with the complexities of family finances, particularly as many of them now involved complicated online procedures.

He tried to imagine the indignity of living a life demeaned by irregular and low-paid employment, low-quality housing, and constant form-filling to claim social security benefits. It troubled him that the parents of a significant minority of his students operated within the jungle of emotional and material poverty, but there were too many variables for him to assimilate who was at fault for this reality.

Tony Tranter's welfare, at this moment, was of paramount importance. The helplessness he felt in the case of the boy's suffering disturbed him and, despite himself, he dwelt on the boy's plight. He taught Tony three times a week and studied him closely in the classroom. He also found himself hoping that the child wouldn't be absent, an indication that his domestic situation was worsening. The possibility that he'd been bullied by an older student he entirely dismissed.

Archie had agreed that Pat's photograph showed the latest bruising clearly and could be used as hard evidence, should a case ever be made against Mrs Tranter's new partner. If only her son could be encouraged to tell the truth, his safety might be ensured.

There had been no new injuries since the bruise on his cheek, but Tony had continued to be subdued and unresponsive. Was the child's father aware of the daily abuse his son was experiencing? The idea had occurred of trying to contact him, but he'd dismissed it.

The next time Tony arrived late for English, Biggsy was so relieved he issued no reprimand. A smile greeted the young boy instead of a frown as he took his place next to Noah Mintern, his classmate. The latecomer was struggling to concentrate on the lesson, staring into space when he should have been listening or writing. Just before the last buzzer of the day was due to sound, Tony began talking to Noah, explaining something that caused his friend's eyes to widen.

"Could I have a quick word with you, Noah, before you set off?" he called as the class departed.

Noah was usually the last to leave, so the request wouldn't delay him.

"I saw that Tony seemed a little unhappy during today's lesson. Can you tell me what he said to you just before he left?"

Noah looked up, lips pursed, uncertain as to how he should answer. An honest lad, telling untruths would never become a ready tool in his behavioural repertoire.

"He told me to keep it a secret, sir. I can tell you because you're his favourite teacher. He said he wasn't going home and he was going to run away."

Alarm at the revelation was tempered by relief that he'd asked the question and that Noah had answered it truthfully.

"Did he say why he was running away or where he was going?"

"He said he can't go home because he's frightened. He didn't say where he was going."

"He really did say he was frightened? Why's that?"

"There's a man living at his house who hits him. It's not his dad, though."

"Has he ever said anything to you before about running away?"

"No. It's the first time he's ever said that."

"Did he say where he'd be going?"

"No, sir. Didn't tell me. Do you think he really has?"

Biggsy was worried. He needed to find Tony.

"Not sure. You've done well to tell me all that, Noah. Thank you. Now off you go."

"OK, sir."

He hurried the small boy out of the room, locked the door and ran down the corridor towards the school exit.

****

As he ran, he barged into a boy carrying a rucksack with the words 'I'M NOT IN!' inked in above the strap. Calls of 'No running in the corridor, sir!' rang out behind him. He had no time to turn and smile.

"Sorry, lads. Emergency!" he shouted, by way of explanation.

He reached the school gate, where Archie Matthews was on duty. By chance, it was his turn to ensure good behaviour as boys left the site. There would also be a teacher a hundred yards down the hill, policing them at the bus stop. He stopped for a moment to apprise Archie of the reason for his haste.

"Can't stop, Archie. Tony Tranter may have decided to run away. His classmate just informed me that he's scared of someone at home who knocks him about. We know who. Can you ring Tony's home and alert his mum to the situation?"

"Poor little sod! Yes, I'll do that now."

"I hope I can intercept Tony before he carries out his threat. See you."

The sessions at the gym were paying off. He ran without stopping once, despite being fully clothed, as far as the bus stop. There seemed to be as many boys congregating outside the newsagent as there were waiting in line at the stop. An ageing local resident in a grubby knotted scarf and grey raincoat huffed and puffed his way through a group of pupils trying to edge their way into the shop.

But there were no sightings of Tony. Questioning younger pupils in the queue produced no results. The boy had been seen by no one. Perhaps he'd changed his mind and was on a bus home already. At a loss as to how he might continue his search, he set off at a brisk walk back up the hill.

Archie's office door was open. He was sitting at his desk, massaging his chin with thumb and index finger.

"Oh, there you are. Any luck down the road?"

"No. Wherever he was going, he was well away. I asked around, but not a sign of him."

"I got through to his mother on her mobile. She played dumb at first when I told her what Tony may have done and the reason he'd given his mate. Then she started to panic, saying that the school had a responsibility of care for her son, and she'd do all sorts of things to us. She was tearful and genuinely worried."

"Once he leaves the school, he's the parent's responsibility. What next then, Archie?"

"I said I'd ring her back in fifteen minutes to find out if he'd made his way home. In fact, it's almost time to ring again. If he hasn't shown up, it's a matter of contacting the police."

"Do you mind if I speak to her, particularly as I'm the one who discovered what he's up to?"

"Be my guest. I'll ring, have a word with her first and then put her on to you."

"Thanks."

Mrs Tranter must have had her phone to hand because she answered immediately. Before Archie had a chance to speak, a querulous voice confirmed the two men's fears.

"He's not come home!"

******

Chapter 10

"Then I spoke to her. She was in a state, understandably."

"What did she say?" Myra asked, her hand rubbing away with a tea towel at a spot on the kitchen worktop as she gave full concentration to her husband.

"Well, she wasn't grateful that I'd raised the alarm. She was angry, as though I were the cause of her son's disappearance. I told her that the school had contacted the police and that they would be visiting her shortly. That really set her off."

"Fingleton wasn't too happy when he was told that a police car would soon be pulling up in the staff car park. A young officer turned up, took our statements then set off for an interview with Mrs Tranter."

"When something terrible like this happens, it's often the case that the wrong person is seen to be to blame."

"I explained what Tony had confided to Noah, the boy he sits next to in class. He told Noah what he wouldn't tell us, that a man at home was laying into him on a regular basis. The man, Vince, is not his dad. I made a point of mentioning the boy's worsening grubbiness over the past week or so as well as the bruising I'd seen on his face."

"Oh, my God! That's awful."

"Yes, it is. But, for one reason or another, his mother didn't prevent it from happening."

"She may not have known. She may have seen the marks you saw and assumed they were the result of knockabouts with boys at school."

"They looked to be serious injuries to me. And the fact that he's not being looked after at home properly suggests she's other things on her mind, temporarily at least."

"She may not be seeing this Vince character for what he is. He may be striking the child when she's not around."

"You could be right. Hadn't thought of that. She said I should have kept Tony behind when I saw that he was upset during my lesson. I told her that he'd not been his usual bubbly self for the past two weeks, not just today. Then, when I mentioned the reason he'd given Noah for deciding to run off, she became tearful."

Myra found herself becoming emotional as she reflected on the boy's disappearance and the mother's plight. Two souls in need of desperate help. She was almost persuaded of the mother's innocence from what she'd heard so far.

"At that point, if she believed what I said, she must have started thinking about Vince's relationship with Tony. For the first time since her new partner's arrival on the scene, she may have found herself thinking not solely of her beau but worrying instead about her boy."

"You hear about situations like this so often. A woman, struggling to cope, takes someone else into her life, hoping for emotional and material support, with little knowledge of how that person will behave towards her children."

"Yet it continues to happen. I don't want this disappearance to end tragically. He must be found. Now that the police have been informed, they may manage to make progress where I wasn't."

"Where could he be?" Myra wondered aloud. "It's cold and dark. Anything could happen to him. There must be one of his acquaintances at school who'd know of places where he liked to spend his time."

"That's a good idea. While there's nothing to go on so far, it should be followed up. But the trouble is we can't do anything at school until tomorrow. God knows what may happen to him in the meantime."

"You don't have to wait until tomorrow. One of his friends may know the sorts of places where Tony goes out of school time. It's only early evening. The police could pay a call somewhere and ask."

"His only friend is good-natured Noah. Nobody else in his class has much to do with him. The little lad has also had to get used to living without his father around. He lives in a high-rise in Brentford. Not the most salubrious area for a mum on her own to bring up a child. I've never met her. No idea what she's like."

"What she's like and where she lives don't matter. A visit to Noah's home is worth a punt."

"You may be on to something. I didn't actually ask Noah if he knew anywhere that Tony might hang out. Should've done."

He wondered how he'd feel if he were Noah's mother, another young woman trying to bring up her son alone, having the police knock on her door at this time of the evening.

"Right, I'll call the police and put your suggestion to them. Noah's mother can't begrudge her son providing any information that could be useful if it saves his little friend's life."

He took out his mobile phone.

****

He'd formed an impression of Sally Tranter, but his imaginings could not have been further from reality. Personal prejudices could be unreliable, as he was discovering. She wore no make-up, had not dyed her hair blue and was not wearing a luminous track suit. Her short dark hair framed an attractive face, and there were no false eyelashes shading her piercing blue eyes. The red windcheater, tightened with a cord at the waist, highlighted her trim build. Taller than average, she cut an athletic figure.

Sitting opposite her in Archie Matthews' office, he felt disappointed in himself that his brief phone call with her the day before had caused him to misjudge her. He guessed that Archie was going through similar emotions as he sat himself down, opened a file and took out a sheet of paper. He looked it over and cleared his throat before speaking.

"Well, I have to say, Mrs Tranter, that we're all very relieved here at St Saviour's. How has Tony been since the police found him and brought him home to you last night?"

"He's fine, Mr Matthews. Just a bit upset, tired and hungry. I can't tell you what a weight was lifted from my shoulders when they phoned me with the news they'd found him."

Her voice, soft now that it was no longer under strain, indicated heartfelt gratitude.

"I wanted to come in and thank you both personally for finding my son. It was wrong of me to be so rude on the phone, particularly to you, Mr Biggs, but I went into a blind panic the moment I realised he'd gone missing."

"To be honest, my wife is the person who deserves your thanks. She suggested early yesterday evening that we get the police to talk to a school friend of Tony's to see if he might know of a secret place where your son liked to spend his time."

"Young Noah's mother was only too pleased to allow the police to speak to her son. Thank heavens she did, and that his friend remembered Tony sometimes went to Brentford Dock. He may not have been discovered so promptly otherwise," Matthews explained.

"I'd no idea he spent any time down there. Boys go off on their bikes to all sorts of places at the weekends. He's always been a bit secretive like that. Never tells me what he's been up to."

"Yes, he was found hiding under a section of canvas in the hull of an old narrow boat. These police dogs are marvellous, aren't they?" Matthews added, smiling before asking his next question. "Has Tony explained why he ran away, Mrs Tranter?"

Both men believed they knew the reason. Did Sally Tranter?

"I think I know why and it won't happen again, I can assure you. All this fuss is my fault?"

Hands clasped on her lap, she looked to the ceiling and sighed.

"My husband left me last summer. He'd been seeing somebody else for a year or so apparently. I eventually became suspicious and challenged him. I suppose the row we had made his mind up for him and he chose to go off with her. It was terrible for me, and Tony took it badly. I've no other children. I know he misses his dad."

She opened her handbag and began searching for something. Biggsy was worried that she would become upset, but Sally Tranter was too practical now for tears. She took a mint from a small plastic container and placed it on her tongue.

"Sorry, since I gave up smoking I live on these."

"I admire anyone who has the determination to drop the habit. I can tell you I found it tough," Matthews consoled.

"Oh, you too. Anyway, I've been a fool. Just before Christmas, I met Vince. He was a bit younger than me and very attentive. Life seemed to be offering me a new beginning. We dated for a while and then I let him move in with us. We got on well, and things were going fine. He was keeping Tony in line, and I thought I'd come up trumps. What I didn't know was that, when I wasn't around, Vince was mistreating Tony, verbally and physically. Tony told me all about it last night. I couldn't believe it. So caring to my face and a monster behind my back. I suppose it was a case of not seeing the wood for the trees."

"I'm sorry things have turned out the way they have, Mrs Tranter."

"Thank you, but I don't deserve any sympathy. I feel like such an idiot. When everything came out last night, I told Vince to pack his things and leave. He pleaded innocence, like all good liars, but he went. I'm having nothing further to do with men. Thank God, Tony's still in one piece."

Her eyes aglow with determination, she sat upright. Both men were full of admiration for her. It took courage to open one's heart to strangers and admit to having misjudged somebody so completely.

****

"You were right, love. Tony's mum knew nothing about the mistreatment of her son by her partner."

"Am I ever wrong!" Myra quipped. "You men are all amateurs in the sphere of human emotions."

"I'd have to argue that one with you, but you've certainly enhanced your reputation as ace detective's assistant. You're a sleuth in your own right now. What might be a female variation of the name Sherlock?"

Biggsy filled his mouth with another forkful of fish pie. He'd grudgingly accepted his wife's decision to alternate meat and fish during the week for evening meals. Fish nights weren't his favourite. Thankfully she'd not insisted he become vegetarian, a dietary change she rather fancied.

"I don't know. 'Sherlock' sounds so masculine, I can't be bothered trying to think of anything."

"Curlylock sounds pretty good."

"I don't think you could have suggested anything more stupid, my beloved. I sometimes think you're going soft in the head the way your mind works."

"Harsh. But, anyway, I hope that young Tranter comes out of all this in one piece. Violent Vince has gone, but the poor lad is still without a father."

"If what you tell me is true," Myra mused, becoming serious, "those boys at your school who now have both parents at home will soon be in the minority. Society is changing."

"That thought had occurred to me. I get the distinct impression that the majority of pupils I talk to you about, particularly the younger ones, keep quiet about their home lives for that reason. There's a kind of creeping father-envy about the place. I've even had boys call me 'dad' in the classroom, which is a bit of a giveaway."

He uncovered two prawns on his plate, balanced them on his fork and placed them on his wife's plate.

He was happy with pieces of cod and salmon in his pie, but he'd never been able to stomach prawns. The presence of one in his mouth created the sensation of chewing on an oversized piece of gristle.

"And I tell people you never give me anything."

"I'm sure it's a potential cause of bad feeling between boys. Most are cautious about mentioning their fathers in company these days. At parents' evenings, most students come to school with their mothers only."

"You wonder what all these bloody men are doing!" Myra exclaimed. "Given the choice between their children and a new piece of hot totty, the kids rarely get a look in. Talking of emotions, I think a lot of men are pretty clueless in that department. Most easily fall into the trap of mistaking lust for love."

"I love it when you start generalising so monumentally."

"The media must take a degree of blame. Female nudity has now become obligatory in films, even those with a parental guidance rating. Any young female actor knows she'll eventually be required to do scenes of full-frontal nudity. Males, on the other hand, only give us girls the pleasure of watching them undo their top shirt buttons in steamy sex scenes."

Biggsy laughed aloud at Myra's sudden shift from the deadly serious to anarchic hilarity.

"I can't keep up. So, we've shifted to an analysis of female exploitation in the film industry?"

"Correct. It's called lateral thinking."

The conversation was interrupted by an incoming call on Myra's mobile phone. The frown on her face as she looked at the screen disappeared and became a look of surprise.

"It's Neil's mum," she mouthed, as she pressed green to connect.

"Neil who?"

"Hello, Jan," she said, giving her husband a dimwit-of-the-year grimace. "How are you both?"

"Oh, that Neil," he muttered to himself.

"Yes, it was a lovely evening. We've not been out since. You can probably guess why."

The final comment, totally unwarranted in her husband's opinion, sent him into a bout of excessive eye-rolling.

"You have? Easter, you say. Well, I can't imagine a better time to get away from our perpetually gloomy shores."

Her nose wrinkled as she listened to the details of the Thompsons' holiday plans. Then her eyes widened as she took in news to her advantage.

"Jan, that is such a generous gesture. I can't quite take it in."

She paused for breath. A minute later, after which time her face had become radiant with pleasure, she spoke again. "Absolutely! I'd love to. Or, rather, we'd love to."

He was becoming agitated. The look of controlled glee his wife was giving him signalled a magnanimous gesture hinted at when the two couples had last met. He guessed it was an offer Myra would not let him refuse. A free holiday. His eyes widened and he shook his head gently from side to side. Ignoring these silent gestures, she turned to face the cooker.

"Of course, I could join you for a coffee Saturday morning at Nero's. Eleven, then. Can't wait, Jan. See you then."

Myra ended the call, an expression of bliss fixed on her face.

"No, Myra. Besides everything else, the Easter break is when I do all my GCSE admin. I can't afford to lose two whole weeks then."

"That's all right then because we'll only be away for a week. Don't worry. No need to press the panic button. I'm only going to see what Jan has in mind."

"I am panicking. The next thing you'll be saying is we're almost family anyway."

"Hadn't thought of that one, love. You'd better hurry, or you'll be late for whatever it was you were going to do."

"What was it I was going to do?"

****

Where he avoided confrontation, his professional adversary had the reputation of thriving on it. He had no alternative but to face her down on this occasion. He was still head of English, and one of his colleagues was being bullied. Whatever the consequences, he had to act.

The possibility of permanent damage to a working relationship and the risk of looking foolish didn't trouble him. In this situation, the first of those considerations might not apply. According to Andy, Toner was looking for a new post and could be at another school by September. By the time he was a working member of the management team, she'd be gone.

A person desperately seeking promotion, to his reasoning, should not risk blotting one's copybook. She should be showing herself at her best as headship material, and he might tell her this. She'd hardly raise a stink, should he upset her, by running to the head to complain if she were targeting the glowing reference she desired. Then again, Fingleton might have reached the point where he'd be pleased to see the back of her. But who would manage the school curriculum if she departed?

"The new deputy head of curriculum, you doughnut!" he said aloud to himself.

Top Tip No. 12: Nobody, but nobody, is indispensable to a school staff.

There was little possibility that this interview would result in public embarrassment, whatever he said. With that comforting thought, he pressed the button outside her office and awaited green for go. Almost immediately the illumination appeared.

"Good afternoon, Mr Biggs. Take a seat. What can I do for you?"

The question opened up a range of possibilities for him, from handing in her notice to joining a mountaineering team to attempt an ascent of Everest. Seating himself with legs crossed and arms folded, he looked at her steadily. The last time he'd been in this office, things had gone quite well for him. He was confident that he would also give a good account of himself on this occasion.

"I've been led to understand that you're less than pleased with a member of my department for some reason."

"If that were the case, wouldn't it be better for the individual concerned to be sitting there, instead of you?" she replied, narrowing her eyes and glancing at her laptop monitor.

"No. It wouldn't. I'd like to hear what complaint you wish to make about Mr Devlin, as I will be the one to resolve any professional issues with this junior member of the school staff."

"Who has told you that I have any grievance with Mr Devlin?"

The evasion reassured him, signalling the possibility that she wished to avoid confrontation. Time for a note of defiance.

"I'm not obliged to tell you that. As Nick's line manager, I need to know what he's supposed to have done wrong."

She looked at him, placed her elbows on the table and rested her chin on her hands. This studied attempt to appear relaxed wasn't working.

"And I need to tell you that the matter is a confidential one between Mr Devlin and me."

"I'm sorry, but you're going to have to do better than that. You may think you have a divine right to victimise staff for your personal entertainment, but a case of bullying in the workplace in my department is a matter that I propose to pursue with the head and my union representative."

This news brought the deputy head up short. Her change of expression from aloof amusement to the hint of a frown told him that she was uncomfortable. He guessed that no one had ever openly accused her of having thuggish tendencies before, and he was interested in her reaction. The prospect of her becoming angry did not worry him. He'd dealt with the full range of ill-tempered students in his time. The image of Toner as a truculent playground bully almost made him smile.

"I think you should consider your position very carefully here, Mr Biggs. You are making a very serious accusation against a member of the school's management team."

"I suggest that, if you wish to stay in school management, you reflect on your behaviour in this present situation and others that have resulted in accomplished teachers deciding against remaining on the teaching staff at this school."

He was amazed at his audacity.

"Are you implying that I have been responsible for members of staff choosing to leave St Saviour's?"

This response was far too quick for one innocent of such malpractice.

"Now there's an interesting line of inquiry that would also require investigation by my union. This situation could blow up in your face, with very unpleasant long-term consequences. I don't give a monkey's whatever about my career. I'm rapidly tiring of having to deal with people like you in education, and I'd be better off out of teaching. But your career would be going nowhere, should everything I know about your conduct at this school become public knowledge."

A longer pause. He couldn't refer directly to her after-school activities with Aaron Aimes in the old gym changing room, but he hoped that she might begin to wonder exactly what he did know. The words 'professional misconduct' would be worrying her. She could be asking herself if he'd had any involvement in the staff Christmas meal incident. He wasn't worried on his account if she were about to question him on this matter because, most importantly, Fingleton knew he hadn't. He hoped there would be one overriding query troubling her. Why is this ordinarily even-tempered nobody taking me on at my own game?

"If you really do wish to know why I have had cause to pull Mr Devlin up on a few occasions recently, it's because he's not marking children's work as often as he should."

"That's a criticism you could level at almost every teacher here, and in the UK for that matter. I suggest you raise the issue with the whole staff rather than pick on one junior individual. You should ask yourself whether your attitude towards Nick is merely one of spite, arising from personal, as opposed to professional considerations. That said, I have no interest in discussing this matter further with you."

Giving her no opportunity to get the last word in, he rose from his chair, maintaining eye contact the whole time. Before leaving, he had an ultimatum to deliver.

"I'm going to give you some valuable advice before I go. If you don't get off Nick Devlin's back, your whole house of cards here could come tumbling down."

****

His armpits were damp, and his head was buzzing. Although he'd not lost his temper, he felt aggrieved that he'd been forced to adopt a threatening posture. This consideration outweighed the sense of satisfaction he experienced at his controlled performance in Toner's office. All he had to do now was wait. If her vendetta against Nick continued, he would have to be as good as his word.

What had he to lose if he unleashed a storm at St Saviour's? He wasn't a careerist. There were no personal ambitions to satisfy. The house was paid for, but money would be needed for Ella's university fees and accommodation down the line. Then there were the holidays abroad. He was confident he could get a teaching assistant job somewhere, but there would be no urgency to do so. He and Myra had money in reserve.

Hazel Frears had alerted him to Nick's distress. It was Hazel, therefore, who should be told of the latest developments. He went to her classroom before starting his lunchtime playground duty. She deserved a confidential conversation with him, but there was rarely enough time in his day to do everything he would like.

"Hello, Hazel. Do you have a minute?"

"Yes, but only because it's you," she laughed.

"Sorry, but I have to be outside on duty, so I can't go into the detail I'd like. I saw Toner and gave her the low down. Either she stops victimising Nick or all hell breaks loose. That's about it."

"You decided against the subtle approach," she laughed. "Good for you."

"I kept my temper but made it clear that I'd be prepared to go down with her if she carried on."

"How do you mean?" she asked, pulling the lid off her plastic lunch box, and removing a package wrapped in aluminium foil.

"I explained that I'd play as rough as she's doing if necessary. There's much I could disclose about her unprofessional style, even if it meant me being finished in this place, but I'd prefer not to take that line. The truth is, I can no longer work with her as things stand. She is now in no doubt of that fact."

As he spoke, it struck him that there were now two people with whom he would choose not to work at St Saviours. Either middle age was changing him, or he was beginning to open his eyes and see beyond the piles of exercise books waiting to be marked.

"I hadn't imagined you'd take such a stern line, Biggsy. You're always so measured in your approach to all situations."

"Could be why people take me for a soft touch. But don't tell my wife that, or I may be in trouble. I'll keep you posted if there are any developments. Thanks again, Hazel. See you later."

Was he telling Hazel too much? Could he be accused of being unprofessional? He didn't care at this moment.

Rushed communication with colleagues was to be avoided, but he had to get outside and be visible on the field. Somebody on the senior management team would be sure to be on lunchtime walkabout, checking that he was doing his patrol. Another change in his circumstances suddenly occurred to him: he would be doing that very job from next term. Andy would also have less free time when he became department head, as he would be required to do regular lunchtime duties. To date, his second in department had avoided all voluntary tasks of this kind, arguing that those with a full teaching timetable should be excused from further impositions on their time. It amused Biggsy to think that he could well be checking on Andy's appearance on the school field in the future.

As he walked to his favourite spot on the far side of the field, a boy he recognised approached him. Alan Treadway, nonchalance personified, ambled alongside him.

"Dunno if you're interested, sir, but a blue car like the one you were on about is parked outside the school, just up the road a bit."

"Of course, it's Friday," he blurted, thinking aloud. "Thanks for telling me, Alan. Can you do me a favour? Without making it too obvious, can you wait here by the railings and, if the car comes along this road, make a note of the registration for me? Will you do that?"

"Don't see why not."

"Just up the road from the back car park, is it?" Biggsy asked, anxious to be off.

"Yeah. That's what I said, innit?"

Amused by the student's disdainful manner, he was certain Alan would do as requested. He set off at a brisk pace, hoping not to attract undue attention. No students could be seen in the car park. Almost as soon as he'd exited the school site, he heard a car ignition. The Polo pulled away at speed, giving him no opportunity to distinguish the full registration plate. He made no attempt to chase the vehicle but waited to ascertain the direction it took at the junction. Sure enough, it turned left.

He took his time heading back in the direction of his spy. Alan was where he had left him, leaning against the railings as though he were the teacher on duty.

"Did you get it?"

"Yeah. What's it worth then, sir?"

"Somehow, I knew this wouldn't be straightforward with you, Alan."

****

It was well after one o'clock when Myra returned home from her Saturday morning coffee date with Jan. She was abuzz with good humour from the moment she breezed through the front door. Something more than coffee must be working on her mojo.

"You must have had a good time, love. How's Jan?"

"She's great. Do you know, it's amazing how she and David have suddenly come into our lives, all through Ella?"

It was a worry how far Neil's parents were going to come into his life. They could come as far as they liked into Myra's, but he liked to keep those outside the immediate family at arm's length. His wife may well have been right when she ascribed this inclination to his being on the autistic spectrum. Whatever degree of autism he may or may not have, he was happy with the way he was. His world view was that if one gets too tight with people, something of oneself gets lost. Close friends were for those who liked closeness. He didn't.

"You both hit it off then?"

"Hit it off? It's as though I've found my long-lost twin."

He was on his guard whenever Myra used extravagant language when talking about her emotional responses to people.

"Lovely. You must have had plenty to talk about then?"

"Oh, yes! We never stopped. How long were we in that coffee shop together? Over two hours!"

Unable to stop himself, he had to know if his wife had thrown in their lot with the Thompsons and committed the family to Easter in Menorca. His whole work routine over the two-week break would be upset if he were anywhere but at home.

"Did Easter breaks and Mediterranean villas come up?"

Myra was not to be deterred by the obvious direction of his questioning. She considered toying with his anxieties but decided against wasting time.

"You must be genuinely psychic. As it happens, those were the main topics of conversation."

"They must have long-term friends who can go with them?"

"I'm sure you're right, but obviously nobody as important as us. Like I said, Jan and I get along famously, despite the fact we've only recently met. What I can't understand is why David was so taken with you on first meeting. He, apparently, was in entire agreement when Jan suggested the holiday arrangements to him."

For the moment, he put aside irritation at having his fears compounded. He found himself in new territory. The fact Myra considered it odd that he should have interest value for others didn't trouble him. But David Thompson did puzzle him. Not since his school days had he found himself in the market as having pal potential. The status quo of having few, if any, close male friends was something to which he'd become accustomed. Family was enough for him.

If Jan were trying to convince Myra of the sincerity of her offer, there was no reason to add the detail of her husband's enthusiasm for a new male companion. Myra was already hooked. On the other hand, Jan's astute powers of character analysis may have detected that a special inducement might be necessary to get the one fly in the ointment on board. That thought, of which he should obviously feel ashamed, could be doing her a gross disservice. A Kafkaesque image of himself as a fly thrashing about in ointment produced a wry smile.

Misinterpreting his expression, Myra interrupted his reverie.

"There, that's cheered you up, hasn't it? Somebody, besides me of course, doesn't think you're a social liability."

"No, you don't quite get it. I need that whole two-week period to sort out exam admin."

"Well, I don't need you to spend Easter, yet again, buried in paperwork. Anyway, there's one very important fact you're overlooking."

"What's that?"

"You won't be head of English after Easter. Remember? Somebody else will be you, doing what you think you have to do. And that you will be Andy. Or had you forgotten?"

There was something in what his wife was saying. She was questioning his assumption that he would be responsible for every aspect of his department's public examination preparation up to the very start of the summer term. Why hadn't he?

"I can't leave it all to Andy. Anyway, there's the other point I made when the subject of this holiday offer was first raised: I can't risk accepting such a gift from the parents of a student at my school."

"No problem there either. I'm accepting it."

****

Chapter 11

This would have to be done with caution. Experience told him that boys of any age do not discuss personal matters with any teacher, whatever the situation. He hoped that he could be the exception. A fortuitous encounter on the school field was his first plan of attack. Searching through the faces of the players in each of the four separate football games in progress, he saw no sign of his prey. A visit to the basketball hoops might prove fruitful. Strolling in that direction, unable to stop himself, he picked up a handful of empty crisp packets en route. As he emptied them into one of the waste bins provided, invisible to most pupils, he spotted a small group of younger boys loitering near the cycle shed. Tony and Noah were amongst them.

The pretext he chose for separating Tony from his friends was failsafe: first contact requires the officious approach.

"You boys should know better than to hang around near this gate. With bikes going missing as often as they do, we've got to keep the area out of bounds. I know you're all as good as gold and wouldn't so much as take sweets from a baby, but somebody else might think you look suspicious. You'd better make yourself scarce, lads."

Relieved at being allowed to take themselves off with no threat of a demerit mark in their diaries, the boys prepared to disperse.

"Oh, Tony, could you hold on a moment? I need to have a word about your homework."

"See you in the library in a minute, Noah," Tony called over his shoulder.

"Your homework's fine, Tony. Just wanted to check you're doing OK."

The boy gave his teacher a nervous glance and then looked down at his shoes. "S'alright, sir."

"You've not had an easy time of it. Nor has your mum. She had no idea what was going on and was so worried when she thought she'd lost you. She thinks the world of you, and things are likely to get better for you now. Trust me."

He was relieved that Tony didn't try to hurry off, embarrassed that a teacher should know all about his home life.

"I want you to know that, for the rest of your time at this school, I'll be a friend to you. I may come in handy to you one day. You can rely on me to be in your corner if you need a hand. I've not made a promise like that to any other pupil I've taught. Is that fine with you?"

He'd made a commitment to a pupil that circumstances might undermine. Wasn't he thinking last week that his time at St Saviour's could be drawing to a close? If he were to retain any integrity in this youngster's eyes, he'd have to stay for half a dozen more years yet.

"All right, sir," came the whispered reply.

"As well as the fact that your mum needs you to stick around and be strong for her, there's one other important thing you need to know."

"Yes, sir?"

"You'll soon be a teenager. Then, before you know it, an adult. What you do with your life then will be entirely up to you. All children have difficult things to deal with, at some time or other, but you're not a child for very long."

"Yes, sir."

Tony didn't seem convinced as he looked up at the face of this disconcerting middle-aged man.

"Off you go then, but don't forget what I said."

Had his words made any impression? If so, would Tony attach any credence to them?

Thinking about his own childhood, he recalled a primary schoolteacher who'd left a mark on him. At eight years of age, he'd somehow been aware that this kindly old lady, with a grey bun knotted tightly at the back of her head, had a special interest in him. She always had a warm smile, never told him off, and often gave him duties and responsibilities that other children craved. He would regularly find himself sitting passively, surrounded by children waving their hands wildly above their heads in the hope of being given the 'special job' that needed to be done. Many had been the time that Miss Collier had ignored the pleas and pointed directly at him.

There was one occasion when she set the class a story-writing exercise. The title was 'How the ladybird got its spots'. The task completed, he was surprised when she read his effort to the rest of the class. He vaguely remembered the storyline involving a red ladybird flying underneath the ladder of a shop sign writer and being showered with spots of paint. He'd told his mother about this minor triumph but was amazed at what followed. The story long since forgotten, he'd found himself the recipient of an even more unexpected accolade than the teacher's special praise.

His teacher stood before the class one morning holding up a large envelope and a package. They were for him. Glowing with delight, she asked him to come to the front of the class and made the presentation. The package contained two colourful summer shirts, one light blue, the other yellow. There was a ladybird design on the label inside the collar of each. Inside the envelope was a certificate with his name printed in the centre. How the class clapped! He was pleased with his prizes, but Miss Collier was overjoyed.

Thinking back on the episode, he wondered how the competition organisers had known his shirt size, particularly as he'd been small for his age. Miss Collier had, it seemed, taken a lot of trouble on his behalf.

He could be Tony's Miss Collier.

****

"Lads! Lads! Lads! This is just an artful diversion to waste time. We need to get on with the text."

The study of Chaucer was a challenge, and *The Miller's Tale* was no exception. His concern was redoubled: getting through the tale was taking longer than he'd planned, and Colley's unique brand of populist literary criticism was, as usual, one of the reasons. The boys could have their few minutes of fun and then he'd insist they resume serious study.

"There's something I can't get my 'ead around, sir."

"What's the problem now, Chris?"

"This book, sir. You say it was written over six hundred years ago, yeah?"

"That's correct."

"Well, what goes on in this story is good fun. No problem with that. But this stuff is twenty times worse than anything you see on those old repeats of Benny Hill. How come Benny got the push from the telly because everybody thought he was politically incorrect, and Chaucer is allowed in schools – for children to read?"

"Very astute of you, as usual, Chris. I am, of course, interested that you describe yourself as a child, but what you need to understand is…"

171

Colley wasn't prepared to be deterred from his rant by any teacher flannel. He wanted to cut to the chase of the nitty-gritty.

"I ask you. Not only does this Nick grab Alisoun by the you know what, but 'as 'is wicked way with her. Next minute she's sticking 'er backside out of the privy window for another geezer who fancies her! I ask you, is this sort of material suitable for young scholars like us? What sort of people at the exam board think this is acceptable for schoolchildren to study?"

General laughter erupted. Somewhere, in the not-too-distant future, he could imagine Colley doing a stand-up routine with just this sort of material at a comedy club venue. He found himself unable to answer the student for laughing aloud.

"What I was about to say before I was interrupted, was that scatology has always been a staple of English humour, back even before Chaucer's day."

"Scat who?" Bellchambers asked, biro hovering above his A4 pad.

Biggsy wrote the word on the whiteboard as he enlightened the class.

"It means toilet humour, traditionally that involving human excrement."

"You mean shit, sir?" Bellchambers inquired, with a look of distaste.

"Yes. When Nicholas sticks his bum out of the privy window and farts in Absolon's face, who is kissing what he thinks are Alisoun's lips, that's an example of scatology."

"Can't imagine Jane Austen included this in her bedtime reading, sir," Dixon chuckled.

"Probably not."

"Not very romantic either, is it, sir?" Gibson added, joining the discussion.

"It's not up there with 'An Officer and a Gentleman', I grant you. But you have to remember that all of Chaucer's tales are narrated by people of different social classes, many of them ordinary people."

"Just ordinary perverts, sir?" Quickfire Colley asked.

This last observation had the whole class rocking in their seats. He leaned so far back that his chair almost toppled backwards. A smart readjustment on the student's part prevented what could have been a serious accident. Or a humorous one, from the others' perspectives.

"We've been through all this before. *The Miller's Tale* is one of the twenty-four tales Chaucer wrote, and this one happens to feature low comedy. He presents a varied range of characters from different social strata, all of whom recount their stories in different styles. The miller just happens to be a rough and ready character, and his tale fits his character."

"Just filth really, innit, sir?"

Despite himself, Biggsy laughed again at Colley's pithy assessment.

"Anyway, getting back to my original point, sir," Colley persisted. "Benny Hill got kicked off the telly because, supposedly, he was too smutty. And yet, here we are, reading this scatology and it's classic literature. Where's the justice?"

"I can see you're not going to let this go, Chris. Chaucer employs many narrative techniques throughout *The Canterbury Tales*. He wasn't a one-trick pony. And besides being entertained, you're learning Middle English at the same time."

"I'm with you now, sir. So, if Benny Hill had written all 'is comedy sketches in Middle English, he'd be seen as a genius like Chaucer."

"That's one I'll have to think about, Chris. OK, guys. Fun's over. Let's get back to work."

****

Conflicting emotions were unsettling him. He was experiencing a growing sense of alienation from St Saviour's as an educational institution. The causes, he believed, were a combination of the circumstances surrounding relinquishing his position as head of English and the dramatic deterioration in his relationship with Andy. The open warfare with Toner contributed to his professional malaise, but she, hopefully, would be leaving the school soon. Yet his career trajectory, far from plummeting into oblivion, seemed set for a dramatic rise.

The irony of his situation set him thinking about working life in a way he never had before. Was this the secret of success in one's career? Was it possible to rise to the upper levels of a hierarchy once the seeds of contempt for it had been sown? The expression 'selling out' presented itself. One consoling factor convinced him that he could never be guilty of such cynicism: he was dedicated to the students.

Here he was, sitting in the headmaster's office, his feet planted in the thick carpet pile, about to state terms for his new school role.

Fingleton was explaining the details of what he expected from his new head of sixth form, and soon-to-be assistant head, after the Easter break. There would be all manner of additional responsibilities Biggsy hadn't reckoned on, including chairing the school council that met once a month in the library. Overseeing this important institution of school life could not be taken lightly.

"Students' views and requests must be taken seriously," Fingleton stated, "though within reason."

The role would not be the easiest to undertake. Pupils must be given a voice, but the senior member of staff chairing the council had to know when and where lines had to be drawn. The boys must not be given to believe that their every whim would be taken seriously. The power of the chair's veto would have to be applied whenever unreasonable demands were made.

It came as a surprise to the new sixth-form head when he was then informed he'd be required to introduce a new dress code policy. The head wanted the students in suits, not the jeans and trainers they preferred, and wheels would have to be set in motion to achieve this policy change. The realisation of the risk involved quickly dawned on Wheelhouse's replacement. He would have to accept the prospect of sacrificing a degree of his popularity amongst the boys.

"If anybody can make progress on the suited and booted front, you can, Mr Biggs."

He was uncertain how he felt about this issue. He did sympathise, to a certain extent, with Fingleton's intention. Indeed, he'd recently decided to become one of the suit-wearing fraternity himself whilst at work, but getting people like Christopher Colley into a whistle would take some doing. There'd be all manner of protests from his year group at having to wear a suit to school in their last term at St Saviour's.

This final unexpected instruction was a worry. Most definitely a tall order, but some form of quid pro quo might make the challenge a little more palatable.

Biggsy was learning to be nobody's dupe. He had conditions of his own that would need to be met if the uniform initiative were to be accepted. Before naming them, he reminded himself of the defiance he'd shown towards the head who'd been so dismissive of one of his students the previous term. Failing to turn up at his office with Dixon, a member of his tutor group who was prepared to offer an apology to the head for assaulting a rugby player from a rival school, hadn't impressed Fingleton one bit. But he'd ridden out the head's disappointment in his head of English.

Time for some horse-trading.

"A baptism of fire, so to speak. That would be a radical departure from the status quo, headmaster. I would be prepared to start the ball rolling, but I would ask you to consider accepting two conditions. I'm sure you won't have a problem with them."

Fingleton saw something in the demeanour of the man before him that both discomfited and pleased him. He waited.

"I would ask you to promote Sarah Clifton to second in English, officially, and to begin the process of installing a hot drinks machine in the sixth-form common room. I should be grateful if you would implement the second request soon after the start of the summer term, so that Dave Wheelhouse can announce its imminent arrival before he retires."

"You certainly think fast on your feet, Mr Biggs. That's a quality that should serve you well when you join the management team next year. The first request I have no problem with whatsoever. Sarah is an asset to your department. She's developing a reputation for being something of a mover and shaker. Is it true that your department's tuck shop was her idea?"

Nothing got past the head. There was no way of ascertaining the vast number of eyes and ears Fingleton had around the school, and they were all highly effective. There was no point in stating anything other than the truth.

"Yes, she saw a failing in the department's teaching and learning, owing to a lack of basic course texts, and decided to do something about it. I gave her my full support, in the knowledge that we would only have two or three months at most to raise funds for the textbooks we needed before pressure from other departments would cause us to be shut down. Sarah was also aware of that probability, but insistent that we would be able to buy the essentials we needed within that brief time frame. She was right too."

Fingleton leaned back in his chair and gazed at the ceiling.

"Yes, I had no choice but to accede to pressure from several curricular areas, though I was reluctant. Their objections arose, of course, from envy. You have to admit, though, that I did give your department a few extra weeks before I effected the closure of the tuck shop."

"We were very grateful for that flexibility on your part, headmaster."

"So, on to your second request. The little matter of the hot drinks machine. I had initially given Mr Wheelhouse to believe that such an installation would prove to be manageable. However, there were various setbacks. The necessary contractual agreement with a hot drinks provider proved to be the main obstacle.

I hadn't imagined the cost implications to be quite so prohibitive. I'm still of the same mind."

"There could be a way around that. Setting up a school tuck shop, providing the same healthy snacks that we've been selling, could generate a significant profit for the school. A proportion of that money could go towards the running of a drinks machine, couldn't it?"

"That would work in theory," Fingleton conceded, "but I'm not sure that I want large numbers of staff giving up what little free time they have here supervising a school tuck shop. I know that, with the closure of your venture, there have been student demands for it to be reinstated. That could only be realized, as you have surmised, as a whole-school initiative. Not keen on that at all, whatever the boys say."

"Your main objection being...?"

"As you've asked, I might as well be frank. School tuck shops may have been a feature of schools in the past, but they have no place in the twenty-first century."

The head did have a point. He was right, of course. Thinking about it, there was a whiff of Greyfriars about the concept. But then Fingleton took him by surprise.

"However, I could consider moving forward with the idea of an automated snack system, which would be more appropriate for a modern secondary school. I'll do a bit of research. There must be companies that offer schools both hot drinks machines and those that dispense food items. Leave it with me and I'll get back to you."

****

"The head's office is becoming your second home."

Myra hesitated before taking another bite from the slice of cheese on toast he'd prepared for her tea. Another Saturday was drawing to a close all too soon. Before he knew it, Sunday evening, that dreadful time of the week would be upon him. He wondered if those in other lines of work experienced the same degree of anxiety that he did about the prospect of starting another week of work. The enjoyment of interacting with the boys was still there, but the bureaucracy was becoming intimidatingly unmanageable. The older he got, the worse the fear became. Larkin's toad of work was well and truly squatting on his own life.

"I thought you and he didn't get along all that well."

"We have to these days. There are no flies on him. He's priming me for next term and beyond, setting out the blueprint for the rest of my career at St Saviour's. Yesterday afternoon, he itemised the list of my official duties, not to mention others that go under the school radar."

"That won't be to your liking. You've never been the devious sort. By the way, you've surpassed yourself with this cheese on toast. There are certain things you're good at around the house."

"I do specialise in one or two domestic areas. Putting things under the grill is one of them. Getting back to Fingleton, he's easier to get on with if you're one of his team. That's what worries me. I naturally recoil from the idea of being on easy terms with management."

Despite the welcome distraction of her toast, Myra took in the full import of what her husband was saying and added a useful qualifying quip.

"Not that surprising because you recoil from being on easy terms with me."

"You noticed? Anyway, I've a bit of a reputation on the staff for being something of an anti-management maverick. And suddenly, I'm looking to be one of the head's poodles."

"He's clever," said Myra, striking a serious note. "Having you on his side will make his life a little easier. You've just got to stick to your guns on the issues you believe in."

A groan escaped him at the trotted-out cliché. Trite as the sentiment sounded, he began thinking how easily beliefs could be discarded in one's middle age. What on earth would he be like in old age? He pictured himself as the family curmudgeon, a permanent fixture glued to his worn-out armchair in the corner of the room. Then he thought of his mother. She was anything but a grumpy misery. There was hope. He prayed he'd inherited her contentment gene.

"I'm worried that I may be losing sight of the few remaining principles I believe in, Myra. At management level, it seems, those I still cling on to might have to be shelved, as and when necessary. Running a school is often more of a pragmatic than a principled process."

"You don't imagine you may be overthinking this business, do you, love? People routinely make compromises in their working lives. The more responsibility you have, the more you're required to compromise."

He considered his wife's logic. She was the realist, more grounded in the everyday world than he wanted to be. Did that make him naïve? Hanging on to his adolescent inclination to want everything out in the open and above board was going to be even more problematic next term.

"We should switch jobs, love. You seem to be able to rise above the dross that constitutes the daily round."

"I don't dwell on things over which I will never be able to exert any control. I don't fret about apparently insoluble situations and long-term plans like you do. I'm more a person who enjoys sensations, and looking forward to them keeps me afloat."

"What sort of sensations are you particularly geared up for at the minute?"

"I suppose the thought of pushing my toes into warm sand on a sunny beach, with the sound of the breaking surf in my ears and a gentle breeze caressing my face."

"I shouldn't have asked. You've got Menorca mania."

"And why not? You did ask. Just get used to the idea."

The idea was becoming a hard fact. He'd presented his objection to the holiday offer. It had been rejected.

"My job at St Saviour's could well be at risk if word gets around that I've had a free holiday, courtesy of the parents of one of my sixth-formers."

"That could be a good thing. You've gone on and on since the start of the school year about not being happy there. Anyway, there's no need to worry on that account: Neil's been told never to mention the subject of his parents' villa at school. They don't want to risk him being victimised for coming from a wealthy background, so he's hardly likely to mention you as his new holiday chum, is he?"

It was Custer's last stand all over again. Myra had broken through his last line of defence and nailed him. There was nothing more to be done.

****

"I always recommend this short story to any student intending to study English at university. What did you make of it?"

Simon sat opposite him in the office. The young man rubbed his chin, pursed his lips and exhaled slowly.

"It was a lot easier to get through than *Howards End*, obviously because it was so short, and I found it quite powerful."

"Didn't you find *Howards End* powerful?"

"Well, yes, but you don't imagine a short story being able to hit you in the same way as a full-length novel."

So, *The Celestial Omnibus* had made an impression. Conscious of the fact that literature study at school risked turning students away from reading for pleasure, he'd offered Forster's short story as an antidote to, what often became, the laboured analysis of literary texts.

The unnamed boy in Forster's story possesses a curiosity for life and a passion for literature that his father ridicules. He believes the only good thing for a child to do with a poem by Keats is to learn it by heart. When revising for A-level in English Literature over thirty years ago, Biggsy had been advised to memorise Hamlet's soliloquies. There were still teachers who insisted that every study text be memorised backwards if examinations were to be passed.

"The boy's supernatural journey to heaven took me by surprise," Simon continued, "then I began to realise it represented his imagination opening up to literature in an emotional way."

"Is that concept alien to you? Do you ever experience it when you're in lessons?"

"I can't honestly say I've been affected that way yet by any of the books since I started the A-level course."

He wasn't surprised that Simon had answered the question honestly or that he'd yet had no experience of literary excitement since starting the subject. The teaching to which many children became accustomed, it seemed, was more likely to induce boredom than excitement.

"Fair point, Simon. I felt the same when I was studying for my A-level, until a student teacher named Mr Ball started taking us one lesson a week for a full half-term. He was a geeky type who generally went through hell with the teaching groups he was given. In one of my A-level lessons with him, whenever he turned to write on the blackboard, boys threw ripe blackberries at him. By the end of the lesson, the back of his white shirt was dark red. I wasn't involved, I hasten to add, but my classmates thought it was very funny."

Simon's expression turned to one of distaste. He knew what the student teacher must have felt.

"Children of whatever age can be cruel, as you know, but they don't always realise the effect such behaviour has on their chosen victims. The pursuit of adolescent fun can justify all manner of vindictiveness. Most online trolls, I'm sure, have limited awareness of the pain they cause others. The emotional immaturity and personal insecurity of such people do untold damage to the innocent souls they target. Bullies of this sort can carry the habit through to adult life."

Sensing Simon's growing discomfort, he decided to get back to Mr Ball.

"Anyway, this student teacher gave us the task of selecting three novels to read by any one author of our choice. We then had to write an essay reviewing the works. I chose Graham Greene – no idea why – and had the kind of literary awakening the boy in this story has."

"The first time I experienced that in a book I had to read at school was in Year 9 with *The Nature of the Beast*. I was looking at the language the writer used, not just wondering what would happen next."

"That comment makes me feel pleased the department chose the novel as a class reader. Anyway, Mr Ball connected with me, if he made no impression on any other boy he taught at my secondary school. I'll be forever grateful to him. Without his influence, I may never have discovered the joy of reading. It was no longer a study chore. I loved Greene's books. I didn't have to take exams on *The Power and the Glory* or *The Quiet American*', but I found them memorable in ways that the set texts weren't."

"I suppose *King Lear* could be having a slightly unexpected effect on me. The language the king uses in his mad ravings works on me, and the Fool is a revelation. But there isn't always time to interrupt Mr Orchard and discuss language. I couldn't do that in front of the rest of the class, anyway. I'd be too self-conscious – afraid, I suppose."

Biggsy paused, wondering how any teacher could respond to such a disheartening admission. He wouldn't ask Simon to talk again about the frustration he'd lived with since starting at St Saviour's. Being a gifted student could be a curse in the state education system. Simon knew it, and he knew it.

"Students of your ability make enormous compromises. You grew out of the classroom experience years ago, but you still have to turn up and sit in class lesson after lesson. You're also going to be hamstrung by the nature of the teaching you receive, which has to accommodate students reliant on being spoon-fed, the teaching method to which many have been groomed."

A frown appeared on Simon's face. He said nothing.

"Students of your talent cope as best they can with the teaching limitations to which they're exposed in the secondary school system. I know you must be doing this already, but I'll spell it out for you. Allow your imagination to be fired by literature, whatever way it's taught here. Resist falling into the trap of allowing your opinion of writers and their works to be coloured by the way their books are taught. I often wonder how Shakespeare would have reacted if he had known that his plays would become the staple diet of children's English lessons centuries into the future, butchered by tens of thousands of teachers down through the ages. I imagine he'd have thrown himself over a cliff."

Simon allowed himself a wry chuckle.

"I'm going into church sermon mode, so I'll shut up now."

****

"It's wonderful."

"I know. Mobile phone technology has come on leaps and bounds."

"I'm not talking about my phone, jughead. I'm talking about what I've got on it."

He looked up from the dining table on which he was marking exercise books, lowered his glasses and squinted in the direction of his wife. Seated in an easy chair beside the glowing gas coal-effect fire that had cost hundreds of pounds, and that he didn't believe was worth the expense, Myra was peering in delight at her phone. She insisted that, at weekends, he did his marking downstairs to keep her company on the day of rest. He acquiesced, on condition that the volume on the radio be turned down. Trying to concentrate on the vagaries of students' written expression was difficult when Motorhead was booming away in the kitchen.

"These photographs that Jan sent me of the villa are lovely. They bought the place twelve years ago and have done wonders with it. It's a single-storey property, but there's so much space. Looks so bright and airy. Beautiful off-white floor tiles throughout, four bedrooms, a sun deck and a pool big enough for a proper swim."

She stretched out her arm, inviting a perusal of the images on her phone. Readjusting his glasses, he glanced at an image of a sunlit terrace with a shimmering pool in the background, smiled, then returned to his books.

"Don't know how people can afford such an expense. The upkeep must cost a fortune."

Myra had lived long enough with her husband to ignore the habitual indifference of his depressive personality. There were people on the planet who were demonstrative in their enjoyment of life, and she was one of that number.

"They've a circle of friends out there who keep an eye on each other's properties – pool maintenance and that sort of thing."

"You obviously consider that we've now moved into their circle. Do you think it will last?"

"What do you mean?" Myra asked, looking up from her phone in mild consternation.

"Well, if Ella and Neil end their relationship, how does that leave us with his parents?"

"You're so pessimistic. If there's a chance to kick the can of negativity, you'll do it."

"I'm just being realistic. You've already got our daughter married off and her in-laws with their feet on our mantelpiece," he stated in a barely audible monotone as he returned to his work.

"Whatever becomes of their relationship, I would like to think that the friendship we've formed with Jan and David will be a lasting one. No reason whatsoever why it shouldn't."

As he thought about his wife's last statement, he folded his arms, hugged himself and threw his head back.

"On this one occasion, let me decide what's best for us. We're not getting any younger and we need to ease up a bit now. If it were left to you, we'd never do anything beyond the daily grind. There comes a time when one has to step off the roller coaster of life and undizzy your mind. You'll find the concept alien at first, but you'll grow into it."

"That's a new one – undizzy."

"You know what I mean. Your head's a clutter of career crap. Nothing else gets through to that cranium of yours."

The thrust of Myra's argument was not lost on him, as it might have been in the past. Her tone was solicitous, not irritable. He understood that she was being protective of him, an instinct he was apt to overlook.

"You've worked hard for thirty years, love. You've earned the right to pass the reins to someone else from time to time."

"I suppose you've got a point. Wouldn't be the end of the world if anybody got wind of this freebie."

"That's more like it. Remember how we used to do things spontaneously when we were young?"

"Just about. There was that time we missed the last train back from Brighton and slept on the beach. Can't believe that was us."

"How could I forget!" Myra replied, standing up. "By the way, where did you put the laptop when you last used it?"

"It's by my side of the bed. Why?"

"Oh, I've just got to book some flights."

****

Chapter 12

"Well, if you're set against moving, Mum, you could at least treat yourself to a new armchair. This sofa's seen better days, too."

"I'm not wasting good money at my age, son. There are years left in this suite. Anyway, tell me what you've all been up to."

Snugly seated on the sagging sofa, Biggsy, Myra and Ella sipped tea from Aynsley teacups. Barbara Biggs was in good spirits, this being the first time since the previous summer that the whole family had visited her. Wearing her new heavy-knit cardigan and smart black jersey trousers, she was excited about the rare prospect of being taken out for lunch. The occasion would be even more special because Sandra, her daughter, would be meeting them at the restaurant with her teenage son, Mark.

The Sunday traffic on the M4 had been light. The family's early arrival meant there was a good hour to have a chat over a cuppa before going off to The Globe. Other than the good food served up there, the restaurant's log fire made it that little bit special.

"Well, you won't believe it, Mum, but we've a holiday abroad booked up for the Easter break," Myra replied. "All of us are going. I managed to twist your son's arm and get him to spend a week in Menorca when he'd rather be doing examination work at home. First time ever."

He smiled, not in anticipation of the 'first time ever' Easter holiday, but at his wife's keenness to share the news of her success.

"Dad works so hard, Gran. He really deserves a proper holiday," Ella added.

"Ooh, Menorca. How lovely! If I know my son, he must have taken some persuading. He'd work himself into the grave if somebody didn't take him in hand."

"Yes, Mum. It's difficult trying to keep him away from his school stuff."

Myra didn't look at her husband to check his reaction to her confirmation of Barbara's opinion. She knew he'd be feeling uncomfortable at being talked about.

"When he was a boy, he was just the same. One track mind. He'd either be out playing football or indoors reading or doing homework. You wouldn't hear a peep out of him – wouldn't even know he was there. Even had to call him down from his room for meals. Never hungry like most boys. He didn't cause me a day's trouble."

Myra compared this version of Biggsy to the one she knew. He was still much the same, locked in his own world at home, patiently wading through tedious paperwork that would send anyone else to sleep. She had long ago rationalised her husband's professional devotion by concluding that there were people who simply have inordinately high boredom thresholds.

"Did he have lots of friends as a boy, Barbara?"

"There were one or two I remember who used to come knocking for him, but not that many to be honest. He was a lad who was happy in his own company. Don't know where he got that from because his dad and I had friends galore."

"Ah, poor Dad! Sounds like such a lonely childhood. Was he a happy boy, Gran?"

"Funny question to ask, Ella. I couldn't honestly say he was loud or happy-go-lucky like the rest of the children on the estate. How can I put it? He always seemed to be in a kind of dream, though I'm not sure what was on his mind. Playing football and reading books. Busy, busy! That was your dad as a boy."

"I was just quiet. Took me a while to come out of my shell, that's all."

"Oh, he was very quiet. That's true. Worried me a bit sometimes. But Dad said he was just different, a thinker more than a doer."

"Dad had it about right. We can't all be shouting and bawling our way through life. I just kept myself to myself."

"Never had a temper like some of them. But if anybody upset him or let him down, he'd go into a mood, a real silent grump. Sometimes lasted for days. Probably because he'd never dream of letting anyone down himself. If he said he'd do something, he did it."

"Well, it's fun sitting here in the psychiatrist's chair, folks, but I think we need to be setting off to enjoy this family meal we're all looking forward to."

"I'll just go and powder my nose then, son, if that's all right with you?"

His mother hoisted herself out of her armchair and brushed imaginary dust off her cardigan. She turned towards Myra and Ella, fixing them with a conspiratorial look.

"He can be very masterful, can't he, girls?"

****

Ella arrived home from school to find her mother engrossed in two travel guides on Menorca. Legs tucked under her on the sofa and sipping from a mug of tea, she looked a picture of contentment.

"Hello, love. Just treated myself to some light reading. Besides soaking up the sun by the pool, there's loads to do on the island. The nightlife in Mahon looks exciting. Doesn't usually get going till midnight apparently. They love their gin – I'd better control myself. Don't want to let everyone down with our generous hosts."

"Yes, not long till we're off. What is it – three or four weeks? I so want to tell my friends about it, but I'm keeping quiet."

"As per your father's instructions, Ella, not mine. If he'd had his way, he'd have sworn us to secrecy on the Bible."

"I can see why he doesn't want anyone at school to know about it. Neil won't say a word."

"They don't come any more secretive than your dad. He doesn't give much away – to anybody."

"From what Gran was saying, he's always kept himself to himself. I wonder what makes someone like that?"

Myra looked up from her reading material and gave her daughter a quizzical look.

"He's been that way as long as we've been together. It's as though he holds himself tight inside. I'd love to know what he's like with the kids at school because he's an introvert when it comes to mixing with adults."

"He did let himself go a bit at Christmas with Grandad when they started drinking."

"And look where it got him – in casualty at the hospital. Typical! He lives life expecting something to drop on him from a great height at any moment."

"I know what you mean, Mum. I love Dad to bits, but I hope I don't marry someone like him."

Myra smiled at the admission. Ella was a socialiser, towards whom others were instantly attracted.

"Your dad's totally dependable – a one-woman man. Just a pity he's a bit lacking in the getting-your-rocks-off department. One thing to remember with relationships: you don't get everything you want from one person. It's all about compromise. Don't fall for all the sentimental slush you read in teen magazines."

"Now I come to think of it, there are some things about Neil that remind me of Dad."

"What exactly?"

"He's a bit of a loner too, I suppose. Self-contained. That's one of the reasons I was attracted to him."

"He sounds like someone who's not going to follow the crowd. Has a mind of his own. That may come from him being an only child."

"Yes, and I get the feeling Neil's someone who needs looking after."

"Oh my God! And they say lightning doesn't strike twice."

"What do you mean?"

"Nothing at all, love. Just enjoy each other's company and let time do the rest. Incidentally, on that subject, I'm assuming you and Neil will be sleeping separately in Menorca. I hope his parents are in total agreement on that fact."

What you get up to besides that is your own business, thought Myra.

"Of course, Mum. They're not new agers."

"Just play safe at this stage. There's all the time in the world to get carried away by the other."

"The other what, you two?" Biggsy asked pushing open the lounge door.

The two had been so focused on their conversation that they were taken unawares by his appearance.

"Nothing you'd be interested in, darling."

****

"How's everything going with you two these days?"

Tony Tranter was all packed up and ready to depart, but he was hanging on for Noah Mintern who, as was his custom, took an age to put his belongings away after a lesson.

"OK, thanks, sir," Tony replied. "Mum's just bought us a new telly but she doesn't know how to work it. I do so I'm in charge of it."

187

"That doesn't surprise me. There's not much you don't know."

"Just waiting for Noah. He's coming round to mine to watch it till his mum picks him up."

"It's good to hear you're both such good mates. It's not the easiest thing to find a friend you can trust."

Having put everything where it belonged, Noah zipped up his jacket and hoisted his rucksack over his shoulder.

"Ready, Tony. Sorry I took so long."

The two boys scuttled off, their excited exchanges on their planned viewing echoing along the corridor.

The final buzzer had sounded only ten minutes earlier, and the English corridor became silent. As he was collecting up the piles of year seven coursebooks from the end of each row of tables, Andy sauntered into the classroom.

"So, she's on her way then, mate," he said.

"Yes, I'd already picked up on that news. They'll be advertising for a replacement soon."

Biggsy had always considered himself lucky, but he believed that Andy had the luck of the devil. Not only had he landed the job of Head of English by the skin of his teeth, but Toner would be long gone by the time he took up the post next term. He'd be spared the torment of working under the woman he'd publicly humiliated. Where was the fairness in that?

"The head of a nice little girls' secondary school in Reigate. They don't know what's coming to them," Andy laughed.

"Let's hope the next deputy head is more to your liking. You never know – could be somebody worse."

"Might even be you one day down the line. You never know."

"Not a chance, Andy. Fingers is happy for me to keep the sixth-formers sweet, but he wouldn't want someone like me having any curriculum responsibility in the school."

"Just thinking aloud. Anyway, it's not possible the person could be any worse than Toner. Believe me. On another tack, do you think young Aaron will still feel the need to get away?"

"I'd like to think he believes he has a future here."

"The two of them were a mismatch all along, as far as I could tell. She's hell-bent on getting to the top and he strikes me as somebody who actually enjoys teaching."

"I'm afraid I'm not an expert in the love stakes, so I wouldn't know what's going on in Aaron's mind. What's going on in yours as regards leading English next term? Wholesale changes?"

"Are you kidding? Everything's running like clockwork."

Whilst Andy busied himself in the office and he was piling textbooks up on a worktop at the back of the room, he decided a little probing was called for.

"Have you seen the head to discuss your new job since the interview?"

"I've an appointment with him next Monday. He must have a few words of wisdom he wants to pass on."

There was no doubt Fingleton would also have a full dossier of curricular imperatives for Andy, besides the news that Sarah was likely to be lined up as his second in department.

"Have you given any thought to who'll be your number two?"

"Yes, I'd prefer Sarah, but I'm not sure she'd want it. Last term she said she was set on taking the pastoral route to promotion. She wanted the job you've landed."

"That's true. It'll be interesting to see what transpires."

"I can't believe the changes we've experienced since Christmas. Let's hope it all works out, eh?"

****

"Your undercover man was right. JB08 WMY."

"Alan Treadway's proved his usefulness, but it came at a price."

"What do you mean?" Archie Matthews asked.

"I quickly had to come up with some fringe benefits – several merit marks to counter his demerits – in gratitude for his spotting the registration. No flies on that boy."

"He's a card, that lad. I see a fine career before him as a copper's nark."

"Have the police found the Polo?"

"Yes, abandoned in a car park at the back of Twickenham High Street. They'll eventually go over it, I suppose, and see if they can get any print matches or whatever."

Archie Matthews had invited him into his office to discuss developments on the in-house drugs matter. The deputy head looked weary, or wearier than usual.

"Have one of these to keep your strength up."

He produced an open packet of chocolate digestives from his drawer. Politeness decreed that the biscuit should be taken.

"Abandoned, eh! No surprise there."

"This must be a serious operation if they ditch their transport the moment they discover it's attracting unwanted attention."

"The police informed us of their find this morning. They think the dealers are from an out-of-borough network for reasons they didn't explain. It looks as though we'll have to start all over again and be on the lookout for another car parking up at the back of the school. Anything of any interest your end?"

"No. This is one situation where the boys will be in fear for their lives. Anybody who knows or sees anything will keep shtum. I've spoken to Jermaine, in his capacity as head boy, only to alert him to our concerns. I felt guilty doing that, bearing in mind his brush with death last term."

"This is one problem we must confront head-on. These people are ruthless."

"I'll involve Treadway no further. Can't take any risks whatsoever from now on."

He thought of Myra's warning. She was right, of course.

"On the surface, things seem fine at the school, but I'm not sure I'd be able to identify every boy involved in substance abuse. I often wonder about the scale of our problem. I'm sure the actual number of offenders would terrify me. I won't use the word 'addicts'. I remember I liked the smell of that glue you'd get with those plastic aircraft kits. Never dreamed it could be fatal. Apparently, glue kills more people than hard drugs."

"The whole mind-expanding scene of the sixties probably seemed like a good idea at the time," Biggsy mused in an undertone.

"Yes. Timothy Leary and the like have a lot to answer for. If they could only see the human wreckage that's resulted from their delusions."

Matthews took another biscuit from the packet, sweeping away crumbs that had accumulated on the desktop with a brush of his forearm.

"Who'd be a parent!" he exclaimed. "We were never able to have our own. I guess there are some consolations in being childless. Changing the subject, how's young Tony doing lately?"

"He's back to his old self since his mother gave Uncle Vince the order of the boot. It's a terrible thing to see a small child living in constant fear."

"Well, there's one happy ending to celebrate," the deputy head concluded, returning his biscuits to the drawer. "Protecting our boys from an organised gang of drug pushers won't be so easy, though, I'm afraid."

"Frightening."

****

For every teacher at St Saviour's, the fear of losing one of the few free lessons on one's teaching timetable, owing to staff absence, was a constant worry. That time when the marking mountain could be blitzed was priceless. Those in middle management also had the concern of being on call from the school office to deal with classroom emergencies, a time-consuming but essential practice that could result in the loss of a whole free period.

The office phone rang. He picked up to hear the tremulous voice of Gill, the secretary responsible for putting classroom callouts through to staff. The knowledge that she would be disrupting a teacher's valuable catch-up time always caused her a degree of anxiety. As one of those who taught her son, James, he was on friendly terms with the secretary. Knowing what was coming, he had no intention of giving her a hard time, whatever he might be thinking.

"So sorry, Biggsy, but there's a request for you to go to Mr Baker's maths lesson, just around the corner from your room. There's a bit of trouble with his year nine class."

Shit! Shit! Shit!

"No problem, Gill. I'll get right along there. Thanks."

"Thanks so much. Really very sorry."

There had been an increase in callouts over the past week or so. His explanation was that, as the public examination period approached, teachers were inclined to become more edgy, often without realising. Students were quick to detect and react to slight increases in staff members' stress levels in the classroom. Thus, teachers could become the architects of increased pupil misbehaviour, or perceived misbehaviour. The teacher, to whose aid he was hurrying, was a prime candidate for inciting classroom mayhem at this time of the year.

Alan Baker's educational priorities were antithetical to his own. He would have hated being taught by the man who had the widest range of methods for browbeating and humiliating students. Mathematics teachers were in very short supply in secondary schools, which might explain why Baker was such a conceited pedagogical tyrant. Much as it pained him to bail the bully out, he had no alternative.

The first sight that greeted him outside the classroom was a tall, heavy-shouldered boy peering through the glass panel in the door. As well as making faces to his mates inside, causing general laughter from the class, he gave the door a hefty kick.

"Pack that in now!"

The last syllable was bellowed, with the result that the word echoed down the corridor.

Having, quite possibly, the loudest voice in the school, he kept it in reserve for occasions such as this. It could be relied upon to take any boy by surprise. Every teacher has his or her own particular attributes. The taller ones can be overbearingly intimidating. Others, highly attractive or strikingly handsome, can twist even the most recalcitrant reprobates around their little fingers. Biggsy was a little below average height but was blessed with two gifts. The decibel level of his optimum bark could induce anything from spontaneous tears to a bowel evacuation, if the rumours were to be believed.

The boy jumped visibly and turned. Glaring at the disgruntled adolescent, eye to eye, he had no intention of blinking. The second gift, total control of eyelid movement, could be guaranteed to unnerve even the most troublesome pupil.

"What's your name?" he asked in a milder tone.

"Thomas, Barry Thomas, sir."

"Can you tell me why you're out here playing the fool when you should be in there developing your mathematical knowledge?"

"It's 'im in there, sir. Keeps picking on me," the boy protested.

"Right! So, you're telling me that Mr Baker suddenly became bored teaching the class and decided to suspend the lesson so that he could concentrate on having a go at you?"

Barry screwed his face up, whilst attempting to work out what had just been said. He gave up and decided that attack would continue to be the best form of defence.

"Baker's always 'ated me, sir. You ask any of the other boys."

"It may surprise you to know, Barry, that teachers are so busy we don't have time to hate pupils. It takes a great deal of time and energy to hate someone."

Although not convinced that what he was saying was true in Baker's case, he continued.

"I'll go and ask your teacher myself why you're out here kicking his door before I decide what to do next. Is that all right with you?"

Thomas gave a non-committal shrug. He seemed to have cooled down and reconsidered his interest in being of further nuisance value.

"You may be right, and Mr Baker will break down in tears and admit that he couldn't control the urge to make fun of you. You never know."

This comment brought a smile to the student's face.

Result! Being bad cop and good cop in the same person took special skill.

Leaving Barry in the corridor, he knocked and entered the room. The boys rose noisily to their feet. Mr Baker looked in his direction, grim-faced.

"Thank you very much for that show of politeness, boys. I won't hold your lesson up for any longer than necessary."

The class sat down in silence.

Right, you bastard, what the hell have you done to wind this boy up?

"Morning, Mr Baker. May I have a quick word with you about Barry Thomas?"

Expecting to be taken aside and spoken to confidentially, he started to approach Baker's desk. However, the aggrieved teacher stood up and began shouting, with the intention of informing the whole class of what was on his mind.

"Thomas is an imbecile who is intent on disrupting my lessons the moment he walks into the room. I'm sick of the sight of him and I'm done with him. He's the most insolent boy in the school. The only punishment appropriate for such a young man is a fixed-term exclusion. Take him away and don't bring him back."

Judge, jury, and executioner. It was a struggle to remain tight-lipped. Although not accustomed to being ordered about by junior members of staff, he did see the funny side of the situation. If the class detected any hint of the amusement he was experiencing, both men in the room could be in professional hot water. He decided it best to adopt the speedy and formal approach. Baker wouldn't cool down for at least another hour, so he'd be wasting his time trying to get any sense out of him. Thanking his lucky stars that his own temper fuse was of the inordinately long variety, he made a terse statement, as much to the students as to the teacher.

Top Tip No. 13: Never betray to a class that a particular student, or teacher, gets under your skin.

"I can see how unhappy you are with Barry, Mr Baker. I hope that, after he has been dealt with, he will be able to offer you an apology."

"I've no intention of ever seeing the boy again!"

Although Biggsy had a little sympathy for fellow teachers prey to losing their self-control when dealing with children, he felt even greater concern for Barry Thomas. Here was a student whose attitude to learning would be coloured by regular contact with a teacher who despised him. Most boys learned to bend like reeds when buffeted by stormy educators such as Baker, but increasing numbers were adopting an inflexible stance when subjected to casual classroom taunts. None of the educational approaches on which Dickens' Gradgrind relied had a place in twenty-first-century schooling. Baker was a disciplinary dinosaur who could do with a fixed-term exclusion himself. The consequences for schools of allowing adults like him to have daily contact with children could be dangerous for all concerned.

Avoiding further eye contact with Baker or any of the pupils in his room, he withdrew.

****

Having decided it wouldn't be a good idea to take the hapless Thomas directly to the withdrawal room, the temporary prison for juvenile reprobates only a short walk down the corridor, he decided on a friendly exchange of views in his classroom. Thomas was amenable to the suggestion, so they set off. Once inside his room, the door was left open, a precaution that had to be taken nowadays when talking to individual students. An expression of bored resignation fixed in place, Thomas sat staring ahead of him and waited for the lecture.

"The visit to your maths lesson made me feel depressed on three counts, Barry. I was disappointed that the learning that should have been taking place in the classroom had been interrupted. I was saddened to see a teacher losing his temper with one of his pupils. And I was upset that you felt unable, or unwilling, to take advantage of the education paid for by your parents. Can we take each point in turn?"

At mention of the final point, Thomas frowned, unaware of his parents' financial involvement.

"All right, sir," he conceded.

"Right. You do see that your behaviour affected every other boy in the classroom. Whatever their opinion of what was going on in Mr Baker's lesson, they were prepared to accept the arrangements in order to develop their mathematical knowledge. But your outburst interrupted their learning. Accepted?"

"S'pose so, sir."

"And would you agree that shouldn't happen?"

"Yes, sir, but..."

"No need to qualify your answer, Barry," he interrupted, in a measured tone. "I'm pleased to hear that. Now let's consider the effect on your teacher. I gather that you and Mr Baker don't get along. Would you say that's true?"

"You can say that again. I know it's gonna be terrible every lesson."

"I see. There's bad feeling between you both every single lesson. Do any of the other boys have problems of that sort in their maths lessons?"

"I know nobody likes 'im. They've told me."

"But they don't get on the wrong side of the teacher the way you do. Let me ask you a really difficult question. Do you think you should allow your feelings about a teacher to affect the progress of your own learning, which will affect how you live the rest of your life?"

Thomas paused for thought. Thinking about a connection between his school behaviour and what sort of life he was going to lead was new ground for him.

"Knowledge is a bit like money. The more you have, the easier it is to get through life. At least, that's the theory. The more intelligent you become, the more opportunities life has to offer. So, your feelings about any teacher who is providing the learning should be unimportant, wouldn't you say?"

Guilty as he felt about presenting such a utilitarian view of learning, he was justified in this case. Presenting learning as a valuable commodity was a strategy that could appeal to the immature mind.

"Well, yeah. I get on OK with all my other teachers."

"I'm glad you agree, Barry. What you learn is a thousand times more important to you than how you feel about the teacher. The final point may be one you've not thought about. A large amount of the taxes your parents pay goes towards providing schools and teachers. Do both your mum and dad work?"

"Yeah, my dad's a plasterer and my mum's an office cleaner."

The conversation was going well. Any hint of bad feeling had dissipated.

"That means both your parents are paying a lot of money in tax every week. You wouldn't want to think that they were paying for all the other children in your class to get a good education and not their own son. If you decide that you'd rather give up on maths and mess around, then that's what would be happening."

Here he was again, focusing on the financial implications involved in state education. But for children who had not entirely moved away from concrete-operational modes of thinking, such considerations could make an impression. Thomas's brow furrowed, possibly a consequence of trying to work out how much money he'd cheated his parents out of during his school career, to date.

"You don't need to respond to that final point. Now I have to prepare a report for your head of year for the reason I took you away from your maths lesson. I can't avoid that. But, instead of taking you to the withdrawal room, I'll ask you if you'd prefer to work quietly at the back of my classroom for the rest of the morning. Are you OK with that?"

"Yes, sir."

"How do you feel about apologising to Mr Baker just before you go to lunch?"

"Do I 'ave to, sir?"

"Sorry, but that's part of the deal. It takes guts to apologise, but I'm sure you're not lacking in that department."

****

When the last of the year seven boys had left his classroom after the sounding of the buzzer for lunch, he called Thomas to his table.

"Right, Barry, let's go and catch Mr Baker before he goes for his lunch. Remember to keep your eyes on his when you apologise."

Thomas said nothing. This was a scenario to which he was unaccustomed. Biggsy was uncertain about the wisdom of the boy offering an apology to Baker and not sure whether it would be accepted. There was bad blood between the two of them, and he couldn't imagine any sudden improvement in their relationship. But he'd made a promise. He followed the teacher out of the room and around the corner to the mathematics corridor. Although Baker's door was open, Biggsy tapped politely before he and his charge entered.

"Sorry to interrupt you, Mr Baker. I've brought Barry to speak to you, if that's fine by you?"

The expression on the teacher's face suggested that it wasn't, but Barry stepped forward.

"I'm sorry I misbehaved in your lesson today, Mr Baker."

The boy's delivery and contrite expression were spot on, but the glowering young maths teacher did not seem impressed.

"An apology hardly seems appropriate for the disruption this pupil has been causing in my lessons since the start of term, Mr Biggs."

Baker was, and would always be, a 'Mr Biggs' colleague. Conscious of the contempt that the man was demonstrating toward both of his visitors, he decided there was no need to prolong this situation. If Thomas stayed any longer, there was the risk of an outbreak of hostilities between maths and English teaching staff.

"You run along now, Barry. Thank you for remaining in my classroom this morning."

Thomas did as he was told. His moral ally stood before a man who was still not in total control of himself.

"I assumed that Thomas would be taken to the withdrawal room until a fixed-term exclusion was arranged by the deputy head."

"The moment I took the student away from your lesson, he became my responsibility. When dealing with children, I prefer to try reform before punishment."

It would be necessary to box clever here. One of them was at risk of professional misconduct, and he was determined it wouldn't be himself.

"That may well be the case, Mr Biggs, but there are accepted protocols here for dealing with the sort of misbehaviour to which I was subjected today. Exclusion is the only alternative in this case."

I could put forward a watertight case for you to be given a permanent exclusion from this school.

"That's your opinion. Throwing Thomas's apology back in his face is not the way to deal with children. If you wish to insist on exclusion, I suggest you take the matter up with Archie Matthews."

Baker might be able to bully pupils but he wouldn't be able to do the same to Archie.

"I agree, and that's exactly what I intend to do."

****

He caught a glimpse of Angela and Nick at the far end of the corridor. He guessed they'd be making their way to the dining hall for lunch. They looked in good spirits. Since daring Toner to continue the perceived vendetta against Nick, he was relieved that the menacing missives from deputy head to junior teacher had stopped. All was quiet on the Toner Front. He returned to his classroom to fetch his weatherproof jacket before venturing out on playground duty.

Other than completing the numerous predicted grade sheets for all key stages that she'd sent him, there had been no other professional contact with her for a fortnight. The work had all been done online, making the task a paper-free exercise. Good for the planet, of course, but there was not the same sense of achievement he'd felt before the advent of the school intranet. Preparing and handing over a stack of A4 sheets in a brown manila folder, after a ten-hour marathon admin stint, gave him the satisfaction of seeing something tangible for his efforts. Now, any sense of relief at accomplishing the task was offset by a nagging fear that the reams of information he sent down the line might be lost in the ether, through no fault of his own, resulting from a glitch in the functioning of the assessment software package.

The teaching game had moved on over the past two decades. Those days when he was allowed to hold the attention of a class with a stick of chalk and the force of his own enthusiasm were long gone. These days, with the wonders of

Wi-Fi, a lesson couldn't start until a laptop had been connected to a whiteboard. In so many subject areas, the pupils' focus had already become the screen, with limitless amounts of text in fancy fonts and colourful graphics. The screen in all its guises – television, mobile phone, games console, and school whiteboard – was all-powerful.

There was the worry that the teacher could be anyone. The accumulation of knowledge was now more important than understanding how to apply it. In his childhood, he recalled being told that, far into the future, humankind would develop six fingers on each hand. The demands of manual dexterity would see to that. But this fanciful prediction was way off the mark. Two flexible thumbs were the new reality.

Although still a bona fide teacher at St Saviour's, he had a sense of himself fading. Within a short time, he felt, there would be no trace left of him in these corridors. Why should he bother what went on here? The answer that came to him, when in such moods, was always the same: the wellbeing of the children in his care.

His mind returned to Toner. He'd seen her, at a distance on occasions, strutting along the school corridors. The school rumour mill had it that she and Aaron were no longer an item and, despite the happy arrival of her long-awaited headship, he was continuing to look for a teaching post elsewhere. He'd be a loss to the school. Not only was he one of the most popular teachers on the staff, but he'd retained his irrepressible enthusiasm for teaching. Whatever emotional upset he may have experienced, it hadn't affected his zest for the job.

"You got a minute?"

Matthews was framed in the doorway.

"Yes, Archie. Come in."

"Thanks. Thought I'd better pass on the news that the head of maths beat a path to my door and complained about your handling of Barry Thomas, the boy you fetched from Baker's lesson."

"Sorry you had to deal with that. I'm afraid my efforts to get the boy on better terms with his teacher weren't appreciated."

"Quite. Now if you'd had the boy hanged, drawn, and quartered, all would be well with the head of maths. I tried to get Lionel to see sense, but he wasn't having any of it. Said he'd take the matter to the head. Really sorry I couldn't talk him around, mate. Be seeing you."

Matthews, in as much of a hurry as Biggsy, turned and left, shaking his head as he went.

Not such bad news. Lionel could belly-ache to Fingleton to his heart's content. If, in the worst case, the head decided to withdraw the job of sixth-form pastoral head on the strength of this complaint, so be it. He still wasn't sure he wanted the post. For that matter, he wondered if he were keen on continuing at St Saviour's in any capacity.

As he strode out of his room to the school field, the idea occurred to him that any form of promotion in any hierarchy, public or commercial, was a poisoned chalice.

He could go straight to the head's office before anybody else felt the need to complain about him and come clean.

"Just thought I'd better tell you: You can stick your job!"

Immediately, he pictured Myra's eyes-heavenward expression, as she listened to his explanation of that outburst.

****

Chapter 13

"What a pair of pillocks!"

"I agree, love, but the maths department is a rule unto itself. They want the boy's blood, and mine too if they can manage it."

"Pathetic! How can two grown men be so high-handed in their dealings with children?"

He'd thought all this through but didn't want to go into the details with Myra. An acute shortage of secondary school teachers in particular subject areas, as was the case with maths and the sciences, presented the temptation to certain members of staff to assume a regal air about the school. It was no surprise to discover common-or-garden maths teachers beginning to swell with self-importance on realising that the head was in mortal terror of them taking their professional expertise elsewhere. He'd become aware of the management team's extra cosseting of Lionel at staff meetings, as had been the case on the most recent occasion when he'd exploded with indignation that other departments were 'unable to run their ships' as tightly as he did. He was also certain that the maths department had benefited from a capitation bung.

A great believer in karma, he held to the certainty that the head of maths would one day experience a cosmic fall from grace, his reputation in tatters. This belief sustained him and ensured that he wouldn't waste any time complaining about the man, as others were wont to do in casual staffroom conversations.

"I won't bore you with the main reason again, but there's another factor to consider, one that school education hasn't properly addressed since the dawn of the computer age. Curriculum designers are stuck in a mid-twentieth-century rut. The world-class education they believe this country offers is still based on the veneration of academia. Don't get me wrong, my conviction is that we should encourage all children to aspire to intellectual heights in their studies. But genuine education involves more than trying to produce a race of juvenile brainiacs."

"How do you mean?"

"Child-centred education is now a thing of the past. We're all so bound up with school league tables that we now offer a data-centred education. Children's special interests and talents are rarely given serious consideration. Kids should be allowed to spend some of their time in school developing those overlooked areas."

"What? Such as bird watching or computer gaming?"

He knew that Myra would play devil's advocate.

"They're certainly suggestions worthy of consideration. I discovered, by chance, that one of my year nine boys is renovating an old Ford Anglia his father bought him as a birthday present. He's learning everything from points' setting to panel beating and loves it. He should have the opportunity to pursue this interest in engineering at school. I'm the only person there who even knows about his specialism."

"Sounds a bright lad!"

"He is, but you wouldn't call him an academic. Don't make the mistake of assuming that I'd advocate students spending their whole time in school on such pursuits. But, in my view, serious changes need to be made. For too many children, school is a torment. Remember what Kevin, your handyman, said about his own schooling: he spent much of his time being forced to follow courses in which he had no interest. I get the same message from boys thirty years on from their school days. I grant you there are tricky waters they need to wade through, but these can be balanced by the offer of studies relevant to their unique personalities."

"Your assumption that children should enjoy what they're doing at school is one that not everybody would accept."

"Then they should be advised to read *Hard Times*."

He'd said his piece, for the umpteenth time, and wanted to climb off his soapbox. He realised his was a voice crying in the educational wilderness. Whenever he made the effort to rail on, it drained him emotionally, not to mention how quickly he tired of hearing his own voice outside of the school setting. Myra had previously advised him against 'pissing in the wind', on the rare occasions that he expressed his passionate ideas about schooling in the future. She didn't use the word 'flaky', but he suspected he was intended to draw that inference.

"Anyway, my advice is to leave the mathematicians to it. Rise above their enmity. Let them complain as long and as hard as they like."

Taken aback by the fervour of his wife's utterances, he gave her an appreciative double-take smile.

"Funny, but that's how I'd decided to play it."

"What a relief. Now, back to planet Earth: the tickets are all booked."

"Oh, are we going to the theatre? What's on?"

"Very funny. You know what I'm talking about – flight tickets."

The prospect of a complete change of scene, with the busiest part of the school year completed, suddenly seemed both welcome and necessary. Unaccustomed to taking holidays abroad at any other time than during the summer break, he found himself thinking that it was time to climb out of the rut of putting school first and last throughout the rest of his career. But he mustn't sound too enthusiastic about the arrangements she'd made.

"Oh well."

"Thank you, Eeyore, for that vote of confidence. You now have my permission to start packing your suitcase. I think Ella's packed hers already, and there are still a few weeks before we jet off."

****

Six inches of snow had fallen overnight. Such unseasonal weather was not unusual now. Looking out of the bedroom window, he saw no separation between the road and the pavements. Getting to work by car today would be hazardous. Two teenage boys walking past the house reached out and swept snow off the roof of his car, dodging around it for protection as they formed snowballs in gloved hands. Wading through the snow, the boys made their faltering way along the middle of the road. As soon as they'd thrown their snowballs at each other, they gathered more ammunition, hooting with delight as they did so. The school corridors would soon be covered with melting ice. The novelty of a snowfall made boys reckless in their desire to pelt each other, inside the school or out. He'd be required to do his lunch duty indoors, keeping the corridors as snow-free as possible.

Unsure if bus services would be affected by the conditions, Myra decided that she'd walk to the hospital. Undeterred by the drifts, she estimated that it would take forty-five minutes at most to make the journey. Unable to talk her husband out of going to school on his old racing bike, she told him not to come running to her if he fell off and broke a leg. He reassured her that he'd be in no danger, the journey being less than three miles. The two capacious bags fitted on either side of the rear pannier would keep his books and laptop dry. If, at any point, he was unable to ride safely, he'd get off and push.

Ella slept soundly on upstairs. She didn't have to be in school until after lunch. He suspected that she wouldn't bother going in at all if the weather didn't improve.

Myra's youthful figure enabled her to look good whatever she wore. Standing at the front door, enclosed in her three-quarter length padded and hooded jacket, heavy denims and hiking boots, she was ready to set off. Checking her handbag and pocket for house keys, she turned to issue last-minute instructions.

"Right, I'm going. Whatever you do, don't take any risks on that wreck of yours. Check that the tyres aren't flat and the brakes work. Make sure you wear your gloves, scarf, and beany hat. It'll be bitter out there."

"Yes, Mummy."

A withering look warned him against further levity.

"I can't believe there'll be staff or kids there even if you make it. But I know you – never miss a day of school. Bye then."

"Don't worry about me, love. Take it easy yourself and text me to let me know you made it safely."

A hurried kiss and clumsy manoeuvring to get her handbag strap over head and shoulder later, she left. A flurry of snow blew into the hallway as he closed the door after her. Wasting no time, he donned his winter jacket and accessories, as instructed, and went out of the back door to fetch his bike.

Opening the shed door involved the effort of shifting a solid mass of snow. He wheeled the bike up the path, through the back door and into the hall. He then cleared up the trail of melting snow he'd brought into the house, before loading up his school paraphernalia. Ten minutes after Myra's departure, he was ready to leave. Waking Ella to say goodbye before he left wouldn't be necessary.

There was no possibility of riding the bike until he reached the high street. The crunch of snow underfoot cheered him, bringing to mind childhood memories of massed snowball fights with mates on the field in the centre of his housing estate. As expected, the main road, gritted the previous evening, was clear of snow but awash with brown slush. He'd be able to cycle, but with extreme caution. Light snow started falling again, but it soon became heavier. Tickling flakes blown into his eyelashes hampered his vision. Looking down at his pedals, he saw a wedge of ice forming on the underside of the hub.

The wind blew full into his face along the stretch of road to Isleworth. He imagined that he must look like a cycling snowman as his dark jacket and beany became white. But he carried on, fingers beginning to feel numb, but grateful that his legs were in good condition as a result of the many sessions on the gym treadmill. Passing the swimming baths, he wondered how well he'd be able to negotiate the increasing half-mile incline as he made his way to St Saviour's.

Once off the main road, staying upright in the saddle became a problem. Packed snow was a far more difficult proposition than slush. Unable to steer, he dismounted and trudged along the pavement edge. His nose needed blowing, but the thought of undoing his jacket and searching for a tissue seemed an impossibility. Nursing his bike along for the final half-mile and keeping warm were more important considerations than his nasal passages.

There was little traffic to worry him on the final push up the hill, and wheeling a bike through fresh snow was less risky than cycling through slush. Two year seven boys, heads bowed and clutching the straps of their rucksacks, laboured along just ahead of him. Although the school day wouldn't be starting for another half hour, he began to query the eerie quiet of the street. Despite not expecting to see scores of boisterous boys on their way to school just yet, he questioned the dearth of stout scholars setting their shoulders against the blizzard.

The school gates came into sight. All was quiet. Reaching the end of the school drive, he stopped at the main entrance. Archie Matthews, sheltering just inside the door, looked up and smiled. Wearing a grey overcoat and rubbing gloved hands together, he looked up at Biggsy's appearance and opened the door.

"What's going on, Archie?"

"Well done!" he called "You're only the second teacher to make it in so far. The boiler's broken down. No heating."

"Can't say I'm surprised. It's ancient, that thing."

The deputy head turned his attention to the two boys.

"Off you go, boys. School's closed today. Your parents will be notified later when we're open again."

Too cold to celebrate their good fortune, they nodded then turned on their heels.

Propping his bike against a large stone flower tub, he shook the snow off himself. It was now time to search for that tissue to blow his nose.

"As I live much closer to the school than the head, he asked me if I'd come in to do the honours and send home any staff and boys who turned up."

"Could be a long school closure then if there's a problem fixing the heating. Wish I'd known about this before I set off."

"You guessed it. Thursday today, so I can't see school opening tomorrow either. I'll have to learn how to operate the switchboard so that I can phone everybody next time this happens."

"If that's the case, I'll have to learn how to sabotage that old boiler. Unexpected holidays like this could be coming along more often."

"You haven't far to go to get back home, thankfully. Do you need a comfort break before setting off again?"

"No, thanks, Archie. I'll just blow my nose and pedal off, fingers crossed. I want to get out of this lot as soon as possible."

"Before you go, the head of maths did go to see Fingleton about your handling of Baker's issue with that boy Thomas. Lionel spoke to me before going into the head's office. He seemed very put out that you hadn't issued execution orders for the pupil. He was very persistent."

"Sorry about that, Archie. You should have told him to 'Persistent off!'"

"I'd like to have done. He and Baker are wasting their time. Some people in this place have a very high opinion of themselves."

"I've no doubt Baker will go far in teaching. New-age education loves his sort. Just glad I won't be around when he gets a headship."

"Well, you'll excuse me if I go back inside, Biggsy. It's perishing out here."

"Right, Archie. See you next week."

He looked at the saddle of his bike before remounting. It was covered in a thick layer of snow.

"Why did I bother?"

****

Once he'd stowed his bike in the shed and warmed up after the journey home, he acted on an impulse unconnected with his job. Thinking of Myra, instead of teaching, he'd pictured her returning home in the same weary condition from which he'd just recovered. He would prepare the evening meal, something special that would revive the spirits and remind her how much he appreciated her. Cooking couldn't be that difficult, surely! After a spot of cookery googling and a quick trip to the butcher in the high street, he had everything he'd need for his cordon bleu surprise.

Myra enjoyed complaining that her husband treated her like a fifties housewife because he rarely tried his hand at rustling up a hot meal. He'd push the vacuum cleaner around the house from time to time and load the dishwasher, but food preparation was a bridge too far. He'd messaged her about the school closure and had guessed she'd believe him to be scribbling his way through piles of exercise books when she got home.

The smell from the kitchen as she opened the front door took her aback. Before entering the house to find out who was at the cooker controls, she noticed dim lighting in the dining room. To compound her state of stunned amazement, she saw the table laid for a meal, with two candles burning in the silver holders her parents had given them as an anniversary gift. Ten years old and never used – till now. Wondering if she might have slipped into a time warp, she opened the kitchen door.

"You sweetheart! What brought this on?"

"Just wanted to surprise you. It was either a case of finishing my lower school reports or cooking a surprise meal for you. You just edged it."

Turning over the spitting fillet steaks in the griddle, he adjusted the gas. *Very professional for a beginner,* he thought, admiring the dark brown lines in the meat.

"So, did you get the recipe from one of my books – that Jamie Oliver one you bought me last Christmas?"

"No, but I wish I had now. They only take thirty minutes. I got this off the internet."

"After the day I've had, this is quite the nicest thing you could have done. I feel quite emotional."

"That bad, eh? How was the journey home?"

"The buses were running, thankfully, so I didn't have to hoof it the whole way. What sort of steak is that?"

"Fillet. Only the best for you, my love."

"Blimey! Where are the smelling salts? And what have you prepared to go with it?"

"Chips, sweet corn and, your favourite, asparagus tips."

"Wow! But what about Ella?"

"My thoughts were entirely on you with this enterprise. She'll sort herself something out with the microwave later if she's not over at Neil's."

"I hope she is at Neil's because you'll be toast if she finds out she's not been included in this. How long before it's ready?"

"You've got about five minutes."

"Right. I'll get out of this lot," she declared, extricating herself from her voluminous jacket, "and powder my nose."

As he put two plates in the oven to warm before serving up, he felt a glow of happiness wash over him. He gave a shudder.

****

"Have you got a minute, sir?"

Turning towards the voice calling to him halfway down the empty corridor, he saw Jermaine Gibson approaching at a jog trot.

With the spell of arctic weather continuing throughout the weekend and into Monday, Fingleton had advised staff and students to leave the site early to reduce the possibility of accidents on treacherous journeys home. The teachers hadn't needed telling twice. They hadn't expected to be in the place at all after the bitterly cold weekend. To their displeasure, the boiler had been fixed but had struggled to keep the school population warm. Although it had taken him only half an hour to tidy his day away, he was one of the last to leave. Even the cleaners were conspicuous by their absence.

"Hi, Jermaine. I'm surprised to see you. I thought I was the only one still in the place."

"I've just finished doing my weights in the sixth-form gym. I saw your light on as I was leaving."

The gym was nothing glamorous, merely a converted storeroom off the main sports hall. Ten students, at most, could use the equipment at any one time. Chris Barker, the head of PE, had acquired the equipment from the health club of which he was a member. On hearing that the club was planning to upgrade its equipment, he'd managed to lay his hands on useful items. The club manager had put up token resistance, explaining to Barker that disposal of the old stock was the responsibility of their supplier. But Chris had managed to twist his arm, metaphorically speaking.

It took the grateful PE staff only a couple of journeys in the school minibus to collect the items made available. The school rugby team made most use of the area, keen to tone up their developing muscle groups. There were two gym benches, barbells with a selection of weights, a working rowing machine, a cycle machine and exercise mats. Gibson had found working out at school physically and emotionally beneficial after the trauma he'd suffered the previous term.

"What can I do for you, Jermaine?"

"It's more what I can do for you, and the school, sir."

This sounded like important news. The head boy was in earnest. He cast a look over his shoulder before continuing.

"I've something I need to tell you, but the information can't get back to me."

"Whatever is it?"

"I can't tell you how, but I've found out the name of the likely sixth-form contact for the drugs gang."

As if Gibson hadn't had his fill of danger this academic year, here he was putting himself at risk again. Both were now looking up and down the corridor.

"Perhaps we should go into my office, Jermaine?"

"No, I'll tell you this quickly then get off home. He's in my year. Gary Treadway."

Gibson's tight-lipped expression made it clear that further discussion was out of the question. The stunning impact of the information on his form tutor ensured that the student was able to make the hasty exit he wished.

"Thanks, Jermaine. Leave it with me. See you tomorrow."

****

"What can Alan be up to? When I asked him to be my lookout for the blue Polo, he surely must have known of his brother's link with the dealers."

"Not necessarily," Myra replied. "It could be pure coincidence that the boy you chose to be your hired help in tracking down the sixth-form drugs baron is his younger brother."

Unable to conceal her mirth, she burst into laughter.

"It's nothing to joke about. This couldn't be more serious," he called from the kitchen.

Without taking off his jacket and clutching the mug of tea he'd prepared, he joined his wife in the lounge. She looked up from the settee on which she was stretched full length.

"I can't believe your luck. Trust you to pick on the boy who's actually related to the villain you want to nail. You must admit, you've got yourself into quite a little scrape here, love."

"It's unbelievable. Jermaine is totally trustworthy. If he says Gary's the one we're looking for, I believe him."

"What sort of boy is this Gary?"

"I've never taught him, but I know he doesn't have a wide circle of friends. Never got himself into any serious scrapes but has a bit of an anti-authority streak. Intelligent boy, though I'd be wary about asking him to post a letter."

"How does he dress? Gucci shoes? Rolex watch?"

She seemed determined not to take the matter seriously. Kicking off his shoes, he extended his legs and placed his heels on the edge of the glass-topped coffee table.

"Hey! Just because you're up to your neck in another school crisis of your own making, you can't start abusing the furniture. Get your feet off there!"

He obeyed but set his jaw in an expression of defiance.

"No, there's nothing that screams ostentation about his appearance. In fact, quite the opposite. He doesn't stand out in any way from his peers – not what you'd call scruffy either. Thinking about it, I wouldn't have said he's the sort who'd take drugs."

"Clever. Whatever he's making on dealing is being stashed away somewhere."

"I can't get my head around this. Why the hell did Alan agree to look out for the Polo, and why did he alert me when it next appeared and tell me the registration number?"

"Could be he doesn't get on with his brother and wants him to get caught. But, if that's the case, he must know that he'd be identified as the boy who shopped him. That's Class-A snitching."

****

"Not sure what to do about this one, Dave."

210

Slumped in his office chair, the head of sixth form looked into the eyes of the man who would be replacing him. The situation presented to him was one about which he'd prefer to know nothing. His decision to stay on an extra term had not worked out well. The issue of drug-taking amongst his sixth-formers was the final straw. He'd been too busy or wary to tackle it, despite rumblings from certain quarters for the past few months. The new man in the job would be the best person to deal with the problem when he took over next term. The revelation that Gary Treadway was the go-to school contact for local dealers came as something of a surprise. Although the upper-sixth boy had not distinguished himself academically, staff didn't perceive him as a villain.

Much as he deplored the thought of any of his students being connected in any way with narcotics, this was one fight too many for him. Getting involved in a high-profile criminal operation was not the way he wanted to end his career. Toner's imposition of the five-minute lock-out rule, instituted the previous term, had done him no favours. He'd had to deal with many disgruntled students, their personal dignity offended, who'd not been allowed into lessons because of lateness, often through no fault of their own. He wanted to be remembered fondly after he'd left St Saviour's.

"Coming from a reliable source, as you say, this information has to be taken seriously," he found himself stating.

"Absolutely."

Biggsy wanted the matter to be brought out into the open and addressed as a management team priority. This was not a situation for one person to sort out, and he didn't want it hanging over him throughout the Easter break. Myra wouldn't want him moping in Menorca about this negative development regarding the new job. Taking on the head of sixth form post and immediately being perceived as the upper school drugs enforcer would make him as popular as a police officer at a student rave. There was his standing as a reasonable authority figure within the school community to consider.

He was concerned for Gary Treadway's health. The student's situation reminded him of Richard Dixon. Young men, whatever the difficulties in which they found themselves, deserved every protection their school could afford them. In the worst case, Gary was setting himself up for violent reprisal from shady business associates, who would not be happy if the source of income from his customers were shut down.

"You seem to be more in the loop than me as far as this business is concerned."

Wheelhouse wasn't directing a slight at his colleague. There was no implication that the English head was encroaching on territory that was out of his jurisdiction. Quite the opposite. He hoped that the man replacing him would infer that he was better placed to follow up this new lead on substance abuse in the sixth form.

"Yes, purely by chance, as it happens. I was on lunch duty on the field a while ago when Archie spotted me and asked if I could assist him. I helped him to identify the delivery vehicle that the pushers were using. Unlikely as it seems, Gary's younger brother, Alan in Year 9, was the boy who picked out the plate for me."

He thought it judicious not to mention that he had conscripted the boy for the operation a week earlier.

"That's a hell of a coincidence."

"Funny – that's exactly what my wife said. Can't believe it myself. It appears the student code has been rewritten: Never grass on anyone, unless he's your brother."

"Why would Alan do that?"

"I haven't spoken to him yet, or Archie for that matter. I thought it best to come to you first about the latest developments. I can only think he either dislikes his brother or isn't happy about him dealing."

"Could be something in that. I think going to Archie with this and getting management on the case is the best course to take. I wouldn't want to confront Gary until we've got Fingleton's take on the whole business."

Biggsy realised that his anxiety about stepping on Wheelhouse's toes was unfounded. He sensed that the sixth-form head was feeling out of his depth and would prefer intervention to come from the highest authority in the school. He couldn't blame the man. Life as a non-combatant in retirement was Dave's main focus now. The thought came that a younger person than himself would be a better prospect for the job of keeping young adults in line. Why had the head ever looked to the English department for a replacement?

"I'll make an appointment to see Archie, stressing that Fingleton be consulted before any further action is taken. In fact, this would seem to have all the makings of a police matter. I never thought I'd find myself in the position of having to draw the activities of one of our students to their attention."

"It may not come to that. I'm sure the police already have the gen on the activities of local drugs gangs. Putting the matter in their hands, without naming Treadway, may scare him off and result in a swift conclusion to all this."

"Yes, let's hope that the tip-off I received will bring matters to a head. I certainly wouldn't take any pleasure in seeing Gary's future blighted by adolescent foolishness."

He'd do his best to ensure that Gary and Alan Treadway came under no scrutiny, stressing the point to Archie that neither boy be mentioned at this stage should the police be contacted. Jermaine Gibson's name would also not feature in any communication with the school management team or the police. A promise was a promise.

****

"If you say you have a reliable informant who claims Treadway's involved, I'm sure I have no reason to doubt it."

The pastoral deputy head was agitated. Arms folded tightly, he leaned back in his chair and studied the ceiling. A thoughtful pause later, he continued.

"So, if your informant's right, Alan, in Year 9, helped us to identify the vehicle that was used to make deliveries to his older brother. Doesn't make sense."

"Dave and I couldn't believe it ourselves, but there it is. Looks as though the two of them don't get on so well. Where does that lead us, Archie?"

He hoped it would lead to a rapid senior management resolution to the problem. Matthews had, to date, shown himself enthusiastic to rid St Saviour's of the blight of drug-taking.

"Without any proof, we're in a bit of a cleft stick situation. If you don't want your man to repeat what he told you to anyone else, we could be relying on Alan to shop his brother. As you've said, that's not an option we should consider either. It's a tricky one."

"If we were to provide Fingleton with hard evidence linking Gary to drug dealing, would he feel compelled to involve the police, or could he just deal with the matter in-house?"

"When I first spoke to him about my suspicions, he gave the impression that he was against any kind of negative publicity within the local community."

This was one of the reasons why drug-taking continued unabated in schools. Few heads would ever have the courage to call in the police immediately, whatever cast-iron evidence they had. The good name of the school would always be more important than the risk of any number of students acquiring a lifelong drug habit. Health and safety procedures in schools were now top priority, except in cases where 'the good name of the school' was concerned. He couldn't be too hard on the head, he supposed. It was one of the unwritten laws of the headmaster's code: don't grass to the police on your own school.

"Understandable. He has a real moral dilemma. His stance may help us to protect Gary – give him a chance to cease his activities."

"We could call the boy in and question him to warn him off further contact with the gang?"

"Who do you mean by 'we', Archie? You and Dave? You and me? The management team?"

A month ago, he would not have dared to be so persistent.

"What do you say to the two of us tackling Gary first off? I take what you said about leaving Dave out of this, out of consideration for his impending retirement."

Archie's reply was what he'd hoped. Gary Treadway must be given the chance to reform. Such a course, however, could incur the wrath of those who were reliant on the market he'd been instrumental in creating at St Saviour's for their illegal wares. Retribution could follow. Drug dealers didn't have a reputation for being reasonable people in financial dealings. The whole scenario was a can of worms.

"But he'll be unlikely to make any admission of dealing. If so, would we put it to him that there's no alternative but to contact the police to handle the matter?"

"My thinking is that we let him know we're on to him then leave him to decide on his next move. I know it's a long shot, but he may be able to put a stop to everything himself. We ought to give him that opportunity."

The worry that this matter would not be resolved before he took charge of the sixth form was confirmed.

Chapter 14

"What you got the 'ump about, sir?" Colley asked. "You got a face as long as that horse that won the Derby."

"How do you mean, Chris? Nothing wrong with me."

"Do us a favour, sir. Somethin's buggin' you."

There were times when he wanted his form group to know that something was troubling him. School business, of course, nothing else. It didn't do any harm to play the martyred soul if you were seeking information. He'd get nowhere if he asked direct questions. Any awkwardness Gibson might have experienced, at mention of the topic he was about to raise, need not be a consideration. He was absent, owing to a hospital appointment for a medical check-up.

"I was just listening in on a staffroom conversation about drug abuse in schools. I sometimes forget how lucky I am teaching in a school where it's not a problem."

"Oh yeah, sir? You must be walkin' around with your eyes closed," Colley corrected.

"What do you mean?"

He looked up suddenly from his laptop, hoping his expression of concerned surprise was convincing.

"Plenty of kids in this place do a bit of stuff," Bellchambers explained, without smiling. "Present company excepted, of course, sir."

"Is that right? If what you say is true, I really must be seeing the school through rose-tinted spectacles."

"It's not a major problem here, sir. But it's got a bit worse since the start of the year."

"Well, I've not come across anything to worry me," he lied. "Mind you, when I was young, there could have been any number of people I knew who had a habit. I suppose I didn't witness anything because I steered clear of anything like that."

"I bet you never even smoked, sir," Dixon said.

"Spot on, Richard. I didn't contribute a single penny to W.D. and H.O. Wills' retirement funds."

"You what, sir?"

"I didn't smoke. I couldn't see the point of spending money on something in a packet that would give me the same experience as standing beside a bonfire."

"Fair point," Padfield volunteered. "But you must have been aware of friends taking dope when you were at school?"

"No. I just assumed nobody else was interested in acquiring a dangerous habit that was difficult to kick."

Another whopper. Pete Yates, the brightest star of his sixth-form firmament, had been a regular user. Universally recognised after O-levels as the boy most likely to gain an Oxbridge place, he hand-painted images of Johnny Rotten on one side panel of his scooter and Sid Vicious on the other. Sometime later, he dropped out of the sixth form.

"If I were so inclined, then, I could contact somebody not a million miles away from the sixth-form common room and purchase something illegal?"

"I reckon you could say that, sir," Colley answered, before anyone else could reply.

There was no hint of levity in the boy's tone as he spoke. Colley's serious side had become more evident since he'd revealed the identity of Gibson's attacker the previous term. Jesting his way through life was no longer the default attitude.

"If that's the case, we've a serious problem. It's only one of the terrible fears a parent can have for a child. I imagine your parents do their best to cope with that fear, just as I do. I sincerely hope none of you ever have to live with that anxiety when you have children."

No smart remarks came back at him. Nobody seemed prepared to take the conversation further. Then Padfield broke the silence.

"Do you think the world is any more dangerous for bringing kids up in than in the past, sir?"

Padfield's expression of concern was genuine. He wanted his tutor's opinion, and the buzzer would soon be sounding. Abandoning his idea to fish for information about Gary Treadway's activities, he switched to surrogate parent mode.

"I'm going to apologise in advance of answering that question, Ian. You've asked it and I feel I should respond honestly. But you may not be reassured by what I say."

"That bad, eh, sir?" Bellchambers quipped.

"Bringing up kids in this world? That's a big issue, Ian. You'll get a different viewpoint from anybody who attempts to answer that question. My take is that, in terms of physical health, the world has never been safer, particularly in the affluent West. The chances of another world war are slim, lessons having been learnt from the two in the last century. But the damage we're doing to the planet has reached a critical phase, and we may not be able to undo that. Another negative I see is that there are far more enticements for individuals to get hooked on risky lifestyle habits. Drug abuse is one, obviously. It could be argued that certain branches of the commercial world, supported by the media, are creating ever more sophisticated ways to control individuals' lives through addictions: alcohol, gambling, sex, violence, football, online social networking, designer clothing even. You can control people's lives if you can dictate how they occupy their time and spend their money."

"I'll take that as a 'No' then, sir," Padfield replied.

"Not entirely. As I said, the prospects for the physical health of humanity are good, especially for the likes of everybody in this room. I apologise if you find my perspective of emotional health depressing, Ian, but these are the facts of life. The media, through television advertising particularly, paints a picture of life for us all that is misleading. You will not transform your life if you upgrade your phone or change your brand of deodorant. Leading a healthy and fulfilling life can't be achieved through focusing on material considerations alone. It's more likely to result from improving your intellect – what goes on in the space between your ears. That's why I'm a teacher. I think I can help children to understand that."

"But if you live your life with what you've just said going around in your head all the time, doesn't that make you a miserable git, sir?" Bellchambers queried.

"I can't reply to that with a smart answer because it's such a profound question. I don't subscribe to the ignorance-is-bliss approach to life. It's a serious business and, yes, dwelling on the significance of why you're here and how you live can have adverse effects on your wellbeing. But appreciating the complexity of human existence can also heighten your life experiences in ways you may not

217

be able to imagine yet. There's far more in the world to delight and enthuse you than there has ever been in the past. If school education works properly, it increases your capacity for reflection and develops the ability to discriminate between cheap and worthless goals and experiences and those that are valuable. You shouldn't go far wrong in life if you learn to do that."

He was getting tired of the sound of his voice again.

"Sorry if you think I went off in lecture mode there, but I felt Ian deserved my honest answer. By the way, you don't have to agree with it."

Top Tip No. 14: Choose the right moments to offer reasoned opinions to children, especially the scarier ones.

****

"Let them find out for themselves. Life's depressing enough for them without filling their heads with predictions of doom."

He followed his wife into the kitchen with the empty coffee mugs, rinsed them under the tap and placed them on a tray in the dishwasher. Myra did the same with their plates and cutlery, put a wash tablet in the compartment, closed the door of the machine and switched on.

"Washing up is such hard work," she said drily.

Pragmatic to the point of being hard-headed in her attitudes and viewpoints, she was in total disagreement with him on this issue. Surprised at her reaction to his account of the earlier conversation with his form group, he developed his case.

"If a young person asks me for my opinion on one of the most important aspects of life, I've no option but to respond honestly. That's why I'm a teacher. My job is more far-reaching than simply getting kids through exams."

"I think children should be left to find out for themselves how tough and awful things can be. They don't need you making them as miserable as you are."

That stung.

"Jackson Browne gave young pop fans the same message with 'The Pretender', but no one complained that he was a misery guts."

"Who's Jackson Browne?"

"I wouldn't be as frank with the younger ones, but these are old enough to cope with such information. If they weren't, I wouldn't have been asked that question."

"I see your point but, from what I read of educational thinking at the moment, everything's going potty. The movement for teachers having to deal with sexual relationships is growing. Suddenly, all children are supposed to become sex experts. I'm not keen."

"That's another issue, as far as I'm concerned. But you're right. The sex genie is coming out of the bottle. So much of what children are exposed to on television now has a sexual content; I suppose it's inevitable that it finds its way into school curricula."

"The whole subject was taboo when I was at school. No adult ever told me anything about the subject, not even my parents."

"I can believe that. Can't imagine your dad giving you the heads up before you went on your first date."

Deepening his voice and furrowing his brow, he began a fatherly tirade in role as his father-in-law.

"Whatever you do, keep the little blighter at arm's length. I'm talking about this young man of yours, of course, not his...whatever. They're only after one thing, all of them. I should know. We don't want you being taken advantage of. Your mother will tell you what that means. If he gets too free with his hands, give the beggar a swift kick in the privates."

"You'd be surprised at just how accurate that little performance was."

"Getting back to Padfield, though, life's big issues are just as likely to be overlooked by teenagers unless their adolescent fears and anxieties are acknowledged and addressed by adults, namely their teachers."

"What about the argument that we're increasingly taking away children's childhood?"

"Their loss of innocence, yes. I take your point. Don't get me wrong, I don't dive in with doom-laden forecasts for my classes as a matter of course. I answer difficult questions plainly when they're put to me. And I obviously take the age of my listeners into account."

"So long as you promote their happiness as well, I don't have a problem."

"Ah, happiness! Every child must be protected from not being happy. It's a very over-rated concept these days."

"Well, before you set off on that tack, let's wind up with any other business."

"What do you mean, love?"

"The first AOB item: have you started packing?"

"Why? Am I leaving?"

"No, you numbskull! You break up for Easter in a week, and then we're straight off to Menorca. You may have noticed that my suitcase is on the floor in the office and that it's already half full. I hope you don't intend to leave your packing till the last minute."

****

"Your days as head of English will soon be numbered, Biggsy. How does it feel?"

It felt a bit like being an astronaut engaged in a spacewalk at the International Space Station and suddenly discovering that the safety line had become disconnected. He was floating off into the abyss, with the prospect of becoming yet another piece of space debris circling the earth forever. He preferred not to dwell on this disturbing feeling of disorientation.

"I'm coming to terms with it, Andy. Thanks for asking."

He had just conducted his final department meeting, the highlight of which had been a surprise iced cake, in acknowledgement of his sterling work as 'the best department head ever'. Everyone had also signed a good luck card. He picked up the plastic figurine of a teacher in mortarboard and gown that had stood next to the farewell message on the cake. He'd put it in his man drawer at home, where he kept other pieces of school memorabilia and photographs accumulated over the years. Myra regularly alarmed him by claiming that she would be cleaning out the drawer, but she had yet to do so.

He walked into the office, Andy following. The surprise awaiting his second was not one he would have wished for himself if their roles had been reversed. But Myra was right. All the English documentation, however intimidating, was now Andy's, not his. Andy's admin – the phrase had a pleasing ring. He might not be playing as much golf with Mags, his wife, over the next few weeks as he'd planned. Biggsy stopped his thoughts. He didn't want to venture into the realm of vindictiveness towards someone who'd once been his closest ally.

"I've been keeping up to speed with all the responsibilities I'll need to get stuck into straight after Easter, as you can imagine. Archie's given me a stack of sixth-form paperwork to work on over the holiday. On that tack, I've put together a file of stuff for you to get your teeth into."

He indicated two mounds of manila folders, plastic files, and loose sheets of paper on the coffee table. Andy raised his eyebrows at the unexpected holiday job his head of department had organised for him.

"That's yours on the right, and mine on the left. We've mountains to climb."

"You can say that again!"

"The admin for the GCSE English controlled assessments will occupy quite a bit of your time. I thought that could be your main induction task over the break. Hope you agree. As you can see, there's a fair bit of copy to occupy both of us."

He thought it wise not to mention Myra's part in this stratagem. He wished that she could be a fly on the wall at this moment. Andy was a great teacher. He'd now have to learn to be an equally good administrator.

Secrets.

No mention had been made to anyone in the department of his Easter holiday in the sun. Besides his desire for absolute school secrecy as far as that subject was concerned, he didn't wish to risk becoming the target of Andy's enmity. Shovelling a huge amount of unexpected work in his second's direction was bad enough, and it wouldn't do for Andy to know where his boss would be whilst he slaved away over essential departmental paperwork. A plastering of powerful sun cream throughout the week away would be necessary to conceal any evidence that he'd been sunning himself in the Med. His holiday priority, other than enjoying himself as immensely as Myra expected, must be taking every step to avoid the risk of unwanted questions at the start of the summer term. A glowing suntan was a definite no-no.

"I see what you mean. Well, it's got to be done, I suppose."

Andy looked less than impressed at his pile. His reaction had the effect of hardening his boss's resolve to be rid of it.

"The problem with promotion is that it takes you further away from the kids because the paperwork mountain gets higher."

The most important thing Andy should concentrate on for the foreseeable future is how fortunate he's been to acquire the head of department job in the first place.

******

"How's it going?"

He looked away from the locker into which he'd placed his civvies. Steve approached him, dropped his kit bag on the bench and began getting changed. They were the only two gym members in the changing room.

"Hi, Steve. Not so bad thanks. You?"

"Good, yeah. All the better for getting here this evening. Thought I might not be able to make it. Had to finish a bit of landscaping I'm doing over Esher way."

"Has that always been your line of work?"

"No. I've worked for a construction firm for thirty years or more. I'm going for early retirement though. Landscaping's a sideline I've recently taken on."

Not being one given to delving too deeply into others' personal lives, he would usually have switched to less intrusive conversational matters. But his curiosity was aroused. He probed further.

"So, you're opting to take early retirement?"

"I am. Getting fed up dealing with some of the flaky personalities I've had to work with."

"Sorry to hear that. By coincidence, I'm finding myself in a similar situation with the prospect of another ten years before I can retire. Not sure if it's the world that's changing or me."

"Yeah? You talking about the difficult kids you have to teach?"

"No, they're the good part of my job. The staff are a different proposition. It's almost the end of a long term, I suppose, and one or two of my colleagues are getting a bit testy."

"I thought it was the kids that wound you lot up, not the other teachers," Steve replied in amusement.

"Don't you believe it! The boys are straightforward once you let them know you're on their side, but you need to tread carefully around the egos of fellow professionals."

Steve raised his eyebrows. He was interested, and Biggsy was in a mood to offload. It wouldn't do any harm to confide professional frustrations, so long as he didn't mention anybody by name.

"I'm going because the job's become more hassle than it's worth. Too many obstacles are being placed in the way of what should be straightforward working practices. A polite way of referring to back-stabbing colleagues."

"Sickening, isn't it? Teaching's not what it was either. Every which way you turn, there are assessment objectives to be met and jobsworths looking to trip you up."

Having given way to the temptation of making wholesale generalisations, he became aware that he was treading on thin ice. Best to end the conversation now and concentrate on his workout.

"Ah well, I'd better get organised. I'm off to renew my friendship with my trusty treadmill. That won't let me down."

"It's gotta be done. A physical workout is the best way to sort your head out."

"Agreed. Nothing better for exorcising the demons of the daily grind."

"In the final analysis, it's just a job," Steve advised. "That's one of the most important facts of life."

"You must know my wife," Biggsy laughed.

****

"Blimey! Never thought you were paying any attention to me!" Myra exclaimed, pretending to support herself by grasping both sides of the door frame, and then wiping a hand across her brow in a parody of an attack of the vapours.

"Perhaps, on reflection, I considered it advisable to start packing a few things as I thought of them," her husband replied, affecting an unconcerned air.

"What! You mean your red pen and laptop?"

His open suitcase was on their bed, and he was rummaging through the drawers of the unit on his side of the bed. Myra was amazed by the sight of a layer of underclothes and T-shirts, evidence that he really was serious about packing.

"Very funny. I was thinking more of personal items. I can't find my Kindle. You haven't seen it anywhere?"

"Can't think of anything more personal than your red pen. I was thinking of surprising you with a gold-encrusted one next birthday. Anyway, your Kindle was in the office cupboard the last time I saw it. Are you telling me that you're intending to read for pleasure on holiday, as opposed to reading students' homework scripts?"

"Could well do. You'll be pleased to hear I took your advice and shunted all my Easter admin in Andy's direction. He wasn't best pleased."

"No reason why he should be. You never looked a picture of elation when you slogged through it year after year."

"It had to be done."

"Hold on, though. I'm still struggling to get my head around this. You're packing for our dodgy holiday, and there is still a week to go before you break up. What's come over you?"

"Just thought I'd opt for a stress-free Easter this year, whatever the chances I end up losing my job."

"Now that sounds more like the man I married. Thought for a moment you'd OD'd on happy pills. To change the subject, I've arranged to go round to Jenny's on Saturday afternoon because a long-time friend is visiting her. She wondered if I'd like to meet him. He's a medium."

His wife was full of surprises, but this one did catch him off guard.

"Seriously? A medium? You do mean someone who gives readings?"

"Yes. His name's Barry Shand. He's worked with the police on serious crimes, even helping them with murder inquiries. Although he's a friend, Jenny invited him on a professional basis for a reading. He charges forty pounds per session. If I'm interested, she'll ask him when he arrives if he can fit me in."

"And you've said you might be?"

"Yes. Never considered doing anything like this before, but why not?"

Why not? He was a fatalist, with a conviction that one's life is predestined. This belief had been tested over the past few months, but it remained intact. If the course of an individual life is preordained, why shouldn't it be possible for those with second sight to pick up on future outcomes? But his wife wasn't a fatalist, so why was she spending a significant amount of money on something in which she didn't believe?

"I didn't imagine Jenny being the type to dabble in that area, and certainly not you. You're a mistress of your own destiny, so you tell me, like Ella. Why waste money on something that you have no time for?"

"Oh, it's just a bit of fun. Don't be such a killjoy."

But he didn't see that what she was intending to undertake could be termed 'fun'. Ouija boards tended to be viewed in the same light. Fun. The possibility of being given a handle on future events could not, from his perspective, ever be viewed as fun.

"Don't get me wrong. I've no intention of being a killjoy, but I do have one question for you. If it's possible to know future events, should we allow ourselves to find out what they are? Or should we leave well alone?"

"I'm not sure what you're getting at."

"Foreknowledge, if such a thing were possible, could have a harmful effect on one's personality. If this Barry knows that you're going to be hospitalised in six months' time, and he tells you, how do you respond?"

"Oh, you're scare-mongering. Jenny says he only tells you good things."

"Well, I came to terms a long time ago with the belief that, if it is possible for my future to be revealed, I prefer not to know about it."

Myra folded back the duvet and plumped up the pillows, whilst maintaining a resigned expression.

"Why do you have to be so analytical about everything? I've already said it's just a giggle. Forget I even mentioned it to you."

"All I'm doing is explaining my position with regard to…"

"And all I'm doing is trying to wash the bedding. Get your suitcase off the bed and put it in the office next to mine for now."

"I'll never get the bed in the office, love," he jested.

"Give me strength…"

****

"A few final words then about revision over Easter, guys."

The term's end was approaching for his A-level group. The sense of relief that he'd covered all the set texts was heightened by the fact that, on triple-checking, he discovered they were definitely on the syllabus. Every year, at about this time, he found himself beset by the fear that he'd taught the wrong books to his students. He'd wake in the early hours from an anxiety dream two or three nights a year, convinced that he'd done so. In a hot sweat, he'd have to get out of bed, dig out the relevant syllabus and confirm that he hadn't made the most embarrassing professional gaff possible. Only then could he try to get back to sleep.

Sitting bolt upright in his seat and pouting in disgust, Colley informed his tutor that other arrangements had been prioritised.

"What are you on about, sir? I'm off to Ibiffa for a fortnight with the lads. You're not expecting us to take Chaucer along with us, are you? Mind you, he might prefer a change of air. Better than trollin' off to Canterbury every year."

"I pray to God that you're winding me up again, Chris."

"Course I am sir. What d'you think I am – a muppet?" Colley asked with a reassuring wink.

Relieved at the student's about-turn, Biggsy continued.

"The most important thing to remind you of is that the examination is not set to catch you out. It is simply an opportunity for you to show what you know."

"That won't take you long then, Chris," Bellchambers joked.

"That's just where you're wrong, matey. Isn't it, sir?"

"Absolutely, Chris. Joking apart, one of your strengths is your ability to analyse relevant themes in a lively manner. Talking of which, A-level is all about the exploration of themes in literature, as well as character and plot development. You all know that, of course. Silly me!"

"What's your advice for revising over Easter, sir?" Padfield asked, doing his best to control rising anxiety levels.

The word 'revision' was guaranteed to have a sobering effect on most examination candidates, Colley excepting.

"I can't give cast-iron advice that would necessarily suit everyone in this group, but I can give you pointers, all of which I found useful when I was studying."

"Don't suppose these pointers would include you getting your hands on the exam paper and telling us what the questions are?" Bellchambers queried.

"Sorry. No can do. Anyway, the first piece of advice is simple. If you haven't read through any of the books completely on your own, do so. You're being assessed on what you know, so you can't rely on my reading the texts aloud to you in lessons. You need to have a thorough knowledge of each."

"I won't be able to read eight books in two weeks, sir!" Colley spluttered. "I will need to spend some of my time sleepin'."

"Very funny, Chris. As most of you have bought your own books, I can recommend using different coloured highlighters when re-reading. Considering the four or five main themes we discussed when studying each book, highlight lines or phrases as you read that focus on relevant themes, using a different colour for each. But don't spend your whole time highlighting. A dozen or so highlights for each theme."

"But we've already got loads of GEQs you told us to write down, sir," Dixon protested. "Why do we need another lot?"

"I don't want you to think that good examination quotes are the guarantee of A-level success, but you may need a selection. And don't complicate your lives by thinking that you must quote whole sentences or stanzas of poetry. Sometimes a pithy phrase is all you need."

"Wish I had a photographic memory like Jermaine," Padfield groaned.

Gibson shrugged at mention of his name.

"Anyway, it's good that you wrote them down, Richard. I didn't say you had to. But if you did, you'll all have the same ones that I drew to your attention. Reading the books again, with all the knowledge you've acquired of each, will result in you coming up with some of your own. That will result, hopefully, in each of your examination answers being different. Think of the poor examiner, who'll need a bit of variety in your written responses to avoid a deadening of the brain through terminal boredom."

"Talking of photographic memories, there will be candidates who have even greater powers than that. A tiny minority of those with whom you will be competing for high grades are so interested in literature that they will need to do next to no revision. A-level English Literature may have encouraged their reading habit. Terrifying, isn't it?"

"I can't imagine that," Dixon admitted.

"I also found that difficult to imagine when I was your age because I hadn't developed the required levels of interest or intelligence. I was a slogger who did everything the hard way, just as one or two of you may have to do."

"If I 'ad a brain like that, I'd be scared it'd explode," Colley concluded.

Expressions of mild amusement on the students' faces indicated that now was a good time to close the subject of Easter revision.

"Well, on that bombshell, let's assume that you've got your revision programmes sewn up. Oh, before I forget, have any of you looked online at what literary critics have written about the study texts?"

The spontaneous collective groan caused him to laugh aloud.

Top Tip No. 15: When examination time comes around, it's as well to remind students of the level of competition they'll be up against.

Chapter 15

"Before going home, I wanted to ask you how you're feeling as you approach the end of your hugely successful time in charge of the English department?"

Beth had taken him by surprise, walking into the office half an hour after the final buzzer. He was on his haunches, returning a pile of books to their niche on a low shelf. He turned and smiled up at her.

"It took me a while to get down here. Now I've got to try and get back up."

"The suffering you have to endure for the department!" she joked.

"Now you couldn't have said a truer word," he answered, dusting himself down with both hands. "This office has been a kind of sanctuary for ten years, and I know I'm going to miss it. Besides missing all of you, of course."

"You'll still have us by your side, though. Won't be so bad, will it?"

He walked across the office to the window to stand in the sunlight.

"On the one hand, there'll be that feeling of losing a kind of second family. Next term, I'll be left entirely to my own devices – on my own, as it were. But then, I know I can always come crying to you lot when I need a bit of support."

"Yes, I suppose you will be feeling a little isolated in that tiny office attached to the sixth-form common room. But the students next door will make enough noise to keep you company, I'm sure."

"You've got a point there, Beth. Dave often says how it's a bit of a rodeo there when they're all in school. That'll make me unpopular, having to tell them to keep the noise down every five minutes."

Beth put her bag on the table and rooted around for something inside. She took out a small, gift-wrapped parcel and handed it to him.

"Just a little goodbye present as a thank you for being such a great boss," she explained.

"How considerate of you!"

"You haven't seen what it is yet."

"As long as it isn't a sex toy, I'm sure I'll love it, Beth."

She smiled, recalling the events at the staff Christmas dinner.

"How lovely, a framed photo of the department. That was one of us all after last term's Ofsted at the pub. I do look a bit tired, I must say."

"I think you mean intoxicated."

"You may well be right. Look at the sign Bridget's making to the camera. Shameless!"

"Yes, she was in her cups that night but, to be honest, we all were."

****

Manchester United would be winning another Premier League title, but he was more interested in the rugby results. Searching through teletext, he was dismayed to see the result of Bath's afternoon home match, a heavy defeat at the hands of Leicester. As he was assessing the team's chances of finishing in the top four of the table, he heard the front door opening.

Myra wandered into the room, an expression of wonderment on her face.

"That was unbelievable!" she exclaimed. "What an incredible experience!"

"It went well then?" he asked, switching his mood from gloom at the rugby result to genuine interest in what his wife had to report. Much as he hadn't wanted to subject himself to an interview with a medium, he was intrigued to hear what had transpired next door.

"What sort of person was this guy, then?"

"Not someone you'd look at twice in the street. Short, tubby, grey hair and with glasses which had really thick lenses. But he had these bright blue eyes and a winning smile."

"Harmless-looking sort of bloke then?"

"Yes, but what he told me was amazing. Barry uses tarot cards. First off, he asked me to shuffle them. I was so nervous and the cards were so big I kept dropping them at first. Then he asked me for a personal item that he could hold during the reading, so I gave him my watch, the one you gave me for our anniversary. You'd better have a look at it."

She handed over the watch and waited for a reaction.

"It's stopped. Look, it says ten past four."

"I know. That's the time I handed it to him. And when he gave it back, it was icy cold. Do you think it's broken?"

"Can't say, but I'll see if I can get it going again."

As he fiddled with the expensive timepiece, Myra continued her account.

"He placed the cards on the table, and I had to cut them every now and again. Each time I did, he explained what the card I uncovered meant for me. The first thing he said was that I was a pure person, whatever that means – a candle in the wind."

"Really?"

"Watch it! He said others looked to me as an example of how to lead their lives."

"Impressive. That's quite a compliment. Did you believe him?"

"What d'you mean? He also told me I was a worker, not a shirker. He knew I'd been promoted recently and said further advancement would be coming to me within the next two years. He knew I worked in a hospital and how tough things have been for me recently."

"I'll bet he knew you were going on holiday soon as well. Jenny must have told him all about you."

"Not true. She swore she told him nothing. He didn't even know I'd be seeing him until the last minute when Jenny asked if he could fit me in."

Biggsy had been holding the watch tightly in his hand while he'd been questioning her. Opening his hand and looking at the face, he noticed that the minute hand was moving.

"That's strange. Your watch has started again just from me holding it."

"How amazing! What do you think about all this now?"

He set it to the right time and handed it back. She took it gratefully and peered at the face.

"He did know that I was going on a family holiday with people who would become lifelong friends. How about that?"

He pretended to appear sceptical but was genuinely interested. Having an open mind on the subject, he would never discount the possibility that there were those who could access future events as easily as those that had passed.

"Did he mention anything about us moving any time soon?" he asked, affecting a light-hearted tone.

"No, but he did say I need to organise an MRI scan for you."

****

230

"The earliest I could book a GP appointment for you was eight o'clock this Thursday, the day before you break up. You'll just have to be a bit late for once."

"Thanks, love. That's good of you. Do you really think it's worth paying attention, though, to something a medium told you?"

"Better safe than sorry, that's what I think."

Drying up the last of the breakfast things, he stood over the cutlery drawer looking at the tea towel he was using, the one he'd bought at Headingley when he'd spent a day watching Yorkshire playing against Somerset. Printed on it were images of scrawny men in flat caps, heavy women in hair nets and housecoats, and examples of Yorkshire dialect. The one he wasn't sure about was 'G'I THISSEN UP THI GINNEL'. It sounded rude, possibly a form of rebuke. One day he'd google it.

"I can't believe Barry's only reference to your husband was to do with his health."

His vanity was offended. Surely there could have been mention of his professional ability and/or future career prospects.

"Like I said, it seems you were a sudden afterthought at the end of the reading. Good job you were!"

"Very flattering, I'm sure. But this guy doesn't know me from Adam. Was there any reason why you should have taken his instruction so seriously?"

"I cut the pack for the final time and, when I turned over the card, he became very insistent."

"Can you remember which card it was?"

"I'm not absolutely sure, but it might have been that dancing skeleton. That would make sense because the first thing you think of with a skeleton is medical matters."

"A dancing skeleton? That's the death card. So, you turned over the death card for me. Charming!"

Myra began laughing, so much so that she had to sit down on the bar stool to compose herself. Having settled herself, she found she was able to speak.

"You're such a hypochondriac. You were the one who didn't want anything to do with Barry, and now you're getting your knickers in a twist over one silly card. Anyway, I'm doing as he said, and you've got an appointment. All sorted! This may be a warning."

231

"You never know. If Paul agrees to refer me for an MRI, how long do you think it'll be before a hospital appointment can be arranged?" he asked, tidying up the spoons and forks in the cutlery drawer.

"Up to six weeks maximum, I'd say, but you could be seen more quickly if there's a cancellation. The equipment's so expensive they like to keep it in constant use. I'll keep my ear to the ground and check on any gaps that may come up in the MRI department's patients' list."

"I suppose it does no harm to follow this up. I must admit my prostate has been playing on my mind these last few months. Could be a blessing in disguise."

"That's right. We don't want anything nasty happening to my hunky hubby."

He gave her his how-long-have-I-got? expression, the one that made him look like a miserable bloodhound. Instead of becoming impatient, she put her arms around his waist and gave him a hug.

"What time do you expect to be coming home tonight?" she asked, hovering by the kitchen door before going upstairs to make final preparations before leaving for work.

"I've finished all my reports and done most of the work for the handover to Andy, so I might go for an early getaway today."

"Really! But who will they get to put the school lights out if you're not the last one to leave?"

"Good one. Anyway, what about booking a Sunday evening slot at Benito's to celebrate the end of term? Our favourite table in the corner?"

"You mad romantic fool!" she exclaimed, looking to the heavens in feigned amazement at the audacity of his suggestion. "I'll get onto it."

****

The local Holiday Inn was the Saturday evening venue for the special end-of-term meal, a formal dinner organised by the head as a fitting occasion to say goodbye to two senior teachers. Every member of staff was present to wish a fond farewell to Dave Wheelhouse. Had he not been retiring, there would have been a much smaller gathering to wish Ms Toner adieu.

He was denied any of the feelings ranging from euphoria to relief at the prospect of the deputy head's departure from St Saviour's. The reason was that he was preoccupied with his own farewells to the English department. Not only that, but he was also firm in his conviction that he could well decide to leave the school himself if he found his new sixth-form role unsatisfying. This thought he had not shared with Myra, but his mind was made up. If the job's not to your liking, get the hell out. She'd understand. When fate gets seriously stuck in, life makes decisions for you.

Fingleton expressed warm gratitude for Dave Wheelhouse's countless contributions to St Saviour's, but his gushing praise of Toner's impact on the school sent Biggsy scurrying to the bar for a malt whisky. As he was being served, Sarah arrived at his side.

"What would you like, Sarah? Sorry for hurrying away from the table like that, but I came over a little nauseous during the final speech."

"That bad, eh? I'll have a white wine spritzer if you're offering. So, you don't think our esteemed deputy head deserved such fulsome praise then?"

He'd had a few glasses of wine at table and knew that he'd have to curb his tongue from this point on in the evening, to whomsoever he found himself speaking.

"It's not just her. I've allowed myself to get fixated on the woman when it's what she represents that's getting to me. She's just one of the new breed who'll destroy teaching as we know it, Sarah."

"She's certainly a systems operative, but people like us can choose to resist all the nonsense, surely?"

"I'd love to think you're right. But she's swallowed the assessment lie hook line and sinker, like every other management team all over the country."

"What do you mean by the assessment lie?"

"That assessing is more important than teaching. Assessment of every aspect of the teaching process is now our main responsibility, and also – don't be mistaken in this – the key to career success."

"Can I help you, sir?"

A tall, dark-haired young man in a crisp white shirt and claret waistcoat stood beaming behind the bar.

"Yes thanks, a double of that malt whisky you've got up there and a white wine spritzer, please."

The drinks produced, he searched in his wallet for a twenty-pound note to replace the ten he'd initially proffered to the bartender. He passed Sarah her drink.

"Thank you, kind sir."

"I hope Andy cuts the mustard for you all next term. I don't want to hear of him making any concessions to the higher-ups. I'd be happier knowing you were taking over from me. Oops – shouldn't have said that."

There it went. His tongue was running away with him. In his current mood, the consequence of two swift glasses of red, he wasn't that concerned. But he knew he would be in the morning. A burst of laughter caused them both to look up at the source. Chris Barker and Andy Orchard were engaged in lively conversation at one of the tables. Biggsy looked to see if Aaron Aimes was in their vicinity but couldn't pick him out.

"It's strange how this year's worked out," Sarah ventured. "If you'd told me the department would be in this situation at the start of the year, I wouldn't have believed you."

"Me neither," he answered as he savoured the peaty aroma emanating from his glass. "I'm going to drink this, then be on my merry way."

"You do make me laugh, Biggsy. I can't imagine you ever going anywhere on a 'merry way'."

"Now, that's where you could be very mistaken, my dear," he grinned. "In a few days' time, I shall be soaking up the sun in a Mediterranean bolt hole, with plenty of this to hand, the company of my good lady wife, and…"

"Secrets."

He was almost certain somebody whispered the word in his ear.

"Really? You've kept that to yourself. Where are you off to?"

"Oh, just a week in Menorca Myra organised. She's sorted it all out, bless her."

"That sounds like just the break you need. Good for her. I've got my parents coming for a long weekend. The older I get, the more I realise how much I rely on them."

"I suppose we teachers need looking after. I'm lucky that I've always had Myra pointing me in the right direction."

"What a lovely thing to say! But I want you to promise me you won't be leaving us permanently. We need you now more than ever. I'm worried you just see this sideways move as a temporary filler before leaving the school for good."

He smiled at Sarah's intuition. She could have been reading his mind.

"I will if you remember to keep the promise you made to me: keep a watchful eye over Andy from here on."

****

He'd wondered why Myra had insisted on him wearing his suit. She'd gone for a smart casual look that was more smart than casual. The flower-print dress and red pashmina were only brought out for extra-special occasions.

"Hope you don't mind, but I've organised a surprise."

His suspicions had been aroused by the fact that Benito hadn't shown them to their corner table. Instead, displaying his usual bonhomie and charm, the restaurant manager ushered them to a table for four.

"How do you mean?"

"I was about to make the booking when it occurred to call Jan first to see if she and David might want to join us. Sure enough, she was only too pleased at the invitation. They'll be here directly."

"Would you like to see the wine list?" Benito asked, hovering at Myra's side.

Armed with two folders, deep red in colour and with matching fussy tassels, he handed them with a flourish to his customers. Coupled with the fact that the atmosphere and food quality were excellent, Myra appreciated the fact that this was one establishment where she could rely on being warm during the colder months. There was no point in eating out, however good the menu, if you were shivering throughout your stay.

"Thank you so much, Benito. We'll browse the drinks whilst awaiting our guests," Myra said.

"Oh, I thought we could enjoy a little time together for a change."

"That is a nice idea, and I do appreciate it, love. But we'll all be off to the villa next week. I thought this evening would be a perfect opportunity to discuss important details about the holiday."

"Is there anything that needs discussing? Don't we just turn up on Menorca, dump our suitcases and head for the sun deck?"

"That may be the way men behave when invited to stay with friends abroad, but women have a host of other considerations requiring one's attention. You can't just turn up and take everything for granted. For starters, we need to discuss what sort of things to pack; food provisions during our stay; arrangements for exploring the island; and how we contribute to various expenses."

"Oh, right. I see your point. Could be a busy evening. I'm surprised Jan and David were free at such short notice, though."

"I suppose, like us, they've kept their diaries clear in the days before their vacation."

"I didn't know I had a diary."

"After all these years, you still don't understand, do you? I am your diary," Myra explained, turning at the sound of a door opening. "Oh, here they are."

He looked towards the entrance and stood up with a start, nudging the table forward as he did so. Myra rose to her feet decorously, giving him a sidelong glance as she did so.

Jan was wearing her brown suede jacket again, this time with a long, silky black skirt and high heels. David looked relaxed in brown loafers, light blue jeans, and a heavy knit dark blue pullover. Biggsy wished he'd insisted on jeans.

"Hope we're not late, you two?" Jan gushed, leading David by the hand.

"Not at all. We arrived early. It's lovely to see you both again," Myra answered.

Benito hurried across to attend to the new arrivals, standing to one side whilst the friends greeted each other. Uncertain about the protocols after shaking David's hand, Biggsy thought to do the same with Jan, as he had the last time they'd met. However, after hugging Myra and kissing her on the cheek, Jan launched herself in his direction and brushed her cheek against his. He flushed at the contact and smiled awkwardly. Myra was now just as effusive in greeting David, who retained his reserved demeanour in the face of her enthusiastic welcome. Benito then took charge of the proceedings, to the relief of both husbands. The manager handed out more wine lists and menus.

Were twenty-first-century English women becoming ultra-demonstrative when greeting male friends and acquaintances? Could it be a continental influence? He'd certainly never seen his mother behave in such a manner, but his sister was heading in that direction.

"What a wonderful host!"

"We love him," Myra gushed, adjusting her cutlery.

"I wouldn't go that far," her husband added drily. "But he runs this place just the way we like it."

"We're also lucky to have a local Italian, aren't we, David? Marco's is only a short walk from ours, and we're regulars there. Fabulous menu! I've been right through it. David usually goes for the same dish every time. Not the most adventurous gastronome is our David."

Jan's husband, smiling at the tablecloth in response to this judgement, had clearly taken the comment in good heart. *It's like looking in a mirror,* Biggsy thought. He could be my doppelganger.

****

The villa was impressive. Built as one of several on an area of raised ground above the minor road that ran alongside the properties, it had the appeal he'd been hoping for. Bright sunlight showed it at its best. The walls must have been whitewashed very recently, and the grounds were immaculate. Well-tended cacti and succulents, glowing vivid green and with sprouting yellow and orange fruits, were interspersed with small trees and red and purple bougainvillea. The Thompsons must pay a fortune to a local gardener for this level of maintenance, he guessed.

"What a beautiful spot for a villa! It's gorgeous," Myra announced in wonderment.

He helped the cab driver unload the suitcases from the boot then paid him. Bronzed and beaming, the islander took the money gratefully. He'd been such good company during the trip from the airport to Son Parc, he deserved his five-euro tip. The contrast between his manner and the dour English cabby who'd taken them to Gatwick couldn't have been greater. The extravagance of such an expensive taxi run to the airport had been justified on the grounds that the holiday stay was, effectively, a freebie.

The hot climate must do wonders for one's general disposition. Biggsy hoped it would work for him.

Myra had immediately picked up on the pride Mano had shown in being one of the fortunate inhabitants of Menorca and had quizzed him about the island's unmissable attractions and excursions. Ella and her father had smiled at each other as Myra did all the talking with the cabby. The Easter break was already working for her.

"Thank you so much, Mano. Thank you!" Myra called from the pavement as he slammed the boot lid shut and, grinning broadly, waved his customers farewell.

"What a lovely man!" she exclaimed. "I've a feeling we're going to have the time of our lives here. Just look at this place. It's like something out of a travel magazine."

"I never imagined anything as plush as this, Mum. What do you think, Dad?"

He decided to whisper his reply.

"Looks good, Ella. You certainly know how to pick a boyfriend."

As the three of them hauled their luggage up the half-dozen steps to the main entrance, the door opened. Jan, David, and Neil emerged from the villa, all wearing T-shirts, shorts, sandals, and welcoming smiles.

Ella dropped her case and gave Neil a hug. He looked older out of school uniform. His designer sunglasses added to the effect.

"Let me take that, Myra," David said, relieving her of the suitcase that was at risk of tumbling back down the steps.

"Come in. Come on in, all of you. You must be exhausted after your early morning start," Jan said, ushering them into the entrance hall.

Colourful canvases of island scenes and glowing floral studies decorated the walls. An ivory marble floor continued from the hall along the passage and into the rooms leading off it. Biggsy anticipated the prospect of walking barefoot on the cooling tiles.

"Let's drop the luggage into your rooms first and then we can relax with a drink on the veranda," David encouraged.

"Yours is the first door on the right, Ella," he added, leading the group along the passage, "and Mum and Dad are in the next one along."

"Bet you two didn't imagine anything as luxurious as this?"

"You're not wrong, Ella," her mother replied. "This is going to be wonderful."

"It's a lovely villa, David," Myra said, peering through the doorway of Ella's room. "Look at that view of the garden."

"The gardener's just been, so it's looking its best at the moment. By tomorrow morning, though, there'll be a fresh fall of pine needles for him to sweep up. That's the only problem having the tall trees at the back of the property," Jan explained.

"If that's all there is to worry about here, you're on a winner," Myra laughed.

"Right, we'll leave you to unpack and get into something more comfortable. Join us outside when you're ready for a spot of liquid refreshment. I'm off to put the coffee on."

As she left the congested hallway, she issued instructions to her husband and son.

"Come on, you two. Leave our guests to settle in for a while. They'll soon be with us."

Father and son dutifully trailed behind Jan into the kitchen. Ella's eyes followed Neil as he turned towards her and raised his arm in a playful wave.

Biggsy surveyed their bedroom, sat on the end of the double bed and sighed. His mobile pinged. He took the phone from his trouser pocket, applied himself to the keypad, then froze as a brief message from Maggy Orchard appeared on the screen.

Andy was involved in a terrible car accident yesterday evening. He was taken to casualty but died this morning. So terrible!

****

TO BE CONTINUED IN CLASS CONSCIOUS